BARBARA MICHELLE

THE DECEPTOR'S CALL
A NOVEL

This is a work of fiction. Similarities to real people, places, or events are entirely coincidental.

THE DECEPTOR'S CALL

First edition. May 23, 2024.

Copyright © 2024 Barbara Michelle.

ISBN: 979-8224782079

Written by Barbara Michelle.

PRAISE FOR THE DECEPTOR'S CALL

"...got so lost in the story I forgot to edit and had to start over!"... Tina Susedik, award-winning author, editor.

"I couldn't stop thinking about the book. I had to stop what I was doing and read to see what would happen next!"... Patti M., NC

"Just as I thought 'there can't be anything more devastating,' the plot twists and turns and delivers once again."... Karen R., NC

"Wild story, well told."... Greg R., NC

"You gave me nightmares!" Theresa Ellett Russ, FL

The Deceptor's Call by Barbara Michelle
Edited by: Tina Susedik, author
Cover Design by: Enchanted Pen Designs

This is a non-AI generated work of fiction. The names, characters, places, and incidents are the products of the author's imagination or are used fictitiously. Any resemblance to actual events, business establishments, locales, or persons, living or dead is entirely coincidental.

All rights reserved. No part of this publication may be reproduced, stored in a retrieval system, or transmitted in any form or by any means (electronic, artificial intelligence, mechanical, photocopying, recording, or otherwise) without the prior consent of the author. The only exception is brief quotations in printed reviews.

The scanning, uploading, and distribution of this book via the Internet or via any other means without the permission of the author is illegal and punishable by law. Please purchase only authorized electronic editions, and do not participate in or encourage electronic (including artificial intelligence) piracy of copyrighted materials.

Your support of this author's rights is appreciated.

Published in the United States of America by
Barbara Michelle

For Jay
You have my heart.
Can't wait to see what happens next...

CHAPTER ONE

Acrid sting of burnt paper tainted the air.

"Sandy? What're you doing?"

Jolted by Elam's unexpected midday return home, I spun my head toward him and the opened side door of the garage. I wished for the ground to swallow me whole as my surging jealousy subsided. Black ash billowed in front of me.

The lighter in my left hand flickered blue. White-yellow flames snaked up photographs dangling precariously between my fingers. Our metal trash bin rested below. His secret wooden box, unearthed from a forgotten corner of our attic, purged of all its secrets with the lock broken and the top flipped open. "You shouldn't have kept these," I said, my voice thin.

Recognition replaced indifference with the widening of his eyes. "My, God." Decades of old letters written on flowered stationery, aged to dull beige, lay open in a pile. Scattered pictures of young, glowing faces in love waited their incineration on the workbench. "Nooo," he yelled. "How dare you." His race to stop the desecration ended in a quick grab of his chest, knees folding like a lawn chair. He gasped out the name of the girl in the picture. "Cam." A pained grunt escaped his lips as his body twisted on the way down. His head bounced against the oil spot on the concrete floor I'd asked him to clean up the week before.

The lighter clattered to the floor. I landed beside him on my knees and grabbed both sides of his head. "Elam," I yelled. My body shook from the inside out as I frantically checked for signs of life. His breath faint and pulse thready, I shouted for help. My voice echoed against the closed garage door. I grabbed my cell phone from my pants pocket and clumsily punched the keys.

"Nine-one-one. State your emergency."

"My husband." Breaths fought to make their way out of my chest. "He's unconscious. I think he's just had a heart attack." As my pulse hammered, the dispatcher asked too many questions. "Yes, he's breathing," I said. "But barely." I relayed the pertinent information. "Send someone now!" Assured that help was on the way, I clicked the speaker key on my phone and returned to the floor by his side. My phone fell to the floor beside me.

"Ma'am," said the dispatcher, "is he still breathing?"

"Yes."

"Stay on the phone with me until the paramedics arrive."

Clutching his jaw firmly between my thumb and forefinger, I shook his blotchy, ashen face. "Elam, wake up." No response. I shook harder. "Try to wake up. Please." Tears blurred my vision and dripped on him.

"Ma'am?" said the voice. "Ma'am?"

I kissed his oxygen starved lips, salty from my tears. "I'm so sorry, honey," I murmured. "Don't leave me. I'll make it up to you, I promise." My head on his chest, loud sobs racked my body. "You're my life. My everything."

"Ma'am? What's happening there, Mrs. Steele?"

A small, fluttery voice whispered around my head, goading me. "Finish her, Sandy." The remaining pile of history lay on the workbench awaiting their fate. The sensual whisper tickled my ear. "Burn." An unseen force tugged me away from Elam.

Tears blurred my vision. Self-hatred scorched through my veins like quicksilver. The last of his first betrothed's pictures and letters drifted in final black tendrils of smoke.

Wishing to reverse the past is a waste. Looking forward is the only option. But not knowing what lay ahead for me—for my family—was a hell-curse all its own.

I waited for the ambulance.

CHAPTER TWO

Moving day loomed on the horizon. Elam's dream life of renting indefinitely in St. Thomas followed by a world tour, and what I pictured for our empty nesting years didn't quite line up. But he'd possessed my limitless devotion for the past thirty-two years. Plagued by insecurity since childhood, I'd always put his wants for the future ahead of my own. I would make this work.

A year after his heart attack, the closing date on the sale of our Midwestern home and an end to an era glowed in yellow highlighter on our Caribbean Islands calendar. I avoided it every time I passed by. Our children, Ed and Shauna, grew up in this house.

I gnawed the pencil eraser. My heart and head battled over the image hanging in the hallway. It represented a glorious weeklong vacation spent years ago in the Sierra Mountains. Keep, sell, or toss? Family fun memories too dear, I scratched *Lake Tahoe painting* under the *Keep* column in the spiral notebook I'd titled *STORAGE UNIT* in black felt tip marker. The tissue box cover crocheted by Elam's aunt landed in the waste basket.

My toe caught the edge of an open box. Catching my balance, I pushed the cardboard box closer to the wall and out of the walkway. The contents inside clenched my heart, Shauna's new comforter for her dorm room for her freshman year of university.

Unable to resist, I rocked in my grandmother's old rocking chair in the corner, I added it to the *sell* column. I'd always envisioned grandchildren frolicking in our backyard, playing amongst the rose bushes I spent years coaxing to thrive. Now the house was under contract, awaiting a new family to move in and create their own memories within its walls. Finished with the hallway, I sighed and moved to the master bedroom.

"Mom." Shauna traipsed in. "My room and the kitchen are mostly packed." She glanced over my shoulder at the notebook.

"After everything's sold, you're not going to have much in the storage unit." The few items I couldn't bear to part with would be stored until we were ready to re-establish a more grounded life.

"That's the idea." I tucked a loose strand of wheat colored hair behind her ear. A near physical replica of me, Shauna embraced life with an abundance of self-esteem and a confidence that eluded my reach for a lifetime. "I'm going to miss you. You've grown up too fast."

She laughed and pecked me on the cheek. "You've already been through this with Ed." She plopped, full bodied, onto the mattress.

I grinned. "That was six years ago. It was hard when he left us for college. In fact, it was awful for me. Now he has his own life and career, as it should be. You're my baby. My last." I withheld the true cavernous depth of my grief and fear of her impending move. Heavy concealer covered the black circles under my eyes from my sleepless nights.

"I doubt you and Dad will have time to miss me. You'll probably make a ton of new friends in St. Thomas."

"It's so far away." I doodled absentmindedly on the top of my notebook. "But he's been utterly consumed with this whole sell-everything-idea since his heart attack last year. It's all he talks about."

She twisted a clump of hair between her fingers. "Aren't you excited, Mom? You guys are going to live out what most people only dream of."

I shrugged. "I'm sure once we finally get going it'll be a great adventure. I just want your dad to be happy."

"I'd love to spend Christmas break down there with you guys."

I puckered my lips and sent her a dramatic air kiss. "That'd be wonderful." I placed my hand over my heart. "Maybe Ed could get an assignment to write an article about the area and join us for a big family Christmas." Our son, named after Elam's deceased father, enjoyed the fast pace and travel as an independent journalist.

Elam leaned into the room. "I'm starved. Want to go out for a bite?" His ragged outdoor T-shirt stretched tight across his sculpted chest.

"Sure," I said.

He moved beside me and peered at my notebook. "Looks like you're finally seeing that we don't need most of this stuff, after all. I knew you'd get there." He twirled me in a dance spin, humming a reggae tune under his breath. "Magens Bay, St. Thomas, here we come."

I tossed the pad on the bed and let him sweep me into his embrace. Nuzzling his sweaty neck, I inhaled his musky scent. "I love you, Elam Steele."

Shauna sniggered. "Disgusting. Get a room, you two." She climbed off the bed. "I'm going out for a last hurrah with the girls. Be back a little later."

He released me when she was gone and made for the door. "I'll get cleaned up before we go."

"Elam, this is all going to work out, right?"

"If there's one thing I've learned in the past year, it's how precious life is. And I have a chance to make everything new. You never know when it's all going to come crashing down." He held both hands out to his sides. "Once this place is passed on to the buyers, all we have to do is show up in our swimsuits." He bit his bottom lip and playfully arched one eyebrow. "Or our birthday suits." He lowered his hands. "Everything down there is ready and waiting for us, including lots of fruity drinks."

Beaming inside, I sauntered closer to him. "Of course, you're right. I'm with you all the way, Wild Man." My hand popped as I smacked his tush on his way to the shower.

BARBARA MICHELLE

I reflected on how his vitality soared after his quick recovery. The heart attack sparked a new craving for adventure. Soon afterward, he organized and successfully completed the sale of the lighting business he'd built into multiple locations over decades. The speed of selling the house and furnishings astonished naysaying neighbors. He joined a gym and lost the thirty pounds plaguing him for the previous ten years. I envied his new outlook on life. Neither of us mentioned the details that led up to his heart attack, as if it were an unspoken curse. *Did he remember?* Guilt swept over me like a tidal wave. I would do anything to keep him happy and focused on the present instead of immortalizing her and the past.

As I inventoried the rest of our art, my deceased mother's favorite oil painting came next. I tensed with the memory it elicited. It was the last thing I saw before I crashed against the brooms in the dusty closet. Though wriggling out of the rope knotted around my eight-year-old wrists and ankles had proved insurmountable inside that dark space, I secretly swore against the prediction of my useless existence Daddy had spat through the locked door. "One. Two. Three." I whispered the count as a distraction and wished hard for Mommy to come home and save me.

The faint scar on my wrist and the recollection of that petrifying afternoon heightened my resolve of the present to just go with the flow and support the drastic changes in our lives. Seeing to my husband's every need and having raised two idyllic children of my own served as proof that I was, after all, "worth more than dog shit."

****

"Sandy, wake up."

A firm hand shook my shoulder. I raised one eyelid. Elam towered over my side of the bed, his salt and pepper curls wound in all directions.

"I found the perfect place."

THE DECEPTOR'S CALL

"You did wha...?" I scratched my head and wiped the drool from the corner of my mouth.

"Get up." He tugged on my arm. "There's still a lot of work to do to finish emptying this place out."

"What time is it?" Slumber lingered in my slurred speech. I yawned and finger-combed my tousled hair as I slid off the edge of the bed and stretched.

"Early." He dragged me by the hand to our reading room. After donating our vast book collection to the public library, the ceiling-high bookshelves appeared barren as a skeleton. He stopped in front of our boxed glass globe, removed it and peeled away the packing paper. He pointed to a spot. "That's where we're going. Palm Isle. Right in the middle of the Caribbean. One-way tickets were a steal."

I rubbed my heavy lids in an attempt to clear the sleep fog and buy myself some time to put everything together. "Never heard of Palm Isle." I leaned close to the globe and squinted. "There's nothing there." I straightened and cocked my head to one side. "Wait a minute." Strange tingling in the air snapped me fully awake. "You seriously changed everything? Without even asking my opinion?"

"I didn't want to wake you." He flipped his hand away nonchalantly, as if it was to be expected that I would fall into line. "Plus, there's not much information about it online."

I hiked my brows incredulously. "We've been married for more than thirty years and have always worked as a team." I gestured toward the glass Earth. "What the hell, Elam? St. Thomas has everything we need."

My chest tightened. "You made a unilateral decision that changes our entire life without even consulting me. That's a little unfair, don't you think?"

"Everyone we know owns a St. Thomas T-shirt." He set his shoulders back. "Since we've never been to the islands, I want to go somewhere different from the usual tourist destinations. Somewhere off the beaten path." He pointed back to the vast aqua-blue area comprised of a ring of Caribbean islands. "Trust me."

"The fact that it's not on the map is one thing," I said. "If you found limited information about the place, that means there's probably not much there. Seriously, Elam. What if your heart acts up again?"

"My health is fine." He stalked to the door. "This trip means everything to me." He shot a reddened scowl my way. "You've never been excited about embarking on this new chapter of our lives. I can't get there fast enough." Elam huffed then stormed off.

"This isn't like you." I tramped to meet him in the half-emptied kitchen. "What were you thinking?"

He whirled around to face me, nostrils flared. "I was thinking how sick and tired I am of your whiny complaints."

"Elam?" Tension pinched between my shoulder blades. "Are you feeling okay?" I touched his cheek and softened my voice. "You're the sweetest man I've ever known. But this morning you seem…different."

"Excuse me if I know what I want and am willing to go after it." He flattened his lips.

I dropped my hand by my side. "Honey, think about it. Everything was booked; the flight to St. Thomas, the deposit on the rental house. I'd finally become more comfortable with the idea of selling the business and uprooting our lives because you asked me to go. You said, 'Sandy, let's see where life takes us.' It all takes some getting used to, Elam. We've raised our family in this house. Now this sudden change of plans makes me feel like I've had the rug yanked out from under me."

A plump vein pulsed near his left temple.

"Not to mention, no home to come back to." I searched his eyes. "Can't you see? It's like you've turned into someone else."

THE DECEPTOR'S CALL

He rounded his shoulders in a defensive gesture. "Does Palm Isle have safe drinking water? Good medical facilities? I'm terrified something might happen. I need to know you'll be safe. Remember, I almost lost you that day." I curled my lips into a well-practiced smile and smoothed my tone, desperately trying to get to the bottom of what precipitated this last minute change of plans. "But, of course, I'd follow you anywhere."

Elam bent over a half-packed box. He grasped an item and ripped off the beige packing paper and let it sift to the ground. He raised my favorite coffee cup over his head.

I shook my head. "Elam, just hold on." I reached up and placed my palms on his chest. "Calm down sweetheart. What's happening to you?"

The muscles of his chiseled jawline ticked, a line creased across his forehead. The cup careened to the unforgiving floor.

I gaped at the pieces scattered near my bare feet, then back to the hardened face of a man I did not recognize. He gripped my shoulders. "This island speaks to me, Sandy. Like none of the others." He lowered his face closer. "Got it?"

I recoiled from him and his sour morning breath. The old house creaked as if uncomfortable with his behavior. "I'm sorry, honey," I whispered. "I just want this to be perfect for you."

He released me, the tight line in his jaw relaxed. "Oh my god." He stared into his palms. "I don't know what came over me."

"I'm worried about you, Elam." I managed a half-smile, my heart still slamming in my chest. "The empty nester thing is probably getting to both of us. Things are happening so fast." I ticked off each point on the fingers of one hand. "The business sold in no time, the house is about to close, everything has been organized for the storage unit, dropping Shauna off at her dorm, selling our car before we leave. It's a lot to come to terms with, the complete overhaul of everything we've ever known."

The corners of his lips lifted into the tender smile of the man I married. "Understandable. But we'll be fine. This is about exploration." He kissed the crown of my head. "I have to get the last of my tools ready. A guy's coming in a few minutes to buy them. Don't worry so much." He winked at me. "After all, the world is our oyster shell. What could possibly go wrong?"

He headed to the garage then leaned back inside. "I've worked hard for this freedom, Sandy. And just so we're straight, I'm going to Palm Isle." He narrowed his eyes. "With, or without you."

I stamped my foot. "Elam, what is going on with you? It's like I'm dealing with a stranger."

As if I hadn't spoken, he disappeared into the garage.

With steaming anger and trembling hands, I grabbed the broom. As men's voices penetrated the wall, glass shards clinked against the dustpan.

Reflecting back on that day and the dark changes in my husband, I possessed no power to refuse the trip and break my promise to make him happy. Within a few weeks the obscure island would unveil its incomprehensible depth of vengeance.

****

The metal landing gear groaned and the jet's rubber wheels lowered as we made our descent. The 737 touched down on the mainland, and we bumped on the tarmac. Condensation from the mix of humidity outside and the air conditioning blew in through the cabin air vents like white party favors. The plane taxied along a narrow strip on a peninsula stretched out into the Caribbean Sea. We pulled to a stop by the squat airport terminal. Sun glinted off the tin roof.

The corners of Elam's eyes crinkled as he leaned across me to my window seat and stared at the expanse of the calm, blue sea. "Travel book pictures don't touch the real thing." His same wide-eyed wonderment had captured my heart thirty-two years before.

THE DECEPTOR'S CALL

"We made it, Elam. I'm the luckiest woman in the world." I slipped my hand into his. "After everything, we made it." He relaxed back into the seat. His gentle squeeze of my hand reassured me that everything was going to be just fine.

Twenty minutes later, we deplaned and found the baggage claim area. After picking our way through backpacks and suitcases heaped on a large wooden table, we made our way toward the exit and a gentleman with long dark dreadlocks. His hand-held cardboard sign said *Elam Steele* in black marker. He flashed a broad pearly smile. "Welcome."

"Feel important, Sandy?" Elam laughed and shook the hand of the taxi driver. We followed him to the white sand parking lot. My humidity drenched hair stuck to the back of my neck. The driver's keys jangled as he pulled them from his pocket. We approached a subcompact new in the nineties. Rusted hinges grated like nails across a chalkboard as he opened the small trunk. Inside, a gray metal tank with a control gauge filled half the space, a connected black plastic hose extended from the gauge to beneath the back seats.

Elam flinched. "What's the tank for?"

"Butane." The driver's friendly smile failed to erase my unease. He reached for my backpack and placed it in front of the tank. "Cheaper than petrol." Spanish-Creole musically accented his English.

I searched my mind for a discrete way to retrieve my bag in case the tank blew up.

He tossed Elam's larger backpack on top, stuffed the edges down tight into the last remaining space, and slammed the trunk shut. He walked to the passenger side door and held it open. Elam and I shared a concerned glance as I crouched into the tight space. Elam's lean six-foot-two frame folded in beside me, his legs bunched up at an odd angle. He winced and rubbed the knee afflicted by an old college basketball injury.

The driver settled in. After four tries, the ignition whined to a start. Reggae music blasted from the radio. Quickly lowering it to a conversational volume, he hummed the lyrics. We bounced and scraped along a highway obstacle course of deep potholes and unpainted speed bumps.

"First visit?" the driver asked conversationally.

Elam leaned forward in his cramped position and placed his hand on the top of the front seat. "It is," said Elam. "And happy we finally made it. We're here indefinitely. Maybe forever."

Despite my private, nagging apprehension, I smiled to myself at his boyish enthusiasm and our new season of life. Lush jungle wilderness and patterned citrus and banana orchards rushed past my window. Soft green mountains peaked in the distance.

"Where are you staying, Friends?"

"Palm Isle. We've rented a great cottage."

"Palm Isle," the driver repeated, as if to himself. "Never heard of it."

I leaned forward as Elam relaxed back. "You've never heard of Palm Isle? Are you from here?"

"I've lived here my whole life."

I pursed my lips and raised my brows at Elam. He shrugged.

"But there are many islands. I'm sure you will have a good time. But I must warn you." He chuckled as if to himself. "Some find life is better here and never leave. The islands can be enchanting."

Settling back into my seat, I decided the driver's knowledge of Palm Isle was not required. I laid my head against Elam's shoulder and took in the view as we sped on.

Exposed rebar, from unroofed, random structures on our way, stretched to the heavens like bent, arthritic limbs. "What's up with all the unfinished buildings?" Elam asked.

"Owners build as they earn money. Sometimes, one brick at a time."

THE DECEPTOR'S CALL

An hour later, we entered the bustling capital city of scarred concrete buildings marred by the fury of past hurricanes. The scenery was a stark contrast to our Midwestern neighborhood of manicured lawns, tree-lined streets, and all the trappings of first world excess we'd left behind. Sticky, sewage-tinged air entered the car as I cranked down the window.

Elam's head and neck bent unnaturally against the roof. He caught my stare. "It's all an adventure, right?"

"Right. It's going to be fun." I forced a smile as heat sparked deep inside my belly. "I can't wait to get to the island and see our rental." Sweat trickled off me as I flicked my shirt front for cool relief.

He lightly pecked my moist cheek. "We're in this together."

"Always, Elam."

****

Delivered in front of a worn water taxi terminal building, Elam hoisted his backpack and stepped away from the trunk. "This place is incredible." He scanned the area.

I reached for my pack. The driver held his grip on the strap far too long, resulting in what seemed like a tug of war. Elam's voice and the parking lot faded into the background as my head went fuzzy. The space around us compressed into a void I shared with only the driver. He tipped his head in a straight-faced nod of knowing.

He narrowed his dark eyes at me. "Some islands choose."

A chill coursed through my fingers then traveled up my arm.

"Enjoy your stay."

Elam's voice returned. "Don't you think so, Sandy?"

The man released the bag. I slung it over my shoulders and huddled close to my husband who'd been unaware of the exchange.

"I'm sorry," I said. "I didn't hear you. My mind was somewhere else."

Elam fumbled through his wallet and paid the fare. Tires spun in the sand. A blast of exhaust and dust billowed in the car's wake.

"Ready?" he asked. "On to the last leg of the trip."

"Ready, babe." I marched in step and let the strange encounter go.

The water taxi terminal buzzed in an alphabet soup of mixed foreign languages. Doors and windows opened to the breeze, passengers drooped under the burden of luggage, faces slick with humidity. People of diverse ethnic backgrounds and ages slogged in all directions, some collapsed onto plastic chairs, in anticipation of the overwater journey. Food and excursion vendors materialized in competition to win our business with the best deal.

Elam checked us in while I chose the last open seats. I scanned the crowd and caught sight of a young woman's head to toe examination of my oblivious husband at the counter. She stood next to her rolling suitcase with a death grip on the handle. Her red shock of hair conjured a flood of memories and the face in the photos I burned a year earlier sprang to mind. The old rush of ripe jealousy returned. My impulsive reaction to the pictures had proven almost as detrimental thirty-two years before, the day of my first and final face-off with the girl. I twisted the gold band seated firmly at the base of my left ring finger.

I exhaled and averted my gaze from the stranger back to Elam. *Forget the past.*

Beyond the open windows, docked motor and commercial sailing vessels dressed in brightly colored canvases crammed the dock. Elam plopped down beside me and handed over the tickets and a cold bottle of beer, an open one in his hand.

"Ah. Just what I needed." I rubbed the icy glass against the side of my overheated neck. "Where'd you get these?"

"I bought them from a redhead selling them over by the counter."

THE DECEPTOR'S CALL

I glanced back to the empty space where I'd spied Elam's admirer. "There's no one there."

"Dunno." He gulped deep from the bottle as he scanned the spot.

"Elam, I saw a redhead over there earlier. She was holding onto a suitcase."

"Then we're not talking about the same girl. I think your hormones are kicking in again."

I tried plastering on a brave grin to spite my churning insides.

A man in pineapple patterned shorts and a deep tan grabbed the seat across from us. His sun-bleached braid snaked down the back of his black tank top. The neck of his scuffed guitar in one hand, he saluted Elam then swung the instrument to his lap and softly strummed a tune.

"I want to be THAT guy," Elam said under his breath then sipped from his bottle.

Grating scratches broke through a loudspeaker. "Palm Isle passengers. Please make your way to the exit."

Unnoticed by Elam, I placed my unopened beer in a garbage receptacle on my way out.

Swept up in the throng, we pressed through the widened door and out to the dock. The engine idled as I stepped across the gangplank and onto the fiberglass interior of the water taxi. We selected two seats by an open window. The sun cast a shadow of our boat through the clear water onto the sandy sea bottom.

Bodies squeezed in around us. I practically wilted in the unrelenting hot, wet air. *This is it. This is really happening.* Exposing my jog bra, I sopped perspiration from my forehead with the bottom of my tank top.

Elam leaned over and surprised me with a light kiss on the cheek. "Welcome to the tropics, Sandy."

BARBARA MICHELLE

My breath caught at his grin as he brushed strands of sweat plastered hair out of my face. God, I loved him.

After we packed in like sardines, the door slammed shut. Bronzed tones of the indigenous passengers glowed healthy and vibrant. I placed my palms flat on my thighs to partially mask my washed out, pale skin and felt homely amongst their exotic beauty.

Beyond the window, the topaz surface danced with a zillion white diamonds brought to life by the sun as it beat down. The sea opened wide and the bow angled upward as the engine roared to top speed. The hull slammed down onto the rolls of water with bone jarring speed. Tiny, scattered, uninhabited islands covered in soft needled pines and twisty palm trees edging their narrow white sand beaches spread as far as I could see. Like fine art pieces, the islands surrounded us in all directions. I was reminded of the Caribbean Islands calendar left magnetically suspended on the refrigerator of our sold house.

All the planning and effort coming to fruition, it was time to let go of my anxiety and enjoy the journey. The kids had their own lives. No house or car to worry about. No turning back. Untethered freedom finally took root in my heart. Elam was right. The possibilities were infinite. Ignoring the past, our unblemished future gleamed ahead. A sliver of hope wedged its way forward; we might find a sense of quietude. I smiled to myself. *Island mysteries lie in wait for Elam and Sandy Steele.*

CHAPTER THREE

Forty-five minutes later, a large island came into view. The bow lowered to the surface as the engine slowed to idle. Coconut tree trunks curled over the water, the fallen fruit bobbled on the surface below. The taxi rumbled to the concrete dock. Flamboyant colored sailboats lazed close to shore. Shirtless men, uniformed in shorts and leather sandals, caught ropes tossed from our boat and tied them on metal dock cleats. After the exit door was unlocked, our mob shuffled out single file across the gangplank.

I accepted an offered hand by an employee with long dreads and reached my foot to step off the gangplank. Chatter waned around us.

His soulful honey-colored eyes oozed calm and secret wisdom beyond my reach. He nodded at me as if he shared the same knowing as the airport taxi driver. He delivered his message without parting his closed lips. His smooth, deep voice rolled in my ears as a sensation. "Welcome to paradise, Sandy Steele."

My sweaty skin cooled at the nape of my neck. "How?" My words echoed in our space vacuum. "How do you know my name?"

He released my hand and assisted the next person in line. Surrounding conversations resumed. Fear ghosted over my body.

I have to be experiencing jet lag. Shaking it off, I inhaled a deep breath and planted my sandaled feet onto the tropical land of Palm Isle. Hints of spicy nutmeg and cinnamon mixed in the tangy salt air steered my focus back to my surroundings.

Snowy seagulls squawked above the buzz of activity. "Whoa," Elam said as he hopped one pace over, nearly knocking me off my feet. Six bicyclers whizzed by, their tiny bells jingling. The swirl of air created by the group brushed my skin. Waxy palm fronds rustled high above in the breeze.

"Just look at this place," he said. "It's like we've stepped into another world."

"I'm sure we have," I said under my breath. An artist's palette of red, purple, and yellow blooms bejeweled the area like tropical garland. Wood and concrete buildings washed in pastels rested on high stilts among the natural beauty. Clammy hands entwined, we marveled at a world unique in imperfect charm. Palm Isle was completely foreign to anything I'd ever known.

****

Studying Elam's hand-written directions to our rental, we decided on the easy way and hailed a cab shooting by at top golf cart speed. The driver, long dreads flying, spotted us and slammed on the brakes. The cart skidded to a stop.

"Welcome to the island." He helped us load our backpacks onto the seats. We settled into the second-row bench, my hand on Elam's meaty thigh. The driver hopped back in and wheeled us away with a jerk.

"Where are you staying?" he asked. His cart rolled closer to our destination.

"1 Conch, please." Recaptured giddiness inside, I grinned at my husband.

He flicked the tip of my chin with a light touch. I grasped his finger and kissed it.

"Our rental is supposed to be out of the village," Elam said.

The driver stopped the cart abruptly, the momentum lurching us forward.

"Jeez," I yelled and leaned back to the seat cushion.

He turned and faced us. "Old Camilla's place?"

"Not sure about the owner," said Elam. "It's supposed to be a little blue house."

The guy hopped out, a grimace crossing his face. He darted to the back of his cart. "Sorry." He removed our backpacks at the same time. "I cannot help you."

THE DECEPTOR'S CALL

"What?" Elam asked. "I don't understand."

"I do not drive there. Out of my range."

Dazed, we climbed off the cart and caught the bags shoved at us. He sped away, the tires spraying a cloud of sand.

"What in the world was that all about?" I asked.

Elam shrugged. "No clue. I guess we'll have to figure this out ourselves, after all." He grinned down at me. "Feeling important now?" He patted me lightly on my bottom and walked on with a snicker.

After all the years together, my nerve endings still tingled with his teasing caresses.

The directions for our rental cottage led us in a wild, unruly maze of colored concrete houses and wooden cabanas. Sea breeze teased the curtains in the glassless windows.

Spray painted boards nailed above entrance doors designated the names of businesses and restaurants; hardware and printing supply stores, a beauty shop, eclectic local art galleries. "Hey, there's a doctor's office and a pharmacy," I said, more relieved than I let on about spotting these.

"I told you we'd be fine here."

An island melody from steel drums drifted out from a cabana window. Feathery flowers plumed like pom-poms from towering tree branches. People rambled over the patterned streets in sandals or bare feet. Triple-benched golf carts loaded with sweaty tourists of various ethnic backgrounds whirred by like a swarm of bumblebees. Customers sipped umbrella drinks under the shade of grass-roofed palapa bars. Exuberant school children in khaki and blue uniforms filed after their teacher like a precious line of baby chicks.

"Thank you, Elam." I clasped his hand.

"For what?" He let go of my hand and placed his arm around my shoulders.

"For wanting me to share this experience with you. For being crazy enough to talk me into it and then making it happen."

He kissed my forehead. "I'm already seeing the world differently. Chasing material goals day in and day out didn't make me happy. I feel like I'm really living now."

"And we've barely started."

"Wow. Check that out."

I adjusted my sunglasses and followed the direction of his pointed finger. "Stunning."

The street's arc followed the natural curve of the island and opened to a tiny harbor, its channel formed between a short beach on the point on one side and a small island at the opposite side. Sleek sailboats slipped by, others bobbed at their moorings a short distance out. Sailors and villagers milled about conversing with one another.

Blood dripping from their gutting knives, leather-faced fishermen sold their bounty from inside fiberglass boats beached on the sand. Patrons with cash in hand surrounded them at boat-side and selected fresh snapper, conch, and gigantic spider crabs.

I glimpsed a grounded trawler in the harbor's center. The rusted captain's bridge protruded twenty feet above the water at a sharp angle to its starboard side, its keel stuck in the harbor floor. No one had bothered to dismantle and remove the eyesore. Activity crooned a stone's throw away from the corroded vessel, avoided and forgotten.

Raucous cries drew my attention upward. Several brownish-black birds of prey circled high above the sunken boat; their long, pointy wings spread wide, beaks stretched into hooked tips. Vampires in flight came to mind.

Pillowy clouds suddenly turned gray and roiled until they blocked the sun. Unsettling gloom replaced my awe. The peaceful harbor breeze strengthened to a strong wind. My hair slapped my

THE DECEPTOR'S CALL

cheeks. Taut ropes banged against tall masts to a deafening decibel, while the wails of a baby filled the air, growing louder and louder.

I covered my ears with my hands against the woeful transformation. The taste of metal tingled on my tongue. Chills raced through my overheated body. My teeth chattered.

A distinct inner tug on my bones and joints caused me to stumble. The stench of organic detritus and wet earth stung my nostrils. I flung my arms out to the sides and righted myself. The ground beneath me appeared undisturbed. I dragged my feet a step away from the spot. My lungs tightened. Stronger than gravity, the pulling sensation remained as if the ground intended to swallow me whole. At the brink of my crushing implosion, the pull disappeared.

What just happened?

An abrupt parting of the angry clouds released the wash of sun on the colorful harbor. The anxious ropes ceased their clangs. The metallic taste vanished. Peace was restored.

"What the heck was that?" I asked between heavy breaths.

"What was what?" Elam's curls remained unfazed. Bantering nearby continued uninterrupted.

"That change in the...air." I removed my shades and shielded my face from the glare off the water to get a true view of the area. Unobtrusive puffy clouds hung in the sky.

"What are you talking about?" He looked around, taking stock of our surroundings.

Strangers moved about seemingly unfazed.

The atmospheric change and Earth's gravitational pull had lasted only a moment. Seconds, maybe.

"Nothing." I pushed strands of hair from my face. "Jet-lag, I suppose."

CHAPTER FOUR

Unrelenting heat dampened our quest for the rental cottage. We left the energetic village for the remote forested side of the island. The lack of dependable street signs made our way an arduous task. As if they'd been forgotten, houses and inns appeared more bedraggled with each turn we made. The more distance we covered, the more my discouragement grew.

Elam pointed out street signs nailed haphazardly into the corners of the few wooden shacks. "Who would have guessed?" One bent metal sign hung from a single nail in the trunk of a tall tree, its coconuts scattered, their thick furry shells matted with dirt and sand. We passed no one on the jungle-lined road. Certain we must have unwittingly embarked on an unending trek, I considered the possibility our plane had landed in the wrong country.

Twenty stifling minutes later, sweat dripped under my backpack. Perspiration formed unattractive designs on my tank top and cotton shorts. The sun burned my scalp.

"I hope we find it soon." I wiped my forehead. "This humidity is killing me." *Is Elam's dream trip too good to be true?*

"We should be getting closer." Elam marched ahead, always the optimist. "This has to be the right way."

"How can you tell?" Creeping plants thickened the woodland. "Aren't we supposed to be beachfront? We seem to be heading farther away from the water."

He virtually bounced in front of me. "The picture from the owner's email showed the sea by a blue cottage."

I questioned his limitless energy.

"The road must curve back toward the water," he said.

Whispers emanated from deep inside the overgrowth surrounding us on both sides. I scanned the trees lining the sand road. "That's weird."

THE DECEPTOR'S CALL

"What's weird?"

"That sound. Don't you hear it?" I motioned toward the overgrown foliage. "It sounds like people whispering in the trees?"

He stilled and cocked his head. "I don't hear anything except the birds." He bounded ahead of me on his quest to find our place. "You're imagining things."

The whispers vanished. "The humidity must be really getting to me." I plodded on. My shoulder muscles ached under the weight of my backpack.

Around a curve of yet another corner, we found a rough plywood shack propped up on stilts embedded in the bit of yard. A gray-haired woman stared down at us from the front porch chair.

I raised my hand. "Hello."

The rickety chair squeaked as her hefty frame worked to stand. She shuffled down to meet us at the edge of her yard. "Hello." Swollen bags hung beneath watery, cataract-clouded eyes. Her wrinkled, tanned cheeks rounded above a pleasant, toothy smile.

"Good afternoon," she said in perfect English. "You are the Steele's?"

"Yes, we are. I'm Elam," He opened his hand toward me, "and this is my wife, Sandy."

"I'm Camilla. I'm the landlord of your rental cabana."

"Excuse me." The high humidity affected me more than I thought. "You *own* the rental?"

"Yes." Her wave beckoned us. "Come." She wobbled between us. "You're late."

We gaped at her back. The faded flowers of her dress accentuated a warped spine.

Elam raced to catch up. "I apologize. Our water taxi left the mainland a few minutes behind schedule."

Dehydrated, I fell in line. My mood improved knowing we were almost there.

BARBARA MICHELLE

Camilla walked another fifteen yards of the rural road and took a right-hand corner. She swept her arm wide like a geriatric showcase model. "For you." Her creased face beamed. "*Paraiso.*"

Tucked deep in a break of waxy-leafed mangrove trees, loomed our temporary home. The ramshackle cottage defied gravity with ill-fitted and warped blue painted plywood topped by a peaked, rusted metal roof. Slightly tilted, the little house rested on eight-foot, timeworn stilts of knotty tree trunks stabbed into the ground. The bases, covered by stagnant water, pooled in the yard. A wooden staircase led up to a tired porch. A square, fabric-covered window flanked the screened front door.

I swatted the swarm of mosquitos. Flat stone surfaces rose above the standing water forming a dry walkway from the bottom porch step out to the sandy road. Twists of mangrove tree roots gripped deep in the boggy ground.

Ripples disturbed the still water between the stilts from the back. A tremendous, mud-covered, black mutt, part pit bull, waded out on his four large mitts. It sauntered its bulk up the steps to the porch with an air of ownership. I scrunched my nose and lips at the swing of unneutered canine genitalia. The dog circled several times beneath the window frame and thudded into a heap.

"That's Frank." Camilla said. "Feed him. Keep fresh water out for him."

A *condemned* sign belonged out front. The place had zero resemblance to the single obviously edited picture on the internet. I faked a cough to break Elam's indecipherable stare up at the rickety hovel. We needed to make eye contact. He didn't budge. I wanted to come up with an excuse and gently refuse the rental without causing the poor woman insult. *Look at me, dammit.* I glared pointedly at the side of his face.

THE DECEPTOR'S CALL

He smiled to her. "Thank you, Camilla." Accepting the key from her knotty knuckled, outstretched hand, he said, "I'm sure we'll be quite comfortable here." He hurried over the stepping stones.

"Elam," I said, louder than intended. He and Camilla stopped and stared back at me. Frank raised his head from the porch, ears perked. I cleared my throat as a second signal to Elam that we needed to talk privately.

He finally faced me. "What?"

I shot eye-daggers to him.

He scrunched his upper lip and nose and tilted his head. "What?"

Mortified, I puffed air through my gritted smile. He shook his head as if I were crazy and gazed back to *Paraiso*.

"It's open and ready for you." The old woman cast me a shadowed glance as she left. "Enjoy."

I dropped my feigned smile. Unsure if the new taste in my mouth was cold metal, I worked my tongue to clear it.

Camilla tottered away around the treed corner in the direction of her house.

"Let's get a look at these sweet island digs." He gingerly placed his feet over the stones.

"Seriously, Elam?"

"Seriously, what?" He didn't slow his steps.

"We can't stay here."

"Why not?" The staircase shimmied under his sandaled steps until he reached the top. The dog stretched his hideous head up to Elam's hand.

I called louder. "Elam. This is, obviously. Not. What we had in mind. I can't believe you'd agree to this."

"Don't be such a snob. This place is great." The door hinges creaked as he opened it. "We're expanding our horizons, remember?" He disappeared inside.

Drenched in sweat, I tried to control the emotions welling inside me. Arguments were the last thing I wanted. And the last thing he needed. Back and shoulders fatigued, I flounced across the stones and up the stairs to join him.

On the porch, Frank's menacing, deep-throated growl startled me. As I made for the door, the dirty black beast hit me with a dog scowl. Instinct drew my hand back from the door handle to my chest. My heart somersaulted. I inched two paces back. The growl exploded to a toe-curling bark. I jumped, ready to dash back to the road. The bark lowered to a low rumble. He extended his neck until the oversized dome was near me.

"He wants attention."

I jerked my head in the direction of the old woman, alarmed by her stealthy reappearance at the woodland edge.

"You must show respect."

Appalled at being stalked and her lack of concern for my safety, I opened my mouth to respond to her with my scathing retort. Under her baleful stare, I instead opted to touch Frank's broad crown with the tip of one finger. The growling stopped. He lowered his head between sprawled paws. Dominance established.

"The island has been waiting for you , Sandy."

"Excuse me?" I glanced up to see if Elam had reappeared on the deck.

"The island knows." Camilla did not wait for my response. She left for her cottage a second time. My fingers trembled as I wiped off a spot of Frank's mud on my shorts.

I crept over the threshold of *Paraiso*. The sharp contrast of outside light to the dim interior left me blinded. "Elam, you have to listen to me." I planned to touch nothing for fear of what diseases lurked inside. My vision adjusted and cleared. I drew in a gasp.

THE DECEPTOR'S CALL

Paraiso's interior bloomed like spring flowers. Lace sheers fluttered over the front and back windows. A ceiling fan spun lazily overhead.

"Lovely," I murmured.

Mahogany ceiling beams and terra cotta tiles held it all together. Shelves of a side-wall cabinet bowed from dog-eared paperbacks crammed and stuffed to fit. Oil seascape paintings and framed dried flora dressed the walls. Peace reigned by the tick of an antique clock suspended on the back wall. The living area opened to a tiny kitchen with a bistro-style table and two chairs. My original opinion of Paraiso's outside character as tossed and worn changed to warm and quaint.

I drew my attention from the scarred trunk used as a coffee table to Elam outside the back wall picture window. He leaned on the railing and faced the clear blue sea.

I shrugged out of my backpack, dropped it next to his by the front door, and went out to the back porch. Approaching him from behind, I snuggled into the crook of his arm and slid my hand around his waist, pulling him close.

Mangroves framed the backyard sloping to a private beach. Tiny waves lapped on the sand. Shade dappled the yard and water's edge between coconut and seagrape trees. A picnic table rested near a hammock strung between trees.

"This is unbelievable," I whispered. "Paraiso is the perfect name. It's so beautiful and cozy. I would never have believed it with the haggard-looking front. I read somewhere that green coconuts were actually the babies. They make the yard look polka dotted."

"There's one floating in the water over there. This place has everything."

Paddles lay beside a pair of upended kayaks. A pair of old bicycles propped against a tree trunk, their rusted chains draping on the ground.

He stepped back from the railing. "Come on. Let's check out the bedroom." He wiggled his brows playfully.

Back through the kitchen, he veered right to enter the only bedroom. I gripped his hand in mine as I followed. The Caribbean shimmered through gauzy curtains over the picture window.

"The air is intoxicating," I said.

"So is that king-sized bed." He wrapped me in his arms and my lips pressed hard into his. Elam planted seductive kisses on my neck. Stiffness melted from my shoulders. All concerns and travel stress seeped from my body and out to the horizon. Within seconds, the white bedcover and our sweaty clothes lay in a bundle on the floor. Passion flowed in our private slice of rented heaven.

****

An hour later I dressed in clean clothes from my backpack and left Elam to his nap on the bed.

After locating pen and paper in a drawer, I rummaged through the kitchen and jotted down necessary items to purchase at the open-air markets in the village. The list completed, I sent a text, encouraging Shauna with her freshman university courses and Ed who worked on an article in San Francisco. Ed enjoyed the fast pace and travel as an independent journalist, the sense of wanderlust he shared with his dad.

Heart pangs hit me with thoughts of Shauna. The memory of her brave smile as she stood in front the red door of her dormitory as we drove away drifted into the forefront of my mind and brought a tear to my eye. I hoped her first days as a university freshman were going well. I had wanted Elam to turn the car around so I could give her one last hug before setting off on our crazy escapade, but I stopped myself. The agony would have only been prolonged for us both. No amount of mental preparation erased the emotional turmoil I faced when my kids left the nest, but we knew they were both ready.

THE DECEPTOR'S CALL

I headed outside to investigate more of the seaside back yard. Warm, crystal water lapped over my bare feet. I perched on a palm trunk bent like a seat over the beach before reaching skyward. A stingray jumped above the surface several yards out, its angular wings tipped up and stinger pointed downward before splashing back into the deep. I tipped my head back. Salt air filled my lungs. "Mm." I leaned down and inhaled the sweet fragrance of a white jasmine bloom.

The touch of something warm and moist on my leg ruined the moment. Frank waited at my feet, his black eyes zeroing in on mine. I snatched my hands up to my chest, away from the repulsive animal, a stain among the natural beauty. His top lip retracted to display pointed incisors accompanied by the low snarl.

"What in the world do you want, you filthy brute?" I jumped up and side-stepped the cloud of dust he shook at me. "I don't speak dog." His powerful frame, and the growl, matched my steps. I knew little about dogs, but his aggressive behavior frightened me enough to reach down with my fingers to barely touch his dirty head. I recoiled my hand.

The lip lowered and the growl ended with another rub of his head against my bare thigh. "Ugh. Stop that." Done with me, he climbed the steps to the deck, his bones thudded as he sprawled into a mass by the chair. He licked his lips then yawned, unashamed of his vileness.

I returned to my seat on the palm trunk and the view rerouted itself in my soul.

"Thought I'd find you out here."

I wrenched my head up, embarrassed at being caught in a private moment. "Sorry. It's just so great out here."

Elam, hair mussed, leaned on the railing. "You'd make a great picture right now."

"How was your nap?"

"Refreshing." Admiration in his gaze, he left the deck and joined me beneath the tree. He took my hands, pulled me to stand in front of him, and lifted my chin with his finger. "You'll see this is the best thing we've ever done. For the first time, we're doing something just for us. Our lives are forever changed, Sandy."

The rest of our afternoon and evening involved books and drinks in the outside hammocks. I checked myself. Elam's zeal to live out a dream, to make a major life change of true unleashed freedom was infectious. We'd worked hard for this day. He'd endured so much. This had truly happened for us. And Elam was still with me, happy and healthy.

****

The cottage had been stocked with provisions and a few homemade items wrapped carefully inside a small basket with a note attached. *Welcome. Camilla.*

"It was thoughtful of her to leave this for us," he said. "There's something special about her."

"Maybe she reminds you of your grandmother. She's obviously mastered the way to a man's heart, through his stomach."

We picnicked from Camilla's basket of homemade bread and butter, mangoes and papayas so fresh the juice ran down my chin at the first bite, locally made cheeses, and homemade wine. Satiated and happy, we retired to bed with a plan for exploration and discovery of island fun the next day.

But the old woman's dark glare haunted my dreams.

CHAPTER FIVE

My disturbing dream of a baby's cry ended when I opened my eyes. The sheers quivered over the open window, the salt air sticky. Relentless mewls from a kitten streamed into the bedroom. I slipped out of Elam's slumberous embrace and eased off the mattress. A thrill passed over me as I dressed and took in our view. I discovered the baby's cry in my dream was the song of an island bird perched on a nearby branch, making the sound of the kitten mewls.

Coffee dripped fragrantly into the carafe while I puttered in the kitchen. A full mug in my hand, I eased the squeaky door closed and settled onto a deck chair. The first heavenly sip of caffeine and calming motion of the Caribbean produced an all-healing power. My whole body savored the moment, opposing my original repugnance to the cottage. "This is magical," I said to no one.

A low rumble by the chair roused me. "Leave, Dog," I said. Frank's massive head tilted toward me. "You're going to wake Elam." He stared me down in stubborn insistence. "Unbelievable." I touched the tip of my pinky finger to the bony top of his head then withdrew my hand. His long black tongue extended over an unending row of razor-sharp teeth. The slimy tongue swiped from my exposed elbow to my shoulder. "Get away from me," I said. Frank set back on his haunches. "Ugh." I wiped off his spittle.

He dropped on my feet. I wanted a bath.

I stared at the dog and contemplated a way to get rid of him. The precious new healing of my marriage did not need to involve Frank and his dirty aura. His removal from the property leaped up on my priority list. I planned to inform Camilla the animal was an unwanted companion.

"Hello?" A sugary-sweet voice drifted through the cottage. "Hello?"

BARBARA MICHELLE

Head cradled on his front paws, the dog closed his eyes. Struck by Frank's lack of response to the visitor, I pulled my feet out from under his mass of dead-weight.

A copper-skinned woman directed a warm, grandmotherly smile at me through the front door screen. "Good morning," she said as I approached. A large metal pail balanced on the top of her scarf-wrapped head, her arms dangling by her sides.

"Good morning." I half whispered, "My husband is still sleeping." I returned her smile. She lowered the pail from her head. The aroma of warm cinnamon and sugar wafted my way.

With a knotted finger, she pulled the kitchen towel back and showcased perfect rows of browned homemade donuts. "One dollar," she said in the singsong lilt. Her left eyelid drooped. "Made fresh this morning."

The purpose of the woman's visit tugged at my heart. "I'm sorry, I don't have any change."

Her smile fell halfway. She elevated her one droopy lid to match the other in a flattened brow of disapproval.

"I'm sorry." I shrugged. "Maybe tomorrow?"

Her crooked finger slid the towel edge back over the donuts. She eased the pail back onto her scarfed head with a grunt. Without a parting word, she hitched her body around and bumped down the stairs, hands loose by her sides, she made her way on the stone path. Taking a sharp right turn halfway on the stone path, she waded through our watery side yard and stopped at the wall of mangroves and banana trees. With a sly glance back at me on the deck, the donut lady darted out of sight obscured by the wide leaves. The balanced pail never tipped from her head.

Why didn't she go to the road? Curious, I bounded down the stairs to the spot where she disappeared and pulled back the long leaves. A sandy path meandered between a split of gnarled mangrove roots. I followed the canopied path. A soft yellow glow expanded beyond the woman and her head cargo. Whispers emanated from the radiant area.

The donut lady walked out into a clearing in the light. Crouched and hidden by thickened bramble, I peered around the edge. A couple in their early twenties lounged at opposite sides of a picnic table. Their garb in bright orange and bulky shoulder pads was reminiscent of my college years, now appearing as Halloween costumes.

Goaded by the donut lady's quick peek at me as she approached the table, I could not turn away. She lowered the donut pail from her head, pulled back the towel, and offered its contents to the seated girl. A bird cried the eerie kitten mewls. I edged a step from my hideout and lurked closer.

The skin of the girl's youthful face bubbled. I blinked hard to clear my trickster vision. The skin of her forehead melted into creased lines between her brows. Her cheeks drooped to jowls as if pulled by gravity. Streaked, gray hair sneaked out from her roots like serpents. I gasped at her instant ancient appearance. The young man kept his youthful ruddiness.

The seated woman reached her knobby hand to the bottom of the pail. Light glinted from an item she cradled delicately. She inspected the mysterious object close to her face. A gold chain with a golden heart pendant slipped out between her fingers. I tried to recall why the pendant was familiar. My breath caught at the suspicious glower the donut lady sent my way.

Facing my way, the old woman clad in the eighties garb mouthed words. I hurriedly retreated into the vegetation. She turned her face from me and continued the whispery conversation with her male companion. A beat later, decayed breath entered my nostrils. Whispers tickled inside my ear as her voice swooshed inside my head. "You killed her unborn child." The woman's lip movement in her conversation with the young man did not match the words in my ear.

Her delayed message sent my mind reeling. The hair on my neck prickled. I dropped the leaves and withdrew farther into the shadows. I backed away and ran back down the path on rubbery knees.

Breathless and shaking, I reached the safety of Paraiso's back yard and slunk up the stairs to the cottage deck. Weariness set over me. I rubbed my eyes. I slid down into the deck chair and peeked back to the opening in the banana trees. No one was there. Frank stretched his head up and yawned long and loud. Laying my head back, I replayed the absurd scene in my head. My imagination had gone too far.

****

"You're up bright and early." Elam said through the screen. The door slammed back in its frame as he set his coffee cup on the unbalanced table. He stretched his age-defying body then took a seat.

"Good morning." I leaned over the table and touched his arm.

"Deep in thought?" His gaze traveled over the tropical scene before us.

"Yes. About everything and nothing."

He sipped his coffee thoughtfully. "Smell that fresh sea air. What a view first thing in the morning."

His pleasure and sweep of ocean to the horizon helped smooth my lingering unease from the pointless panic attack I'd experienced. "I don't believe there are accurate words to describe it," I said

"What do you want to do today?"

"Anything you want, my love. We can relax or explore as we'd discussed last night. Whatever your handsome heart desires." I left him to make breakfast of eggs and toast provided by Camilla.

THE DECEPTOR'S CALL

Breakfast finished and kitchen cleaned, we righted the kayaks in the yard and lugged them into the water before clambering in. Elam in the lead, we paddled a few yards out parallel to the shoreline. The simple act of working the paddle on each side and the peaceful serenity of the area helped soothe my tension like a form of meditation. I wanted to be nowhere else.

As we slipped by the seashore, we passed a tiny cabana lean-to of rusted sheet metal scraps and plywood set back in the tropical wilderness edge. Poles staked in the sand anchored a hidden clothesline sagging under the weight of draped sheets and towels swaying in the sea breeze. A dock, bowed in the center, poked out from the short beach.

Several women frolicked in the water in front of the cabana. Their jolly banter bounced over the surface. As we floated by, one of the women broke from the group. Her companions did not join her. "Go home," she yelled out to us. "You must go home." The other women remained crouched in the water and talked as if unaware of her shouts.

"Let's go," Elam said as if disturbed by her outburst. My breakfast grew heavy and unsettled in my stomach. We worked our paddles faster and redirected our kayaks toward home.

Out of sight from the swimmers, Elam slowed and waited for me to catch up. We floated side by side "Wonder why she would say that. I get the feeling we're going to learn a lot more about this world we live in. We've had no idea how different our lives have been."

"We're supposed to be enjoying this experience." I forced back the bad vibes.

"Agreed."

A school of silver fish jumped out of the water and soared five feet in the air, wing-like fins spread wide, then disappeared beneath the surface. My grip on the paddle loosened with the delightful surprise. It banged on the side edge of my kayak and fell out. I clutched the sides of my boat, the quick movement causing a half roll to the side. Elam grabbed the side and righted my kayak before it took on water. "Careful there," he teased. "Wouldn't want that hairdo to get wet."

He seized the paddle floating beside me.

"Sorry I'm so clumsy."

His playful grin tugged at my heart and reminded me of the night of our first official dinner date in college. As we neared the front door of the diner, the heel of my shoe wedged itself into a crack in the sidewalk. He caught my arm as I stumbled clumsily, the shoe remained in place. Elam wrenched the shoe out of its snare. "Stupid sidewalk," he said. "Shoes are overrated, anyway." Heat burned my cheeks as he watched me slip my foot inside it.

We paddled back and marveled at the abundant sea life moving beneath us. The perfect clarity of the water acted as a window into the world below. Schools of orange and black striped fish darted back and forth. Narrow baby blue trumpet fish glided close to the surface.

"This is amazing, Sandy." He pulled his paddle up, resting it in front of him across his kayak. "See that red starfish? The one clinging to the round purple coral there on the seabed?"

"Yes. I see it now."

"I bet I could discover something new here every day for the rest of my life and never see it all."

****

Back at our cabana, we scrambled out of the kayaks and pulled them back to the tree. Elam speared the paddles into the sand. We played like children in the outdoor shower then hopped along the walking stones across the wet yard to the street. I repeated a chorus of a song under my breath. Frank followed us to the yard's edge and tensed as we left the property. He made no attempt to follow us.

THE DECEPTOR'S CALL

We flirted like teenagers on the long meandering walk to the busy village. Elam lavished me with attentions that had been previously nonexistent for so long. Excited to simply be alive, a level of happiness I'd not believed possible filled me. The past was a distant memory.

I was touched by the warmth and vibrant culture of the local people as broad smiles and waves greeted us by passersby. Perpetual streams of golf carts carried tourists to and from the boat terminal in the village. Pedestrians ambled between rolling rusted bicycles. Flip-flops, bare feet, and bikini tops were in high fashion. The odd jogger darted in and out of the crowds.

"Fish sale. Fish sale." A man stopped his bicycle to unhook the top fish from his catch piled in the basket hanging between the handlebars. A woman rummaged in her purse to pay him, her young son clasping a fold in her skirt.

Metal clanked from a high window frame. I spied a woman at her stove, her gaze transfixed on the ground. "Go away," she yelled to a scrawny dog sniffing for scraps in her yard.

We passed a ramshackle house made of unpainted rough wood planks and corrugated metal sheets. Little girls kicked a ball back and forth on the sandy patch of yard, their hair smoothed into woven plaits. The mother waved to us from a tiny porch swing. A gaunt dog of mixed breeds tottered by the girls, her nipples drooped close to the ground.

Every conceivable business offered services from the quaint weather-worn buildings, from office and building supplies, accounting services, to ice cream. A line formed in the sweltering dampness at the open counter of a coffee shop. We left the village center on a different path that ended at a short, narrow beach. We followed the parallel running street, admiring the few modern oceanfront mansions set between wooden shacks.

The mixture of waterfront homes at our rear, I stopped as a different type of property came into view.

A timeworn and splintered sign hung on the ornate gate entrance door, the letters barely legible. "*Palm Isle Cemetery.* "I can't believe there's a cemetery," I said. "Here. So close to the ocean." Concrete crypts set above ground jammed six square lots overlooking a magnificent view over the water. A larger wooden sign was attached to a black iron fence surrounding the site.

I pointed to the signs. *No Parking.* "Who would think about parking in there?"

"Yeah. Weird place." He advanced in front of me and pulled my hand. "Come on."

"No, wait just a second." I said. "I want to check it out. I've never seen a cemetery like this. Especially not one on prime oceanfront real estate."

"So now we've seen it." Irritation edged his voice. "Let's get a beer. I'm in the Caribbean."

"Give me a minute, please, Elam. I won't be long."

He let go of my hand, eyes darting suspiciously around the cemetery.

"What's wrong?"

"Nothing." He shook his head. "I've just got a weird feeling about this place."

"It's just a cemetery." I passed through the entrance gate alone. "I promise to only be a minute."

From outside the gate, he shoved his hands in his pockets and cut furtive gazes at the crypts.

Large vaults were painted bright blue, green, or yellow, others were faded in concrete black grey with the occupant's names etched on top. Tall statues of a solemn-faced Jesus, his arms held wide, protected the grounds. Tender-faced angels and statues of open

THE DECEPTOR'S CALL

bibles cradled inside giant hands were placed over others. From the corners, exposed rebar twisted upward toward the vast blue skies.

"Would you hurry it up?"

I ran my fingers over glass jars filled with bright fresh flowers and ribboned wreaths decorating the top of each crypt. "Almost done." Fallen coconuts dappled the area. Unnamed crosses angled peculiarly between vaults and rosy flower bushes. Sunbeams speckled the ground through long tree leaves.

A lone wooden cross rose from the sand at an angle with *Baby Boy* RIP etched into the wood. The sight of the child's grave left me sad.

"Can we go, Sandy?"

"Yes. I've seen enough." I met him outside the gate.

"Let's get out of here."

We left the cemetery's gloom in search of fun and an open-air tiki bar.

CHAPTER SIX

Festive steel drums, guitars, and a reggae vocalist in dreadlocks pulled us into a grass roofed, open-air palapa bar. I read the sign over the bar. *Dress code: shorts and bikinis. shirts and shoes, optional.*

"I think bikinis should be optional." Elam lightly pinched my bottom.

The scarred wooden floor led us inside to a glass bar located along the only solid wall. The sun's reflection off the wall mirror highlighted the vast array of imported liquor bottles. The bartender entertained customers lined up on barstools. Electric mixers whirred behind the bar. Patrons from every continent occupied each table, their high spirits amplified by voices vying for an audience. Two couples danced to the band's intoxicating beat holding their pink and blue umbrella drinks above their heads.

We grabbed the last two empty stools at the far end of the bar.

"Good afternoon," The bartender's appealing looks and funky dreadlock ponytail belonged in a paradise commercial. "First time joining us?"

"Yes." Elam moved his head in time to the beat of the music. "We just arrived a couple days ago."

"Welcome to Palm Isle, the land of mystic power."

I found myself swept up in his boisterous laughter exposing perfect white teeth.

"What will you have today?"

"I'll have whatever local beer you have on tap." Elam raised a seductive brow at me and winked. "Ice cold, please."

My mood vibrated with the music. "I'll have the same." I chair-danced with my shoulders. "Thank you."

Minutes later we held sweaty pint glasses teeming with amber-colored beer. Ice crystals hit the back of my throat on the first sip. The heat melted away.

THE DECEPTOR'S CALL

"To Palm Isle and embracing our destiny," Elam said, his glass held high. "May it shroud us in mystery and enlightenment."

"To enlightenment." I clinked my glass to his. "And may you have everything you dream." The refreshing draft cooled my whole system. I wiped suds from my upper lip. Elam spun backward on the stool and took in the festive atmosphere.

I offered a private toast for my guilty conscious. The memory of the woman's warning, "Go home," throbbed in my mind like an abscessed molar.

After another long pull on the cold beer, I placed the glass on the bar and leaned into Elam's side. "Don't overdo it, Elam," I whispered. "Be careful, okay?"

He swung his head around and landed a glare on me. "Stop being such a worrywart." His face softened. "I'm fine. Relax and enjoy this."

Before I could say another word, he turned and struck up a conversation with the couple seated on the stools next to us. I put on a smile and let the fun commence. I joined in and let myself relax, though I was confused with his reaction.

We shared partially recalled song lyrics with our new bar friends whose names we never quite got around to learning.

"I love this song," Elam said.

I accepted his offered hand, and he swept me up into a slow reggae ballad played by the band. His strong arms held me close. He kissed me long and deep, indifferent to the company of others.

I placed my lips close and murmured in his ear. "We haven't danced since our wedding."

Early evening slipped away. We ended the night with open plans to meet our new friends another day knowing we'd not see them again before they traveled back to their home countries.

"I know you worry about me, Sandy, but it's not necessary." He intertwined his fingers with mine as we walked out of the bar. "Really. I'm perfectly fine."

"I'm sure you are, but I'll always be concerned for your heart. I'm glad you enjoyed yourself. So did I. But I can't lose you, Elam. You're too precious."

We ventured farther with an aim to learn the grid layout of Palm Isle's streets. I was taken with the various produce stands, open at the late hour. They brimmed with fresh fruit and vegetable harvests brought in on boats from the mainland farms. Fresh red snapper sizzled outside restaurants on tilted black metal grills.

"Let's get a taxi back to Paraiso." Elam slung an arm around my shoulders and pulled me close. "Are you tired?"

"I'm okay. It's probably a result of too much bar fun and this humidity."

Less than three minutes passed before a golf cart taxi rolled toward us. It slowed down to match our pace. "Easier to ride." The driver motioned to the empty back seat, his broad smile gleamed.

"Absolutely. Thanks." Elam climbed in. I settled in beside him. "1 Conch, please," he said.

Sweat oozed down my face. I was grateful to be seated comfortably on the bench. "Perfect timing. Thank you for stopping."

The driver didn't budge the golf cart. "1 Conch?"

"Yes," I said. "Out of the village. We can give you directions." I fanned the back of my neck with my hands in the still air. Frogs croaked their nighttime symphony in the background.

"I'm sorry. I only drive in the village."

"Oh... okay. But it would only take a few minutes," Elam said. "And I'm a great tipper."

Elam's jovial mood was cut short with the driver's hardened face. "I do not drive to 1 Conch."

"Seriously?"

"I apologize. Get out, please."

Elam shook his head. "I don't believe this. A taxi driver who refuses easy business."

THE DECEPTOR'S CALL

"Come on, Elam. Let's go," I wanted to avoid making waves in an already awkward situation.

Elam slid out after me. "Thanks for nothing," Elam yelled as the driver sped away. "Unbelievable." He offered his bent arm to me. "Forget him."

I placed my hand on his forearm, tossing off the weird affair.

"Let's enjoy a stroll, shall we, Madam?"

The day's explorations concluded, we wandered on the road through the jungle toward the privacy of our cottage. Recounting funny conversations and stories of our trip so far, we shared intimacy that had been absent over the previous two decades. Small touches of our hands and private smiles shared in public made me feel special and desired, far beyond the title of former business partner and mother of our children. We didn't mention the driver's refusal to take us home, but it left a sense of unease in the pit of my stomach.

The full moon splashed a silvery sheen on the road. The twist of the Milky Way ribbon and bright stars illuminated the backdrop for the last fifteen minutes of the walk home. Crickets chirped a nocturnal serenade and set a lover's mood. I smiled to myself at how love made me see the world as a script made for the big screen.

"Have you noticed how the stresses of our supposedly advanced country don't exist here?" Elam's soft tone drifted in the dark. "All the hard work is almost a long-lost memory."

"Having you in my life has been a wish come true." I slipped my hand around his muscled bicep. "Being here with you, like this, is more than I could have asked for."

As we neared the sharp turn toward Paraiso a small dark figure, barely perceptible in the night glow, stepped out in front of us. My heart hammered in the cadence of hidden creatures. I tightened my grip on Elam's hand.

"Having a good evening, Elam?" Camilla's voice cut through the night's music. The night's shadow washed out the details of her face.

"Yes. Thank you," he said. "It's a unique place. You're lucky to call it home."

"It's a home the locals protect."

I opened my mouth to ask her to clarify her meaning but was cut short when Camilla's moonlit form appeared close to Elam. "You're a big strong man. Would you mind helping an old woman with some heavy lifting?"

He released my hand. "Sure." He bent down to me, his face shaded from the moonlight. "If it's okay with my wife."

"As long as you don't think it's too much for you." I let my skepticism ring loud and clear.

"Only a couple of boxes to be moved." Camilla tipped her head up at Elam. "No more than a few minutes."

"Okay." I held my candor in the little woman's presence. "I'll conjure something up for a late supper to soak up the alcohol."

"Lead the way, Camilla," he said.

"Don't overdo it, Elam," I called after them. "Be careful." Their dark figures had disappeared around the forested corner. Heading alone for our cottage in the dark, it occurred to me the landlady hadn't acknowledged or included me in her request for help. I brushed it off and plodded on.

Frank's guarding pose remained exactly as we'd left him at the edge of the front yard, his paws planted in the stagnant, moonlit water. The massive dog dawdled beside me as I splashed to the front steps. My appreciation for Frank's company surprised me. I opened the unlocked screen and flipped the switch near the doorway. Soft lamplight cast a homey atmosphere over the room. It boosted my assurances for our happiness here in the following weeks.

****

By the time Elam arrived, I had set the table with plates filled with chicken and rice. Two tall candles burned in the center by an

THE DECEPTOR'S CALL

over-sized basket of rolls and a large salad bowl. Soft burbles of the sea rolled in with the gentle wind through the open windows. I worried the food would be cold.

"Smells delish." He crossed over and kissed my neck, sending titillating quivers over me. "Sorry. There were a few more than just a couple of boxes." He washed his hands at the sink.

I poured cold water from a carafe into stemmed glasses. He parked himself in front of a ready plate. "It's fine," I said. "I enjoy puttering in this cute little kitchen." I took my seat across from him. "To freedom."

"To freedom." He raised his glass high then sipped. He placed the glass on the table and lifted his fork. Elam shoveled food in his mouth like a starved prisoner.

"What else did she have you do? Rearrange the furniture?"

He swallowed a bite. "She had me move some wooden crates, but not two."

"How many?"

"Thirty."

I held my fork midair. "Thirty? Is she moving in or out?"

"She wanted them stacked against a wall. She mentioned something about holding onto the past."

I sipped from my glass. "She's over there all alone. You're probably her new hero."

"I love being a hero." He winked.

An erotic chill raced through me.

Shielded by the table, his hand slid up my thigh to my panties. "I'm going to be your hero soon enough."

I lowered my stemmed glass to the table.

Dinner was cold when we returned later.

****

"Good morning, Frank." Camilla's unmistakable Spanish-Creole accent lilted through the screen door. "You're a good boy."

The dog's tail thudded on the deck boards out front.

Her presence ruined the pleasant morning sounds of tropical bird calls and the swish of small waves on the beach outside the bedroom window. Her aggressive knock on the front screen failed to interrupt Elam's light snores beside me.

"Hello in there. Elam? Are you here?"

You have got to be kidding me. I slid from beneath the damp sheet. Elam stirred with the movement. I placed a light kiss on his forehead. "Go back to sleep," I whispered. He rolled over, the slumberous breaths returned.

I picked up the shorts I'd tossed on the chair the previous night and yanked them up my thighs.

"Elam?" Three more insistent knocks.

Time to send Camilla a message. I tossed the shorts back to the chair and reached in the dresser drawer. The new red camisole I'd packed special for the trip waited at the top. I slipped it over my head and let it settle in place. The wooden floorboards creaked under my saunter. I unlocked the heavy mahogany door and left the screen closed between us.

Camilla wore a bright, creased smile. Her joy fell when I appeared. She glanced down to my silky negligee. "Oh." She raised her brows, her expression flat. "I'm here to speak with Elam."

I gawked at her audacity. "He's asleep, Camilla." I traced my fingers through my sleep mussed hair. "It's early still. Is there something I can help you with?"

The short woman searched beyond me into the room then let her icy gaze settle on me. "No." The corners of her lips tilted up into a smile. "No, thank you." She rounded her bent frame from me and stooped to pat Frank's head and mumbled words I couldn't hear. She rose up and tottered, one leg at a time, down the steps and across the stones, the dog accompanied her to the yard's edge. Camilla disappeared around the corner of wet, finger-rooted mangroves.

"What the heck?" I said and made my way back inside.

"Everything okay?" Elam asked groggily from the kitchen, wearing only his swimming trunks.

Distracted by the sight of his chiseled pecs, my annoyance fell away.

"All is well, my dear." I wrapped my arms around his bare waist. "Coffee?"

"Mmm." He purred into my tangled hair. "You're the best."

"I'll meet you on the deck."

He left me to the job with the squeak of the back-screen door. I spooned coffee grounds into a filter and thought back to the strange visit. I chalked it up to Camilla simply being a lonely old woman with a probable tinge of dementia. *Best to let the whole thing go.*

Fresh ground java and each other's company amid our tropical heaven resulted in a late morning run along the waterfront path into the village. On our return, he showered first while I dawdled in the kitchen. Singing under my breath, I rinsed off fresh fruit in the sink. Brunch would soon be underway after I showered.

After I entered the shower stall, Elam stuck his head in the bathroom. "I'm going back to the village. There's no milk. Do you need anything else?"

"No, thanks. I think we've got everything else we'll need. I'll toss it all in the pan when you're back."

"Shouldn't take long." The front door's creak and slam reached me through the open windows since the bathroom ceiling was open to the bedroom and living room. I worked the persnickety nozzles and the special nuances of the aged plumbing system. Dribbles of hot water mixed with cold. I found the right flow and temperature and entered the shower stall barely wider than my shoulders. I worked the soap into a thick lather over my entire body.

"Hello, there." Several knocks on the frame of the front screen door followed the stranger's gentle voice. With Elam long gone, my heart flipped at the interruption. He would not have closed and locked the heavy outer door on his way out. "Hello." More knocks. Knowing the stranger had to have heard the running water through the screen door, my anger flared. He should have shown respect for my privacy and left.

The nozzles squeaked as I shut the water off. Vulnerable, though he couldn't see me, I opened the plastic door a tad and pulled the towel from the nearby hook. Holding it up in front of me to cover my soapy body, I willed Elam to show up. "Yes?" My intentional resentment echoed between the small bathroom walls. Suds dripped to my feet on the plastic stall floor.

"Yes, Ma'am," His Caribbean Creole accent floated in. "You like to buy my coconut water? I cut it from the tree myself. Very nutritious."

"Uh-uh...no. Thank you though." I hugged the towel tighter.

A pause followed. The lather itched my skin. A strange electrical current buzzed in the wall beside me.

Footsteps tromped down the creaky steps.

Where were the dirty mutt's menacing growls when I needed them?

I fiddled with the ancient nozzles again and the dried soap slid off my irritated skin with the lukewarm stream from the shower head. Lids closed, I tilted my head back into the stream. My reverie cut short, the tepid water rose to a scalding temperature. I feverishly rolled the handle to a cooler setting. The water grew hotter. "Ouch!" There was not enough room to sidestep the boiling stream. The nozzle loosened at my touch. Steam thickened and rolled inside the narrow space. I pressed on the plastic door for escape. It was jammed shut. The tender skin of my chest and abdomen burned.

A panicked scream ripped from my throat. My frantic twists of the unresponsive nozzles stopped. No room to back out of the

THE DECEPTOR'S CALL

angry splatting stream, I pounded on the door and stamped my feet. "Help," I screamed. White bursts of light exploded behind my eyes.

The spray abruptly cooled without a turn of the knobs. I trembled in the stall. I calmed my breaths. My vision cleared. Blotchy red patches glowed against my pale skin.

As I dressed in the bedroom, the inflamed burn had disappeared but lingered in my mind.

****

Nothing was important enough to dampen my time with Elam. I refused to let myself dwell on the strange shower incident. The bed made and clean clothes refolded, I headed to the kitchen and sliced fresh papaya and mangoes procured from the local fresh market the day before. Arranged in a decorative pattern, I set the fruit plate in the center of the table.

Elam had been gone too long. The trip to the store at the edge of the village and back was a half hour round trip, faster at a run. I waited for him on the couch and sent texts to Ed and Shauna telling them we were safe and having a great time. I requested return texts then filled Frank's dishes with fresh water and food.

Out on the front deck, I checked up and down the street. Where was he? Frank stirred from his curled spot. Disquiet crept into the back of my mind. "He gets five more minutes then I'm going after him," I said to the dirty canine.

Frank lifted his head and cocked it at me. He peered out to the sandy street then back to me.

I snapped my brows together. "Can you understand me?" No one around to judge, I tested the silly thought. "Frank?"

His bold stare zeroed in on my face.

"Where's Elam?"

The monster sized animal faced back out to the street and whined.

"He's been gone too long." I descended the first few steps. "I'm going to the store to see what's holding him up."

Frank knocked me aside as he shot by. I grabbed the railing with both hands to prevent a fall. He bounded down the steps and across the yard, small waves rippling. He stopped, tensing beside the road.

"What's wrong, Frank?" I expected him to answer as I maneuvered around the stepping stones covered by brown ripples. I reached his side. Human-like concern shone in his eyes as he watched the sharp street curve Elam would have taken to the village.

"Sorry I took so long."

I swung my head up from the dog at Elam's untroubled voice. He jogged toward us, a carton of milk and oranges bounced inside a clear bag in his hand. He stopped in front of me and petted Frank.

"I was getting really worried, Elam."

He wiped the dirt from the dog's head onto his shorts. "I thought you might be." He grasped my hand and pulled me through the watery yard. Frank loped close at our heels then disappeared under the house between the stilts. "Let's eat. I'm starving."

We reached the door. "Where were you?"

"My super-strength, manly services were requested, again," he said with a cheeky grin.

I took the bag and emptied the contents then poured a dash of milk into a pan waiting on the stove. While I cooked eggs and bacon, Elam dove into the sliced fruit. The dog watched us through the back-screen door.

"Elam, this is supposed to be a fun trip. Payment for this place is supposed to be a financial exchange, not a physical one."

"Camilla was sitting on her front porch when I walked by her cottage. She said she needed help moving a piece of furniture. So, I was a good guy and helped out. Besides, who can say no to a nice old lady when she needs a favor?"

THE DECEPTOR'S CALL

"She made it seem like she's been here most of her life. I'm sure there are plenty of residents on the island that would be glad to lend a hand with any heavy lifting she needs." I turned off the stove burner. "She's a bit strange."

"I think she likes to keep busy. Not one to sit around all day knitting shawls."

"Finally." I plated the food and snatched the toast. "I'm famished."

Elam stared out to the ocean view from inside the screen.

I set the table and poured juice into small glasses from the cupboard then took a seat. "At last. Breakfast is served, ladies and gents."

He held his blank stare.

"Excuse me, over there." I cleared my throat. "Breakfast."

"Hmmm?" His posture relaxed. "Oh, sorry." He pulled out the opposite chair and settled in. "The bacon smells fantastic."

"You were a million miles away."

"Well, actually," He stuffed a forkful into his mouth. "I was thinking of her."

"Camilla?" I put my juice glass down. "What about her?"

"You won't believe it, but . . . I guess this seems odd," he scratched his head. "She talked while I moved the cabinet."

"About what?"

He glanced up as if the ceiling held an answer. "I don't remember."

"But it just happened."

"Yes, the whole situation was strange. Funny thing, though, I was impressed how young she looked."

"Wait." I swallowed a mouthful of food. "What do you mean how 'young'? She's an old woman."

"She looked younger . . . I mean . . . a lot younger." His tone drifted to a place far off.

I pushed my plate away.

"Twenty. Or, twenty-five, maybe." His fork jiggled with a twitch of his hand. "Her hair was fixed in a long reddish ponytail."

My appetite vanished. "Elam, her hair is short. And gray."

His hand twitching stopped. He glanced back at me with a shrug. His fork clinked to the half empty plate. "You cooked. I'll clean."

He cleared the table. I kept my seat and mulled over the conversation while he tidied the kitchen. Elam's regularly level-headed and focused nature contradicted his comments about Camilla. More relaxation and a deeper release of the past life stresses remained on tap for him. His health depended on it. A direct conversation with Camilla was crucial to put an end to any more solicitations. I planned to explain his medical reason for decreased stress. Including heavy manual labor. She was, after all, an adult.

The kitchen cleaned, we made our way down to our private beach with towels and sunscreen in our arms for an afternoon of fun and sun. We waded out until we could no longer touch the bottom, buoyed by its salted luxury.

We viewed the treasures of the sea below. As if viewing them through a clear glass aquarium, colorful patterned fish scurried around us. A kite-shaped stingray skated over the sea floor looking for a squirming meal. It flapped its wings until he was out of sight. Starfish clung to coral. Huge conch shells and sea urchins drifted in the bottom current along with other unknown creatures. My heart swelled at Elam's unrestrained delight with our new environment and the mysteries held by the Caribbean.

Powder puff clouds dangled in the broad azure sky. I flipped over and floated effortlessly on my back, lids closed. Drunk with pleasure, I welcomed the peaceful mood washing through me. He splashed nearby. "This is so great, Elam. I might be tricked into staying forever." I flipped sprinkles of water up over my body with my hands. Bubbles tickled my sides, my closed lids fluttered. "It's amazing how easy it is to float in the high salt content." I raised my head and squinted against the sun to admire him.

He stood with his feet planted in the underwater sand floor. Elam faced the direction of Camilla's cottage canvased by tight tropical bushes.

A brusque bark from the beach redirected my attention. Frank sat up as he watched Elam lost in another world. Elam's rigid stance in chest high water fired off alarms in my head. "Elam," My voice bounced over the surface. Failing to rouse him, I called louder. "Elam." *How could he not hear me?*

I swam to him until I could stand. Disturbed by his glazed unfocused eyes, I placed a hand on each of his shoulders. "Elam? Darling?"

Frank whimpered from the beach. Elam's stare faded and he peered down on me. "Yes?"

"Are you okay?" I slipped my hands from his shoulders to cradle his cheeks.

"Of course." He scrunched his brows. "Are you okay?"

"I was asking you to float with me." I dropped my hands into the water, accidentally splashing his face and chest.

"Sorry, I didn't hear you."

"Obviously."

"Let's go." He left me and swam back out to the deeper water.

Frank's whining stopped. He circled around several times then plopped into a massive heap. Keeping his eyes on Elam in the water, tiny waves lapped over his paws.

Trepidation clouded my previous exhilaration as I swam back to Elam. I was determined to enjoy the day with my husband. I had to visit Camilla. The little landlord had managed to charm Elam, but she would not be allowed to ruin the headway I'd made in my relationship. Not after everything we'd been through.

CHAPTER SEVEN

Rain pummeled the tin roof from an early morning downpour. Humidity inside Paraiso elevated to nearly unbearable levels through the glassless windows, rendering the cotton bed sheets dewy. Rose-colored light filtered in through the thin curtains and over Elam's nude body. My head heavy and fuzzy after a miserable night of tossing and turning, my lover lay dead to the world by my side. The long night resulted in detailed plans for my upcoming discussion with Camilla.

I rolled to my back and pulled the sheer curtains aside. Purple-orange sunrays bathed my face and neck. I regarded my rejuvenated state as a good omen. Pushing the damp sheet aside, I dressed in a bikini and shorts and headed to the coffee pot. Two cups down and confidence high, I snuck a peek at Elam through the tiny opening of the bedroom door. He hadn't moved. Slipping into flip flops, I headed out, intent on being back in time to surprise Elam with a big breakfast in bed.

Glistening white fangs and a growl greeted me from his favorite place on the deck. "Morning, Frank." I tapped a finger on his head as I passed by. He trailed me to the end of the yard and whined from the street's edge. "I'll be back in a bit. Go wait for Elam." I walked away. *I'm actually talking to that mutt.*

I mentally rehearsed the conversation on the way, short and to the point.

Camilla's weathered bungalow came into view around the corner, undisturbed in the fold of flowered shade trees. Palm fronds waved and tinkled in the wind.

The building seemed to sleep with the front shuttered windows. Propelled by adrenaline and determined to get the discussion over and done with, I crossed the front yard and took the deck stairs two at a time. After three forceful knocks on her door, I stepped back and waited with crossed arms, heart pounding.

Nothing stirred within the little shabbily built house. I stared at the door and considered the possibilities that Camilla wasn't home or she was ill and unable to call out.

"Camilla?" No response. "Camilla, it's Sandy. Elam's wife." I rapped my knuckles a second time. "I'd like to have a quick chat."

An object thumped inside, perhaps a chair or a larger piece of furniture.

"Camilla?" I knocked again. "Can we talk for a moment?"

Metal scraped against metal as the padlock on the door was unlatched. The door scraped open six inches. Camilla's unkempt mass of gray hair framed her tired, creased face. She blinked in the sunlight. "Yes?"

"Good morning, Camilla. I'd like to speak with you." I kept my arms loose at my sides.

"Sandy. I'm busy now." She unleashed a wet cough into her fist. "Another time." The door creaked shut an inch.

I threw my foot on the threshold. "Well. . .this will only take a second." The door stopped. Her imperceptible expression in the interior darkness heightened my discomfort. "I'd appreciate it if you would find someone else, besides my husband, to do any heavy lifting. I'm certain you know lots of strong men on the island who would be glad to help out whenever you need it." I presented her with the sweetest smile I could muster.

"Oh," she said. I removed my foot from the door. She stuck her head out a few inches and scrutinized me closer. The early morning light glinted off a surprising strand of auburn mixed in with the wild head of gray hair.

Under her stoic gaze, I shifted my weight to the opposite leg. I tapped my foot in the awkward, deafening silence. I crossed my arms. "I'm sorry to bring this up, but we, Elam and I, came here to relax." I drove the embellished point home with a raised eyebrow. "And noble as he is, Elam needs this time to fully recover from some fairly recent health issues."

Her flat expression did not change.

"I'm sure you understand. It's simply not a good time for him to help you. His doctor has advised against any kind of strenuous work."

Inferiority burned in my cheeks under her unblinking silence. "Okay. That's all." I pretended to smooth my hair with a swipe of my hand over my head. "Well, have a good day." My rubber sandals slapped loud thwapps on my heels. I sensed her stare burning into my back like a hot poker.

****

The sun higher in the sky, I envisioned Elam still snuggled in the sheets. My nerves were on edge after the uncomfortable one-sided conversation with Camilla. I wanted a chance to get ahold of myself before I returned to him. I moseyed by our cottage with the intent to extend my absence another fifteen minutes or so to explore past Paraiso into the undeveloped half of the island.

Frank jumped at me, sending my heart to my knees. His single severe bark ruined the solitude. "Shush," I said as if I spoke to a child. "You're going to wake Elam." I'd gone a few feet when a cloud of dust rose in my face as the muscled beast had raced to plant himself directly in my path. It dawned on me this was the first time he'd stepped off the property. "What are you doing?" His fierce glower made his intention plain.

He rubbed his massive, filthy head against my thigh. "Stop it." I stepped back as he closed the gap and shook off more dust. He folded his back legs to sit at attention before me. "All right. All right." I huffed through clenched teeth. "But be quiet." I shook my head and opened my mouth to berate him further then thought better of it.

THE DECEPTOR'S CALL

Frank and I wandered in the opposite direction of the village. I kept my bearings on the twisted road canopied in shadows. Bird cries and squawks sprang from all directions within the giant ferns, wild grape, and banana trees huddling over both sides of the road. The jungle tightened, the air suffocating. I decided to go back.

But the tropical forest opened three yards ahead on the left. I changed my mind and we moved to the lighted space. Tall blades of wild grass swayed in an invigorating breeze, cooling my skin. I approached the edge. A narrow footpath hurried through the middle of the small field. I sucked in the fresh air and welcomed the broadened sky.

Farther on, the path ended at a timber wharf sagging over the water, the rough planks bent upward on one side. Frank touched my leg as he waited by my feet. The entrance to the footpath was marked by a wooden sign, set at ground level, and obscured by the grass. I pushed aside the tall blades and read the sun-faded paint. *Welcome All Visitors.*

Interest piqued, I followed the path, Frank in the lead. Before we reached the rickety dock, an inconspicuous cottage appeared to my left in the shambled condition I'd grown to appreciate. Three corners were held off the ground by basketball sized stones. The fourth corner rested firmly on the sandy ground. It set back close to the forest edge, reticent and unassuming. The hovel appeared to be deserted. I recognized it and the surrounding area from our day of kayaking. The woman who passionately yelled for us to go back home had gathered with the other women in the water near the cottage. Frank and I worked our way over the least deteriorated planks to the end of the dock and peered into the sea.

Besides the clearing of the path and cottage, no other structures were visible, no grass trampled by usage. Untouched by progress, indigenous flowers bloomed in the yard of the dilapidated building. Countless pink hydrangeas decorated the base and added to the area's serenity. Trees hugged close to the beach and extended beyond sight. The faded mahogany door was closed. Gingham fabric lined the front window from the inside.

I stepped off the dock, Frank at my heels. As we came level with the little house, a gingham curtain fluttered. A small pair of black leather shoes rested at the corner of the door as if someone had just stepped out of them on their way inside.

A strong sensation of being watched came over me. I called out. "I'm so sorry for the intrusion. I thought the place was empty." I hurried my steps to the end of the path until the cottage was out of sight. Frank's repulsive lurking presence offered comfort.

****

"Sandy?" Elam's voice filtered through the screened door as I reached the top step.

Frank lapped at his water dish outside. I passed him into the dark interior. My blindness adjusted from the perky morning light. "Hi. You're awake I see." I kissed his cheek and joined him at the dining table.

"I was worried about you. We don't know anyone here. You shouldn't leave without telling me where you're going."

"You're right. I'm sorry to worry you." Approaching the stove, I rotated the burner knob until the gas flame caught, then gathered items from the fridge. "But I wasn't alone." Eggs sizzled in the heated pan on impact. "The ugliest dog in the world invited himself along."

"I'm not joking around, Sandy."

I paused my stirring at his brusque tone. "I said I'm sorry."

He rose from the chair. "You didn't need to slip off to Camilla's in secret."

"Seriously? She's already dropped by and told you about that?" The smell of burnt eggs reached my nose. "Dammit." I swiftly removed the pan and set it on a cold burner then turned off the flame.

"You need to leave her alone, Sandy. She lives a solitary life over there. Don't bother her again."

"Wait just a minute. I'm your wife. I'm concerned for your stress level since the heart attack." Close to shouting, I softened my voice. "We're here, if you'll remember, to start our life over with new adventures and relaxation. It makes no sense for you to risk your health doing manual labor for a woman we hardly know." I went back to cooking. "Like I said before, there are plenty of young men on this weird island to help out if she needs it."

"How many times do I have to tell you my heart is fine." He expelled a sigh and his jaw and shoulders relaxed. He crossed the minuscule kitchen and wrapped me in a hug. "I'm good." He released me and stepped back. "Those eggs are beyond repair. Let's go into the village and let someone else make us breakfast." He took my hands.

His forceful attitude and protection of Camilla threw me, but my heart melted under his romantic gaze. "Sure. That'll be more fun, anyway." We left the burnt food cooling on the stove.

Frank's one hundred fifty pounds spilled onto the deck. I let my fingertips graze over his dust covered head as we left, then wiped them off on my shorts.

Elam stared hard at Camilla's cottage as we strolled by.

****

Bacon, coffee, and spices laced the open-air Caribbean Sea and Feed. Bob Marley crooned low from a hidden speaker. We chose a table. Customers seated at the two nearby tables offered us advice on the best snorkel and dive spots found by their adventure club. They shared the names of the best outdoor restaurant where fish was served directly off the rusted grill and beer from a cooler. The exuberant occupants of the next table hushed as the waiter arrived with heaped plates.

Elam took my hand from my lap and held it. "This place is home for me now, Sandy." His softened face focused past the occupied tables to the bustle of the village.

"Why? There isn't much here. I mean, don't get me wrong, I think it's beautiful, of course. But really, Elam.

"It's hard to explain." He returned with a serious expression. "This is where I'm supposed to spend the rest of my life."

"It's a great place for a vacation. But it's so remote. Have you seen a hospital? Or a real health clinic anywhere? And," I leaned closer and whispered, "There's a strange aura here. Weird things have happened."

He dropped my hand. "You always take a negative point of view; the glass half empty. I see things here beyond the beauty. I'm more alive now than I ever was back home." He exhaled a strong huff. "Toiling day in day out, working long hours just to make enough money to keep up with the neighbors."

"Elam, I was there. I helped you as much as I could after the kids came along."

"Still, the pressure was on me to make it happen. But now, here," he opened his hands out wide, "I don't know. I'm part of the island." He inhaled a deep breath. "Take a whiff of those spices."

My nose tingled with a hint of nutmeg.

"The smell of home."

"Excuse me." A deep tanned middle-ager approached our table. "Sorry to bother you." His sun-bleached hair was pulled back behind his head.

Exactly where I'd seen him before eluded me.

"I was passing by to pick up my order." A bulging, paper bag crackled as our visitor shifted it from one hand to the other. "I couldn't help but overhear the suggestions you were given about the best reefs around the island."

"Yes?" said Elam, his expression open and friendly.

He stuck his right hand out to Elam. "I'm Dave."

"Elam." He released Dave's hand.

"Sandy," I said with a slight wave and a formal smile.

"I won't keep you, but I'd be happy to get you two to the best snorkeling spot around here."

Elam glanced at me as if to say, "See. It's all good." He turned back to Dave. "Where is this place?" Dishes clinked in the background. Low chatter hummed around us.

"Everyone wastes time and money going so far offshore when the very best is right here at home. You'll be surprised when you see where it is. It's in the middle of the harbor area. It's a sunken fishing trawler."

I fidgeted in my seat at the memory of the harbor.

Elam's forehead creased as he cocked his chin to the side. "We walked through the harbor the day we arrived. I didn't see any sunken boats. The whole place looked pristine."

Icy fingers of dread shimmied down my spine. "Elam, it's right in the center. You can't miss it."

He looked at me as if I was delusional.

"It's been there forever," said Dave. "Best snorkeling you're ever going to find. Those supposed adventure groups come and go. And they all go to the same popular spots as everyone else. This is special. A hidden gem." He leaned slightly closer and whispered my way, "You'll see things you won't want to share." He tossed his head slightly toward the group's table.

Elam nodded. "Sounds good to me. How much?"

"Are you kidding? There's no charge. Just one local sharing insider info to another. I also heard you telling Sandy how you feel at home here." He chuckled.

"Sounds great. Thank you."

I cleared my throat. "Elam," I touched his arm, "We're still getting a feel for the island. I'm not sure this is a good time to..."

Waving me off, he said, "We'd love to."

"Perfect. How about you two meet me at the pier in the morning. Six o'clock sharp."

"You're very thoughtful, Dave," I said. "We appreciate the offer, but Elam's a late sleeper."

Elam cut his eyes at me. "We'll be there."

"Want to get there before the harbor gets busy. The fishing boats will be gone by then. Quiet and safer." He backed away with a salute. "All the equipment you'll need is on the boat. Enjoy your breakfast."

The braid hanging down his back triggered my memory. He was the musician carrying the guitar waiting with us at the ferry terminal to come to Palm Isle.

"I know what you're going to say." Elam scowled. "But I'm going to meet with him. Why not take him up on his offer? He seems like a nice guy."

"Maybe we should have gotten to know him a little before we agree to get into his boat."

"Lighten up, will you? Adventure. Remember?"

"Right." I hunched my shoulders. "Adventure."

Our waitress approached the table wearing a friendly smile and placed an overfilled plate of an island version of Eggs Benedict. He licked his lips. "A thing of beauty," he said to the dish in front of him. He peered up to her. "This island is the best place in the world."

"So much has changed on Palm Isle," said the waitress. "The elders do not like the newer buildings. Or the countless visitors that arrive on our shores." She placed extra napkins and a bottle of curried hot sauce in the center of the table. "But I like hearing of other places."

THE DECEPTOR'S CALL

"Why don't the elders like visitors here?" I asked. "It seems to me the island depends on tourism."

"They say too many outsiders crowd the deep pulse of the island. Some of us feel like we've been here more than a lifetime. We like to see new faces."

I placed a napkin on my lap. "What does 'the deep pulse of the island' mean?"

She pulled out her pen and order pad. "Where are you staying?"

"We're a little way out of the village. Out on Conch St. It's owned by an elderly woman."

She pursed her lips. She touched her fingertips to her shirt collar. "You stay in the jungle side of the island?"

"Yes. At Paraiso," he said. "The landlady's name is Camilla."

She bit her lower lip.

I exchanged glances with Elam and placed my empty fork on the plate. "Do you know her? We're staying in her rental cottage just down the beach from where she lives."

"I'm sorry." The waitress stepped back from our table. "I have to check on other orders." In her haste, her foot caught a chair stuck out in the aisle. Her slight frame tangled with the legs. A clatter erupted as she and the chair crashed on their sides. The waitress recovered, jumped up, and dashed away. Her flip flops proclaimed her exit like an exclamation point. Her order booklet and sharpened pencil lay strewn across the wood floor, the chair still sprawled in the aisle. She disappeared through a bedsheet hung from the kitchen doorframe. Patrons stared after her as the greasy sheet swayed in her wake.

****

We strolled through the relaxed hub of commerce and play to digest our half-eaten breakfasts.

"Elam," I chose my words carefully, "what if we changed our plans? We could be gone from here tomorrow."

"But we're just getting settled in. And we've already paid to stay a full month."

"Yes." I took his hand. "But I don't feel exactly welcome here. I mean, it's absolutely beautiful in a rustic, bohemian way. But we could see another island. There's something strange here. You seem different sometimes, too. And the rent was incredibly low. It's not like we'd be losing a lot of money, right? We'd still be within our budget."

"You're not giving the place a fair chance." He gave my hand a gentle squeeze. "Relax. Just go with the flow."

Recalling the waitress' strange words and her reaction to our renting Camilla's cottage, staying seemed a caustic choice. I decided to let things go and enjoy the day. Maybe he was right. I was too sensitive. A deep breath and a pineapple slice wedged on an umbrella drink rim might be just what I needed.

****

"My feet are killing me," I said. "We've been walking for two hours. Let's go back for a private swim."

"Anything you want, my lady. You're in an island paradise where all things are possible." He chuckled and kissed my cheek. An empty two-wheeled passenger buggy hitched to the back of a bicycle rolled past.

The driver nodded a greeting and slowed to a stop. "I can take you wherever you want to go, friends. Very cheap."

"Let's do it," Elam said.

"I'm game."

"Okay, yes, thank you." He took a seat then helped me in.

As soon as we settled, the driver pressed hard on his peddles and we were off. A relief to see the village from the comfort of the bumpy carriage, we rolled by the first few shops. We followed the sandy street toward the jungle edge.

THE DECEPTOR'S CALL

"We are staying out of the village on Conch Street," Elam said to the driver.

The bike slowed. "Which cabana?" He glanced in the reflector mirror hooked to the handlebar.

"Pretty much the only rental out there. Number 1." He slowed to a stop. The driver placed both feet on the ground. "My apologies." He glowered at me first, then Elam. "I do not deliver there."

"Are you sure?" I said. "It wouldn't take long."

"Please exit the buggy." He didn't move.

Elam and I shared a look and shrugged then climbed out of the seats. "What is it with you island taxi drivers? Are you too lazy to make it out there?" Without another word the bicycle rushed away.

"I don't get it," Elam said.

Apprehension took up residence once more, in the pit of my stomach on the glum walk back to Paraiso.

****

Late afternoon slipped into evening. We dallied between dips in the warm sea and meanders in bare feet sinking into silky beach sand. We collapsed into lounge chairs stretched out underneath the shade of palms. A metal bucket filled with ice and water bottles lay an arm's length between us. A cold bottle in Elam's hand dripped sweaty lines in the humid air.

I closed my eyes and drifted off into a meditative haze. "You got your wish. I'm going to stop worrying over every little thing."

Recovering from my reflective moment, Elam spoke to the water as if thinking out loud.

"Sometimes I thought I would never be happy again," he said. "True happiness always seemed like it belonged to other people." He shrugged and grinned. "Or maybe everyone else is grinding it out, too."

"Do you mean business stress? Financial stress?"

"Everything." His contemplative gaze remained on the sea. "Life."

I reached across the bucket and touched the back of his hand. "I'm glad you're happy." "It's the most important thing to me." I relaxed back. "And don't forget, we've raised two great kids."

"Yes. I'm proud of Ed. He's definitely on the road to success. And Shauna will get there. Happiness and trust are more important than anything."

Cutting my attention back to Elam's profile, I focused on his statement of trust. I was satisfied he remained untroubled or distracted since his morning edginess. But I knew I'd keep a close watch on him.

****

Groggy in the sunrise hour, my reluctance to get in a stranger's boat and visit his destination niggled at the back of my mind. I hadn't completely forgotten the odd sensation I'd encountered upon seeing the abandoned boat on our first day.

I grabbed at one last attempt to prevent the trip. I tied the bikini string behind my back. "The sunken trawler Dave is taking us to. Do you really not remember seeing it?"

"No." Elam coated himself with sunscreen. "I must have missed it somehow."

I wiped a white spot left on the tip of his nose. "Well, I didn't. And I had a weird feeling when we were there. I tried to ignore it."

"If we honored every one of your weird feelings, we'd never do anything or go anywhere. Enjoy this. What's the big deal? Snorkeling is what people do in the Caribbean. Plus we're up too early to stop now." He picked up the two folded towels I had placed on the bureau and left me in the bedroom.

I pulled on a flowered bathing suit cover over my head and let it fall into place. Stepping my feet into flip-flops, I raced down to the

THE DECEPTOR'S CALL

yard to catch up with him. Frank padded by my side until I stepped into the road. He stared as we turned the corner to the village.

****

The beach devoid of fishing boats, the harbor was quiet. Dave waved from inside his short fiberglass boat secured to the end of a floating dock attached to the pier. I pointed. "There's the old boat." The trawler jutted above the water out in the center.

"I see it now. I would've bet money it was not there that day."

"It looks gloomy. I'm really not excited about this."

Elam's pace picked up.

We exchanged pleasantries and clambered aboard. Dave's idling engine bubbled under the water as he steered us near the harbor's center. "The reef the clubs go to are damaged by tourists. They're clumsy and knock the coral with their fins." He flipped his free hand out to the side. "A waste of time and money. You'll love this one. It's healthy. And the colors are amazing." He cut the motor and threw his anchor overboard. "This is it." He opened the top on a box near the tiny helm. Lifting the contents, he produced two plastic snorkel tubes attached to masks, and two pair of fins.

"Aren't you coming?" Elam asked.

"Seen it a thousand times. Take your time. There's no rush."

"But we've never done this before."

"It's super easy, man. You'll get a quick handle on it." He handed the items to us. "No experience required. Just remember to relax."

He gave us speedy instruction on fog proofing the masks by our own saliva. We applied the masks and fins, laughed at each other's ridiculous looking garb, then slipped off the side of his boat with a splash. After a few unsure moments of breathing through the tubed snorkel, we soon glided over the surface. All my anxiety melted away.

Within no time, my body slinked over the colorful aquatic world of odd shapes and textures like I was one with nature. Elam chanced a dive to the bottom and picked up a giant conch shell, swam it up to me and I gave him a thumbs up. He kicked and replaced it to the sea floor then propelled himself to the reef's edge.

Lured by the unending reef, I moved farther off to explore. Bright striped fish with pointed snouts darted in and out of pink fan-shaped coral. Black spiked sea anemones clung to purple cauliflower shaped coral. A sea turtle inched by as it waved its flippers.

I checked on Elam's position to make sure he was in sight. He floated yards away, lost in his own exploration. The hull of Dave's boat floated just below the surface, a long chain tethered his anchor wedged between the sandy bottom and a sea stone. With reassurance of both men's positions, I aimed to make the most of my time.

Growing more confident, my feet and arms moved easily and my breaths slowed to a natural level through the snorkel. Learning to hold my breath with the rubber mouthpiece in place, I dove deeper to get better sight angles on the lower sections of the reef. I glimpsed a barracuda hunting close to the bottom. Too near the sea creatures, I paddled my fins to the surface and at a safer, more comfortable distance. I glanced around until I saw Elam captivated by the coral yards away.

The sunken trawler came into my under underwater view. The broken-out windows peered like dulled eyes. A sense of familiarity from an unknown source sparked deep in my gut. Building pressure throbbed in my ears.

A shadow moved in my periphery, pulling my focus. I spun toward it, my breath loud in my head. Besides the reef and wildlife, I was alone. Another movement flittered on my opposite side. Obscure water pulses waved out through the windows from inside the darkened trawler belly. Green, snaky eels slithered out and writhed past my head. I paddled by thrusting my arms backward as

THE DECEPTOR'S CALL

fast as they would go. The futile effort failed to move me. I remained floating in the same spot, as if the water around me solidified.

The blackness throbbed like a beating heart. A magnetic force of loss and doom consumed me so forcefully the will to live came into question. But I sensed the loss didn't belong to me. I served only as a conduit for holding a grief suffered by another person, another being. The pulse pulled and pushed me at the same time, as if to drown me in its vacuum of sorrow.

My mind snapped with a spark of defiance, refusing to be lulled into its dreary depth. My lips loosened around the snorkel. I screamed. Water rushed back into my lungs as I inhaled. I lifted my head above water, yanking the plastic mouthpiece out. I coughed until the painful saltwater cleared from my throat. Pulling the mask off my face, I stretched the band taut and placed it on my forehead, the snorkel hung loose by my cheek. The rusted relic remained above the surface. Reeling away, I worked my arms and fins in the opposite direction of the ominous trawler.

"Elam," I called, scanning the area. My husband was nowhere in sight. The quiet early morning harbor and pier sat empty. The ocean loomed out to the horizon unimpeded with the absence of Dave's boat. "Elam?" My plea skipped over the water. Panic gripped deep.

"Over here, Sandy." His voice behind me, I spun around. He waved his arms over his head. Panting, I propelled myself over the calm water, covering the distance until I reached him.

"I called for you several times," he said. "I couldn't find you anywhere," His mask on his forehead, he lowered it to his eyes. The snorkel dangled by his temple. "We'll have to swim to the beach."

I surveyed the area, my heart still pounding. "Where's Dave?"

"He, nor the boat, have been here since I was ready to leave a long time ago. Like an hour."

"You wanted to leave an hour ago? We've only been out here a few minutes."

Dog paddling, he shook his head. "An hour at least. I saw you swim down but you were gone so long I got worried. So I searched all around the reef and couldn't find you."

"I'm really sorry. I guess I was so interested in checking things out, I lost track of time." I decided against sharing the trick my eyes and mind played on me. "Why would Dave bring us out here then take off and leave us like that?"

After swimming back to the beach and removing our equipment, we approached a vendor setting up for business. She displayed her artsy wares on a blanket spread out on the sand, ready to entice expected tourists. Elam described Dave and his boat and asked if she'd seen either. "There's been no one else here. And no boats in the harbor."

Exhausted, we dripped our way to *Paraiso*. "She can't be right," he said. "If we run across him again, I'm going to give him a piece of my mind. Who would insist on taking newbies out and then just leave them?"

"At least we were close enough to swim back." My sick imagination still sizzling with my haunting experience.

"Yeah, and it's not like we were in any kind of trouble." He put an arm around my shoulder. "I guess I should have taken your concerns about him seriously."

****

I attended to his every need as the following week drifted by peacefully. No requests for help came from our landlady, and I appreciated the respect for privacy since my uncomfortable visit to her house.

"Let's do something romantic," I said to Elam's profile. Two feet separated our lounge chairs on Paraiso's shaded beach.

Stretched out with his eyes closed, his head rested on his crossed arms. "I can think of something romantic right this minute."

THE DECEPTOR'S CALL

I traced down the side of his ribs with a fingertip. "I'd like to visit the cenotes we heard about at the bar that first night. Remember that one really drunk woman who sang the loudest? She told us they were water filled, limestone sinkholes. She was adamant that we see them."

"Sounds like a great idea." He yawned, pushed himself up, then propped on his elbow and faced me. "Now you're finally getting into the spirit." He climbed off the chair and stretched. "No time like the present."

Within thirty minutes, we traded the lazy early afternoon for the prospect of a new island discovery. Backpacks loaded with towels and extra clothing, we strode to the village and asked around until we received general directions to our destination.

Because it was on the opposite side of Palm Isle, we ventured on a path cut through the pressing jungle. Overhanging branches and vines brushed and scraped my shoulders like fingernails. Mosquitos and bugs buzzed by my ears and bit into my skin as I slapped and waved them away, mentally second-guessing my grand idea.

Elam stopped at an opening ahead, his body bathed in sunlight. "This is unbelievable."

Sidling up next to him, I gave silent thanks to be free from the claustrophobic forestry hike. The water glowed blue within the lining of a limestone shelf reaching deep into the earth's mystical center. "It looks too perfect to swim in." I recalled the explanation given for the round-shaped sink hole, exposing the underground river.

"Come on. It's waiting for us."

We set our packs on a rock and undressed down to our swimsuits. I bent low and dipped my fingers in cautiously. Ripples spread over the pristine natural pool. Elam stepped onto a smooth limestone edge and dove head first, coming up immediately. "Incredible." He shook his hair out of his face. "Get in. You'll love this."

Invigorated by the sweet fresh water smell from underground, I jumped in feet first. I swam to Elam and wrapped my arms around his waist. "Nature is amazing, isn't it?"

"It's magical." He released me and dove deep, ending in a flip. Mischief reamed his smile as he crested the surface."

I pretended the cenote was our own magical secret as we discussed appreciation for our opportunity to explore. All was right with the world. No weird feelings. No odd looks or frightening events. Satisfied with a new discovery and my own sense of needed well-being ruled the afternoon. We frolicked and competed over the next couple of hours, proving bravery and daring by the deepest dives. Our childish games ended in floating and swimming, while the unspoiled water revived my optimism.

We sat on a smooth section of limestone perfect for two; the water level reached my chest. I kissed his cheek. "You're the love of my life, Elam Steele. I would do anything for you."

He answered my confession by placing his hands on the sides of my waist and lifting me into his lap. He used his expert fingers to untie the bikini strings behind my neck and he kissed the place under my ear that turns me on every time. Thrilled with his touch in open air promiscuity, a throaty moan escaped my lips as he ran his tongue down to my chest. Flames of desire erupted deep inside me. I wanted him then and there. His mouth reached my breast.

"I think we're almost there." The distant unknown deep voice broke the mood like a needle scratched across the surface of a vinyl record. "Yes, here we are," said a feminine voice.

I scrambled off my husband's lap and crouched lower in the water, my back turned from the path opening. My fingers fumbled with the strings until I retied my swimsuit, bringing an embarrassing end to our magic. Awkward silence hung in the air as they tried to look at everything except us.

THE DECEPTOR'S CALL

Privacy concluded, we toweled off, repacked our backpacks, and contained our hysterics until we were on the path.

"I wish you could have seen your face when they showed up. I almost felt bad for them the way they tried so hard to act normal." Elam held his stomach laughing as he led the way out of the jungle. "That was priceless."

"Easy for you." I smacked his bum in front of me. "You weren't the one caught half exposed." I wiped the chuckling tears out of my eyes.

I treasured our closeness and ease with each other. Nothing could ever come between us and break our newly formed bond.

****

Rain fell from bulbous, slate-colored clouds knitted together over the island the entire second week. The moderately dried front yard refilled with rain and formed a new pond of mosquito larvae. Sunshine teased through the clouds in late afternoon reprieves from the relentless heat. We enjoyed Paraiso's coziness for the next several days by nestling together on the overstuffed couch, fingers curled around books, sporadic afternoon delights. Soggy runs to the village markets determined culinary experiments of the day.

I gave thanks to whoever was listening for Elam's return to health. His vibrancy and zest for life had been sorely absent for so many years. His sallow skin had blossomed back to a healthy pink. He rested peacefully as he had early on in our college days. Before everything happened.

"This has been great. Don't you think?" he said from the opposite end of the couch.

Drawn out of the fiction world I'd tumbled into, I peered over a corner of the well-worn paperback. "I wouldn't trade my time with you for anything."

Thunder rolled in the distance. I smacked a mosquito latched on to my knee. Elam rested his hand on my calf. He rubbed his thumb back and forth on my skin absent-mindedly. I lowered the book to my lap.

He stared into the center of the room. "I hate to say it, but," The old sofa springs groaned as he climbed off and stretched his arms above his head. He made a beeline to the refrigerator and cracked the top of a local-brand beer can. Foam fizzed at the opening. He took a swig. "I'm getting a little restless." He tipped the beer can back a second time, his throat constricted with each loud gulp. "And bored."

Frank barked then whined on the deck.

"Elam." I pointed to the beer can. "Careful, there."

"I'm a big boy." He scowled at me. "Remember, Mommy?"

I flinched. Sitting up on the couch edge, my book thumped on the floor. "You just said you've been so relaxed. And happy."

"True. But enough is enough." Another guzzle. "A man can't play Love House forever." He crumpled the empty can in his palm then tossed it to the corner. The tin can pinged in the corner wastebasket.

A knot formed in my stomach at his change. "I'm sure this rain will let up soon," I said. "Maybe we can go out again this evening."

"I can't wait on the weather," he snapped. He popped the top on a second can and chugged it all at once. He flung the empty can aside. It banged as it bounced across the floor.

"Elam, seriously." I eased off the couch. "You don't want to overdo and pass out."

His lips pressed together, he shot a glare my way.

"What's gotten into you?" I asked. Memories of Daddy's anger flashed through my mind.

Rain gushed on the tin roof like an opened floodgate.

THE DECEPTOR'S CALL

"I think it's time to check on Old Lady Camilla. See if she needs a hand." He grabbed his gut and doubled over laughing, as if he pulled the world's darkest joke on his wife.

"No," I shouted. Regret followed the instant I raised my voice. I released a deep breath. "No. Please, don't go over there. She's not your responsibility."

"I'm a grown man, Sandy." His hands curled into fists at his sides. "I'll do what I please."

I shrank back from his new, threatening manner. The back of my calves hit the sofa. I tumbled back into the cushions. "How did this go from zero to one hundred so quickly?"

His cheeks and forehead reddened, and his eyes glassed over. His chest heaved with each breath.

"Please, Elam." I forced myself to calm down. "Have a seat. I promise, when the rain lets up, we'll go for a swim. Or walk to the village. Maybe take those kayaks out. Okay?" I stepped away from the couch. "I can give you a massage."

He sprinted back to the refrigerator. Before I registered his reaction, a third beer can spewed white foam as it sailed across the room. It struck the floor and rolled to my feet. I jumped to the side. Droplets dribbled from the opening; its pungent scent filling the room.

"This is entirely your fault," he bellowed.

"Calm down, Elam." I held my hands out toward him.

Frank whined through the screened door, his nose pressed against the screen as he stared at Elam. Rain rushed off his trembling back.

My husband stomped to the front door. Frank cowered backward. "My fingers are wilted from swimming so much, and I've spent my fair share of this trip walking around with you. Now I'm gonna enjoy a little me time."

BARBARA MICHELLE

The screen door slammed after him. Frank jumped away and barked as Elam passed by. My husband raced down the stairs and across the sodden yard, his short ringlets flattened in the torrential downpour.

"Elam," I yelled from inside the door. "Elam, don't leave."

Frank bounded after him until he reached the street and barked. Without looking back, Elam rounded the curve out of sight.

I reeled at the rapid change in my husband. His ability to remain level-headed under enormous pressure in the past, except for the one fateful moment in the garage, had been awe-inspiring. On many rocky occasions, he served as a beacon in the dark to me and the children. Guilt pressed into me as worry skyrocketed.

The sun peeked around emptied clouds. Frank trotted back to the door and stared at me through the screen. Questions rolled through my mind as humidity pressed in with the storm. I paced inside the small living room as I sought to grasp an answer. Maybe the relaxed environment on the island was too much of a good thing.

I considered Camilla and her curious effect on my husband. She was a lonely, elderly woman who'd done well enough to own two cottages and create rental income. Elam had shown no interest in ignoring the old woman. His strange comment returned. *She looked younger...twenty or twenty-five.*

For me to simply sit and wait for his return was intolerable. Sudden shock had resulted in his heart attack and nearly stole him from my world the year before, the day I had bargained with God to spare Elam in exchange for my being a better person. I swore to attend church and repent for all the pain I'd caused. I vowed to make Elam's happiness my focus and make up for my final act of burning the photos, the cause of his heart attack.

Rainwater and sand rippled at my ankles as Frank and I reached the road. The sky darkened again and the clouds let loose another deluge. We splashed to Camilla's cabana.

THE DECEPTOR'S CALL

The old woman's yard formed a small lake as raindrops pelted the metal roof, the door closed tight against the weather. Fabric covered both windows. The barrage of water prevented me from hearing if anyone was inside. I pushed hair plastered to my face behind my ears and sloshed across the yard. Twice, I stopped and wriggled my sandals from the suction of wet sand. We climbed her slippery steps to her deck. The screened door was open all the way back and cinched on a metal hook on the exterior wall.

Torrential water pummeled and gushed as if buckets were tipped from the eaves. My shirt and shorts clung uncomfortably to my frame. I considered withdrawing, fearful of Elam's reaction to my interference. *What am I doing here?* But, Elam wasn't well. I tapped a timid knock on the door. I pressed an ear to the door and listened hard.

I raised my voice over the deafening rain and knocked harder. "Elam?" Water rolled down my nose. "Camilla?" Frank slung more water on me as he shook vigorously.

No one answered. I grasped the rusted doorknob. It didn't budge. I reached a shaky hand through the window to the soaked fabric. Anger swept over me. We were definitely getting off the island. It was time for me to lay down the law, no matter what Elam said. We'd move on to somewhere more developed. Maybe a European country.

"Enough stalling," I said out loud. I bolted to the window and gripped a fistful of blue and white gingham. I yanked the fabric to the side. *Please let him be okay.* Braced for incensed shouts against my intrusion, I leaned into the darkened interior and gave my eyes a second to adapt. A waft of old wood and dust prickled my nose. I noted one important detail. Surely, my vision deceived me. My heart flipped in my chest.

Loosening my fist, gingham fell back in place. I wiped water dripping off my face. I yanked the curtain back all the way, stuck my head in and leaned all the way inside the window for a second view. No furnishings. No people.

Rain drummed on the metal above Camilla's completely empty cottage.

CHAPTER EIGHT

The curtain slipped from my hand. I shot down the steps. I tripped over Frank and tumbled down the stairs to the sodden ground, landing on my hands and knees. His slimy tongue licked my mud-splashed face. He pressed his side into me as if to nudge me back up. I climbed to my feet and we rounded Camilla's cottage, stopping when we reached the back. Dense bamboo and mangroves rose above a soaked sandy yard open to the rain-pummeled sea, dulled beneath the slate-colored sky. I saw no evidence her cottage had been occupied. Water dripped through planks of the unsteady upper back porch.

Panic boiled inside me. Tension knotted in my fisted hands. My jaw ached from grinding my teeth. I pressed the heel of my palms to my temples. "Think. Think. Where would he go?" Still a new visitor to the island, no answer came to mind. I splashed back around to the front yard and headed for the washed-out road. Frank bounded ahead for home. He might be dependable in the search for my husband.

The screen door bounced into place as we entered Paraiso. Frank investigated nose first. Raindrops passed through the screen and created a tiny puddle on the floor. I'd left the heavy wood door open in case Elam returned. I envisioned him wanting to remedy my paranoia with a strong hug, an apology for scaring me, and a declaration he was ready to leave the island early for the next leg of our world trip.

I tumbled over Frank, settled down in the center of the living room, his head and ears raised. I overlooked his trail of water and mud mottled across the floor. His presence provided a sense of protection, though I had no idea from what.

I located my cell phone, the screen black, hooked to the charger on the kitchen counter. No Wi-fi available, I tried using the mobile hotspot. Manipulating the keys failed to revive the tiny box. "Ugh." I threw it back to the counter. For the first time, I longed for neighbors and friends for help.

The cabana beyond the wild grassy field popped into my mind. It appeared abandoned the day we accidentally found it. But someone had been inside; someone who avoided me.

I debated conducting a search there. I risked missing Elam if I left to look for him. Yet, if I stayed put and he did not return, he could be in danger or lost. Time would have been wasted. I paced in a circle. The curtains flew wild like flags in a hurricane with the wind's yowl. Frank rose onto his back haunches and focused on the ceiling.

"Make a decision, dammit." I yelled to myself. "Do something!" My nervous pacing resumed.

After a few more rounds through the tiny living space, it dawned on me. "Frank." He straightened his back legs, cocked his head, and watched me. I spoke as a general ordering the private. "Stay here. Wait for Elam."

He trotted to the front window and stuck his head out in front of the flapping curtains.

I left a note on the bistro-style table.

Elam,

I was too worried about you to wait inside. I went to Camilla's and found her house EMPTY. Please stay put. I'm searching for you now but will return. I don't want us to miss each other.

I Love You, Sandy.

Changing into my running shoes, I took the umbrella from the tiny pantry off the kitchen and headed out into the downpour, now blowing sideways under a dark, tight quilt of turbulent clouds. I locked eyes with Frank from the road. His head rested on the window ledge. I splashed on for the village.

****

THE DECEPTOR'S CALL

The wet village streets lay nearly deserted. Long-faced customers stared at the weather from under roofed, open-air restaurants, fancy cocktails clutched in their hands. Employees gathered in the entrances of businesses, watching the storm. Palm trees bent, their long leaves wavering in the raging gusts. Whitecaps rolled out to the gray horizon. I pressed on.

I visited every open business, asking if they'd seen Elam, leaving descriptions in case they did. All resulted in shaking heads with promises to tell him I was worried should he be spotted. No corner went unsearched. Each passing minute brought more anxiety.

I ventured into small shack neighborhoods. The rain whipped clothing left on lines strung between front yard palm trees. Disheartened, I trudged home, tugging at the umbrella straining against the blustery winds.

Outside the village, my frustrated tears released like a broken dam until I was empty. "Where are you, Elam?" I yelled. The trees bent close as if watching me. Each pull of my feet in the sandals felt like concrete blocks in the rush of water and sand.

****

At his post in *Paraiso's* window, the fabric flapped around Frank's head with the breeze. He met me at the door. My note lay untouched. I dropped into a chair, the watchdog at my knee.

Forlorn and lost without Elam, a new idea sparked. "Frank." I patted his dirty head. "Why didn't I think of it before? I know where to go for help. Stay on guard for Elam."

Fresh optimism surfaced as I fought the monsoon. My chest on fire, I pumped my legs fast. I stopped twice to catch my breath. Everyone I'd approached earlier gawked at me as I ran past a second time in the downpour.

PALM ISLE POLICIA was nailed over the door of a tiny building. We had noticed the building in the center of the village on one of our precious strolls. Young, officers uniformed in lemon-colored shirts, scurried in and out of the rain. Some kept watch as they leaned on the wall inside the open top of a Dutch door as if expecting an uneventful island day.

I stopped in front of the building, hands on my knees, heaving until I caught my breath.

"Come." A hand rested gently on my arm. "Come in from the rain." The officer nodded his head toward the building. According to the badge fastened to his shirt, his name was Chief Officer Juan. "Come," he repeated in his soft accent. He gently coaxed me inside. All the officers gathered at the open counter. They opened the bottom half of the door and parted as I entered. One dragged a chair to the center of the small space for me.

Nearby conversations stopped. The officers waited. My breathing slowed. I lowered into the creaky chair. Humanity and perspiration hung in the damp space.

Officer Juan towered over me, a cone-shaped cup of water in his hand. "Drink." His deep accented voice calmed me.

I gulped unashamedly until the cone was empty. He took it and passed it on to a younger officer who refilled it from a water cooler in the corner. I guzzled it down again. He tossed the empty cup it into a wastebasket, bouncing on top of the others piled high.

Juan pulled a chair close to me and eased down, his long legs too large in the space. "Why did you run?"

"My husband," hot tears stung my lids. The awful words passed through my lips, "is missing."

"Your husband." He glanced up to the other officers. They bunched in. The space around me shrank.

"Yes." I stopped crying and swiped tears and water from my face with my hands. My words came easier. "He left our cottage and hasn't come back."

"What was your husband's mood before he left?"

THE DECEPTOR'S CALL

"He was angry." Elam's furious expression as he walked out was vividly plastered in my memory. "He was bound and determined to go to our landlady's cottage." Hurt waved over me with the memory.

"Husbands often need a cooling off period after a disagreement. He'll return when he's ready." His subordinates burst with laughter. "We see this often," he said with a smirk.

Officer Juan reached for a clipboard from a shelf near his head. The calm, citrus yellow of his shirt clashed with my anxiety. He chose a pen from a metal can on the counter and settled the clipboard on his thigh.

"Your name, please."

"Sandy. Sandy Steele." He scribbled on the form secured by the board's metal clip.

"Home country? U.S.?"

"Yes. United States."

"Where do you stay on the island?"

"1 Conch."

He stilled his pen. He peered deep into my eyes as if he read my thoughts "You stay at 1 Conch?" The last word was an octave higher. The officers bent near us, their breaths filling the air.

"Yes, that's right. Paraiso cottage on 1 Conch."

He continued in his baritone voice. "Home address in U.S.?"

"We sold our home. We're traveling indefinitely." I crossed my legs and moved my toes up and down anxiously. "Can we get on with the fact that my husband is missing? Please?"

"His name."

"Elam Steele. S-T-E-E-L-E. He's six-two. Dark hair. A little gray at the temples. Fifty years old."

The pen scratched on the paper as he took notes, the process painfully slow. "Clothing."

"White t-shirt. Black shorts."

He scribbled.

"No, no. Wait." My fingers tapped my head for clarification. "Dark blue, I think. I don't remember the exact color, but I'm sure his shorts are dark."

"Where did you last see him?"

"Aren't you listening? At our cottage. He left a couple of hours ago. Maybe three." I spoke quickly as he jotted my words on the paper. "I've gone everywhere to find him."

"Where have you looked?"

"First I went to our landlady's cottage. Her name is Camilla." I searched his attentive face for any sign of recognition. "Her cottage was empty." I drew a long shaky breath. "Completely empty." I detected a slight twitch of his brow.

"Where else?"

"Then I came into the village and asked around. No one remembers seeing him."

Juan spoke Spanish-Creole to the young man closest to him.

"What are you saying to him?"

"He has instructions." I faced the officer, craving assurance and confidence in locating Elam.

The officer maintained his professional demeanor. "You return to Paraiso. We will search." He briefed the men around him in their language. The huddle dispersed and spread out in all directions. The office emptied with frenzied excitement, preventing my protests. A *Will Return* metal sign dangled loose from a thin chain on a nail by the door. Officer Juan shook my hand and escorted me to the door.

I kept a vigilant watch for any sign of Elam as I left for the cottage through the soggy streets. The implausible idea of doing nothing but waiting did not sit well with me.

The pelting deluge had stopped. The rising water already retreated into the sandy earth. My sandals alternated sucking noises in the mud. My heart sank as I reached the cottage with Frank still in

THE DECEPTOR'S CALL

his lookout position. I let him out. He loped to the deck and guarded the street from between the railing slats. The torturous wait resumed.

I paced in narrow circles. No longer comforting, the soft wall clock ticking seemed to echo throughout the space as if it were Big Ben.

Exhausted clouds hung in place. The sea of whitecaps had calmed to low rolls lapping softly on our beach. Ocean murmurs lulled me out to the back deck where I viewed the clean wash of splendor, anxiety and worry soothed from my mind.

The clock's rhythm slowed. The hypnotic tick tock reached me outside on the deck. A daydream of memories I'd fought back since Elam's heart attack wedged their way forward. I tightened my grasp on the wood railing. Images of the year-old sunny day came to mind. The scene in our garage unraveled. His grimaced face when he realized what I was burning. His anger at my destroying documentation of his past. His body as it slammed on the concrete floor.

I did not want to believe he revisited the scene daily. Did his newfound affection for me now serve as a bandage to help deny his discovery? I'd loved Elam fiercely since our first encounter in our college library. He'd clumsily dropped a book on my foot. We became fast friends and confidantes. My devotion had never wavered.

"Stop it, Sandy," I called toward the ocean. "He's chosen to move beyond it. Focus on finding him." I loosened my hand from the railing and walked down to the lush back yard.

My thoughts halted with Frank's ferocious barking from the front yard. I raced up the back stairs and into the cottage to the front door, heart pounding. Juan worked his way over the wet stones. The pilings underneath vibrated the cottage as he climbed the steps. Frank licked at his hands as if meeting an old friend.

"Mrs. Steele," he said through the screen, the chief officer's neutral face unreadable.

"Please, call me Sandy." I opened the door. The sun peeked at a cloud's edge in wait for the officer's news. "Come inside."

He hesitated with a darting inspection over my shoulder at the interior of the cabana. He passed over the threshold, his head missing the top of the door frame by an inch as he searched the room. He opened and closed his fists anxiously. His exhalation brushed my face. "Sandy, we have a witness. A shop owner has seen your husband."

My heart fell. "Where?"

Juan's height filled the room. "The owner saw someone while opening his shop. He believes the man fits the description of your husband."

I pressed a hand to my chest and repeated the words I'd longed to hear. "He said he saw Elam? So, he's okay?"

"A few more questions." Juan continued to scan the living room and kitchen area. He rubbed the back of his neck and shifted his feet.

"Anything." I motioned to the chair. "Please sit down."

"No." He glanced to each corner of the room. "I prefer to stand. Are you traveling with your children? Other friends?"

"No. I told you, it's only the two of us. Why?"

"The shop owner. The man he saw was not alone." He exhaled then closed his lips as if choosing his next words carefully.

"What?" I leaned closer to him. "Who was he with?"

"The man he saw," he paused and scratched his head, "was in the company of a young woman."

My throat tightened.

"Have you associated with anyone else on the island?"

"Besides random people in a bar, no. Well...yes . A week ago, a guy named Dave took us out to snorkel at the reef in the harbor. But he was gone before we were done. We've not seen him since. And

THE DECEPTOR'S CALL

our landlady, I mentioned earlier, her name is Camilla. But she's an older woman." Her labored gait came to mind. "Elderly, actually." I raised both hands out to the sides. "That's all. And we haven't met any younger people besides wait staff. The man he saw can't be Elam."

"Where does this Dave live? Where did you meet him?"

"We met him in a restaurant. He wore his hair in a braid. No idea where he lives."

"The shop owner thought your husband walked with his daughter."

"My daughter is in school back in The States."

"Well, I'm sure he'll return to you soon." He made for the door.

"That's it?" I encroached on his personal space. "Elam is still missing." He pulled back slightly. "You can't be done with the investigation," I said.

His hand was already on the screen's handle. "You say the shop owner is mistaken. We will keep a watch. All fishermen have been notified to keep an eye out, as well. Their boats surround the island."

"But..."

"Your husband will be found, or he'll come back to you. This is a small island." He pulled open the door and joined Frank on the deck. The dog nuzzled his outstretched hand. "Good-day." His descent shook the cottage.

He left me slack-mouthed, alone in Paraiso's quaint space. Elam still remained somewhere out there.

"Where are you, dammit?" I had to figure something out. With nowhere else to turn, I decided to think back over incidents that led up to the present in hopes for a clue.

Camilla and her requests for Elam's help came back to me. She'd said she needed him to move furniture. The furniture turned out to be boxes, according to him. Elam had fallen into strange, faraway moods after helping her out. His last conversation had changed from his normal, easy-going, happy demeanor to angst and frustration.

He'd said the cottage was confining. Happy to be at Camilla's beck and call, Elam's attitude toward me had grown cold and indifferent. But the cottage had been empty.

Officer Juan had cringed when I mentioned Camilla and our address. The memory of the taxi drivers refusing to take us to Camilla's rental cottage popped in my head. I wanted to go back and turn the questions back to him.

Shauna and Ed came to mind. The kids would want to know about their father. My cell phone screen still black, I located my iPad and connected to a mobile hotspot. The simple act of writing an email and bring them into the loop alleviated my fear and frustration. I aimed to send a positive impression. One paragraph completed, the data connection disconnected. "You've got to be kidding me." I saved the draft I'd written in case connection returned. Tossing the iPad aside in frustration, my pacing resumed.

Tropical birds announced an end to their workday as the heavy lavender twilight sky changed to final seconds of pink-orange light. The sky's saddened color palette mirrored the sea and my mood. My childhood memories of being locked and bound in the closet returned as the light dwindled to dark. The sea lapped softly on the beach, a reminder the Earth's rhythm would continue despite Elam's absence.

****

Tired from constant pacing, I settled onto the chair by the window. Time slipped away. Stars blinked as past memories were triggered. My mind wandered back to the article I'd seen in the Daily Gazette newspaper more than two decades before; the morning after IT had happened.

Coroner determines woman's death a suicide after being hit by an oncoming vehicle yesterday. Witnesses reported seeing the young woman in Spring Garden Street as a delivery truck traveled in her direction

THE DECEPTOR'S CALL

at approximately 3 p.m. The driver described his attempt to avoid her. "Before I knew it, there she was, right in front of my truck. She had a weird look on her face." Black tire tracks remain at the site. Evelyn Smith, a witness on her way to work at a neighborhood cafe, stated, "I heard tires squealing in the distance, then there was a thud. I'll never forget it. When I saw the body, and that hair, you can't miss her beautiful hair, I was shocked. We were friends. She'd been so excited. She'd recently found out she was pregnant."

 The thin newspaper slipped from my hands and floated to the cheap linoleum of my college apartment. My knees liquefied as I'd crumpled to the floor amid the papers. Not only had things gone terribly wrong, my self-loathing from what had happened between us deepened with information from the article. Elam's fiancée had been pregnant. As close as he and I had become, he'd not trusted me enough to share their secret. I'd been a fool to think he viewed me more than his good friend. My first choice had been telling the authorities the truth of her fall. And my unsuccessful attempt to prevent it. But Elam would suffer the loss the rest of his life. I had the ability to stop his suffering. I knew him so well. He would have everything he'd ever desired. The secret stowed deep inside, we exchanged wedding vows two years later.

 Three decades of marriage molds and evolves for the sake of happiness, at least to achieve comfortable cohesiveness and relative satisfaction. But eternal guilt made sacrifices and unpleasantness a bearable lifetime punishment. Some of the lessons were simple. I learned to cook his hamburger with the proper amount of pink in the center, not too much, not too little. I smiled when he suddenly decided to entertain friends at home when I preferred to have a low-key night alone to read after the children were in bed.

 Early in our marriage, I learned to play the role of supportive wife. We worked hard as the self-made, multi-store lighting business owners. My role changed with the first pregnancy. I'd made sure our family was admired and regarded as perfect within our small community. I was PTA president for years. The children always used their manners, were top of their classes, and accomplished classical string musicians. I lived only for them. Never trendy, I kept my hair styles and wardrobe timeless. I greeted friends and acquaintances with a cheerful smile. No one suspected the internal toll of my secret.

During college, I'd thrown myself into secretly making up to Elam for the truth he would never know about the part I played in her death. He'd dealt with internal anger after the shock of the newspaper article.

Elam could never be given a reason to contemplate the past, to pine for what could have been. I was his future. Long ago events had gone beyond my initial plan. My only purpose for the trip that day had been to see for myself the luminous eyes and the red hair he'd described to me, his good friend. I had to meet her, the owner of his heart. Nothing more.

I faced him in the hospital after the heart attack. Beside the bed where Elam's weakened and unconscious body rested in a tangle of wires, monitors closely tracked his vital organ functions. My apology for burning the pictures and letters, and the promise of a return of his happiness as the center of my being, went unanswered. I'd come so close to losing him. The guilt, a cumbersome extra limb I'd worn for decades, grew heavier with the incessant beeping of the monitors.

Hours passed as my fear of what could have happened to Elam intensified. I sulked at the table in our rental island kitchen. The notion of leaving to stay with Shauna until he was found passed in and out of my mind as quickly as it came. I chose to remain on the island and endure whatever discovery was made of his whereabouts. "I will not turn my back on you, Elam."

I walked into the cottage bedroom and collapsed on top of the quilted cover. The night's humid heat closed in with my loneliness. I rolled over and cradled his pillow close to my chest, drawing the

THE DECEPTOR'S CALL

scent of him deep into my lungs. Sleep refused to relieve my tormented conscience.

The rental cottage lost its coziness. Pink-yellow split the horizon. Cramped in the suffocating interior, I made a strong pot of coffee and paced on the back deck. My report to the police had come up with nothing. The need to do something productive toward locating Elam burned deep. I brushed aside Officer Juan's order to wait and put pen to paper. I formed a list of questions for the chief.

****

The reprieve from pelting rain ended. I left the cottage, the wooden door open and screen door closed as a welcoming gesture for Elam just in case he returned in my absence. I ignored Frank's bark and nose pressed to my calf in his desire to accompany me, his purpose better served to stay in wait for Elam, once again, and protect him when he returned. Unconcerned with comfort, I left the soaked umbrella dripping against the front porch wall.

Determined to speak to Officer Juan, I forged the drenched road to the village with my list of questions, my effort heightened by worry of Elam's not returning in my absence. His mental state when he left made him unpredictable.

The image of the lone cottage off the grassy lane came to mind. I continued on toward the small, unassuming police building. Yet, the recurrent picture returned like the peevish buzz of a bumblebee, details of the abandoned shack and twisted dock etched into my brain.

The breeze intensified. Whirling, hissing whispers beckoned. As if pulled by a magnet, I changed course and proceeded in the direction of the derelict dwelling.

The water-weighted blades of grass made the makeshift sign easily visible. I sloshed along the narrow rain-drenched path to the cottage, the whispers drawing me forward. My stomach flipped.

What kind of reception would I receive when I arrived? My company had not been welcomed the first time I was here. The deluge made the deserted building more forbidding. Saturated clothing clung to me like an extra layer of skin.

I approached the porch angled by the three house-supporting stones and dodged the rush of rain from the tin roof edges. "Hello?" Desperate for help, I rapped at the door, the whispers in my ear. I detected a strong presence inside. "I'm looking for my husband. He's missing." The still curtains did not move. "He's not well." I waited.

The door eked open a slit. Splashes from the deluge poured like a waterfall from the roof and puddled at the base of the door.

"His name is Elam." My words tumbled out before the door could slam in my face. "He's tall with dark hair." I leaned close and strained to see inside the narrow opening. "He's wearing dark shorts and a white t-shirt."

The door banged shut. I pulled back in time to avoid the impact on my face. Fear of something evil seized me. He must be inside. "Elam." My fists thrashed against the door. "Elam." I gripped the locked handle. The curtain held tight against my grasp as if nailed to the inside frame of the window. "Elam, are you in there?" I leaped off the porch and raced to the back of the hovel.

The back door opened at my turn of the handle. I stepped inside. Flat gray light spilled to the floorboards. My heart hammered in my ears as red and yellow floral patterns sifted in through the fabric window coverings. The unfurnished single room lay bare.

"Hello?" My voice echoed in the space. Dark objects against the far wall were shadowed in the dim light. I clasped the door handle tight, craned my neck, and peered farther into the gloomier side. Weathered wood crates covered the wall. I counted neat stacks of six rows across and five crates to a row.

He had said Camilla asked him to move a couple of boxes, but instead had him move thirty. I had assumed he worked in her cottage

THE DECEPTOR'S CALL

around the corner from ours. I stepped inside and inched closer to the crates.

I blinked. I slapped my hands over my mouth to stifle a gasp.

I stumbled backwards.

All thirty crates were stacked and painted in the same bold black lettering. *ELAM STEELE.*

CHAPTER NINE

My mind and body functioned on autopilot. Without a glance back at *Paraiso*, I ran at high speed as the rain ended. Villagers and tourists slackened their hustle and gawked at me, the crazed woman. I dashed between them, half crying, half screaming between gasps of air all the way to the police department. Officer Juan watched me, a reproachful knit in his brow. Unable to speak, I waved away the chair he offered as my lungs sucked in needed oxygen. I bent over and puffed until I could form words.

"Boxes are stacked," I said between heaved breaths, "in the cottage."

"What cottage?" He crossed his arms and tapped his foot irritably.

"The abandoned cottage," I drew in more air, "at the dock."

"Please, take a breath and slow down. Which dock?"

"I can't slow down. The dock and house where the welcome sign is by the road. Out beyond our place. There are crates stacked in there with my husband's name printed on them. Every last one."

Juan sighed. "What are in the crates, Sandy?"

"I have no idea." *How could he not get it?* "I wasn't there to shop." Every second, I teetered on the precipice of a mental collapse from which I may never return.

Juan smirked, uncrossed his arms then delivered orders to two junior officers, no sense of urgency in his Spanish. I was centered, like a circus sideshow, in the group of gaping-eyed tourists and locals gathered to watch me through the open door. The officers hopped on bicycles leaned against an outside wall and rode away.

He returned his attention my way. "They will go." Then, to a third officer, he gave more orders in his natural language. "Officer Rodriguez," he nodded to the man, "will escort you back to your cottage. You remain there until we have new information for you."

THE DECEPTOR'S CALL

The man reached to touch my arm. I shrugged him off. "If I hadn't gone looking for Elam myself, those boxes would never have been found. I'm going with them." I stomped out and stared the horde of spectators down, daring them to stand in my way. The crowd split like a parting sea and opened a clear path for me. Gossipy undertones followed me.

"Come." His deep voice called. "Ride with me."

I stopped at his authoritative tone.

Juan snatched a key from a nail in the wall by the door and walked around to the back of the building. He returned in a golf cart and pulled up in front of me. "Get in."

I climbed in beside him. We rode in silence until we reached the *Welcome* sign. The cart's wide set tires bounced along the narrow sandy footpath, compressing the wild grass underneath.

The chief braked in front of an undisturbed scene. Crystal water glistened beneath the stretched dock under a brilliant sun. The cottage door stood wide open as I'd left it in my hysterics. Two officer's bicycles lay strewn on their sides near the door.

"Stay here," he said. He removed the key and slipped it into his pocket.

"I can't sit out here and do nothing."

"If you cannot follow orders," he lifted a pair of cuffs attached to his leather belt, "I'll handcuff you to the cart."

Sweat drained from my pores as I paced in front of the golf cart, my attention fixed on the little building. Muffled male voices flowed out from the gaping door. After what seemed an eternity, the three officers emerged. They walked toward me, their expressions blank.

Juan pulled out a pad and pen from his pocket and handed it to the young man on his left with a communicative nod. "Document our findings," he said. The junior officer disappeared inside the cottage. Juan's gaze bore into me. "Sandy."

My jaw tightened as he drew closer.

"There are no boxes."

I shriveled under his glare. His sobering words echoed in my head. They made no sense. "I'm not crazy." I lifted my leg and kicked the golf cart's back tire. "Ouch." Toe throbbing in my sandal I hopped on the other foot and grasped the injured toe. No one said a word. My emotions pushed to the limit, the details of the vision came back to me. I lowered my foot and stood firm. "I saw thirty crates." I approximated the size between my hands. "Large crates. Elam Steele printed on each one."

"There is nothing inside."

"You're wrong. You have to be." I moved from the cart. A young officer placed his hand in front of me.

"Let her go," Juan said.

I raced through the open door and halted in the dim interior, almost losing my balance. I stared at a solid blank wall. Not one crate remained in the empty space. Shoeprints were the only disturbance in the dust covered wooden floor. Dejected, my shoulders slumped and I shook my head. "I can't believe this."

"You need to get some rest, Mrs. Steele." He placed his hand gently on my shoulder. "This has been difficult ordeal for you. I'll take you back to your cottage. You can wait for your husband there."

Any basis for argument and energy for resistance had been removed. I would have to wait the situation out alone. He guided me, his hand gentle on my upper arm, to the passenger side of the golf cart and took me home. He helped me settle on the couch. Frank's thick, wet tongue licked up my arm.

****

Thoughts jumbled in my mind like a shaken box of puzzle pieces. No instruction manual existed for the unexplained events piling up.

Coherent thoughts dribbled to me. My short time in a foreign country resulted in making no friends, a rental cottage without a workable phone, and a missing spouse. The officer said a witness stated he'd seen a man matching Elam's description in the company of a young girl. Then it dawned on me. Elam had said Camilla was younger than her elderly body. One detail about her teased the outer edge of my memory.

"What was it?" I raked my fingers through my hair. "What did he tell me?" With stiffened muscles, I left the couch and walked in obsessive circles. "Dammit, what did he say?"

Then it came to me, clear and bright as a lightning bolt. "Bingo," I yelled, racing out the door.

****

"I remember something." I burst into the police station. "I remember." I panted between words to the cops inside the building. A group of older ladies were in discussion with Officer Juan. I bore down on him.

"Excuse me for a moment," he said to them through pursed lips. He faced me with raised brows. "You have orders to stay at home." Exasperation lined his tone.

"But I remembered something." I would not be dismissed. I leaned in closer to him. "It's important. I should have remembered earlier."

"We are busy here." He cocked his head to the side.

"The witness. The man who said he saw Elam walking with a young girl..." I panted a few more breaths.

"Yes?"

"Did he tell you what color her hair was?" I opened and closed my hands to release some of the adrenaline thrumming through my veins like quicksilver.

Three lines formed on his forehead as his brows knitted together. He reached for his notebook on a desk in the corner of the small space. Opening it, he flipped back a few pages then stopped. He scanned over his notes. "Red. He said the girl had red hair."

"Yes." I clapped my hands together. "Exactly. The detail I'd forgotten. The day he'd gone to help Camilla move furniture, he told me he'd actually moved boxes instead. He was adamant about her age. He said she'd appeared as young as twenty."

Juan's hand swiped at his glistening forehead as he flicked his eyes to the ceiling then back to me. He rubbed his temple.

"I went over there the next morning and asked her to stop using him for heavy labor. I said he needed to relax. She wouldn't come out. In fact, she stayed half hidden by the door. But I thought I noticed a red highlight in her gray hair."

He glanced at his watch. "Mm-hmm."

On the verge of a shout, I grasped fistfuls of hair. "I realize what I'm saying sounds far-fetched, but red is exactly what I saw." I tried to stop fidgeting and stuffed my hands in my pockets.

"Sandy, you're tired. Go home. I am sure your husband will return to you." He stepped closer. In a lowered voice, "I don't mean to cause you unnecessary pain, but tourists go missing all the time. Men come here to let go, have a little fun in the Caribbean. They drink and smoke. Stray from their wives. It happens every day."

I swallowed hard and shook my head at his preposterous supposition. "You still don't understand. You think I'm simply a paranoid, jilted wife. But I'm trying to get this point across to you." I pointed to my chest. "My missing husband told me things. And I saw something. It's an important detail."

Juan stared at me, doubt set in his raised brow. "Why didn't you mention this before?"

"It honestly didn't occur to me. I wish I had." My hand ached as I clenched it into a fist. "Can I rely on your help?"

We squared off inside the newly formed semi-circle of lemon-shirted officers.

THE DECEPTOR'S CALL

His stone face broke into a patronizing half grin. "You came to me. You say boxes were stacked in an empty cottage with your husband's name on them." The smile vanished as he crossed his arms and shifted his weight to one side. "There were no boxes." Juan adjusted his posture. "We are short of personnel. There are not enough people to patrol the whole island all the time. If there is new information, we will investigate."

"Has anyone taken a boat out? Done an offshore investigation? Or attempted to track down a redheaded woman?"

"Yes." He stiffened and bit his lower lip.

My mouth fell open. "Yes?" I breathed.

"I didn't want to frighten you. My men patrolled and searched the surrounding water after you first reported him missing. And again after he was not located on the island. I assure you, we have covered all possibilities."

"What about the Dave guy?" I asked just short of shouting. "Have you searched for him?"

"Yes. No one knows your Dave."

I cleared my throat. "Listen." I spread my hands wide. "I understand you and your men are busy here. And I appreciate everything you've done to help." I wanted to appear collected. "I don't mean to seem ungrateful. But I'm terrified. And alone." I lowered my voice. "Some weird things happened days before Elam went missing. I didn't think they were important during the emergency of him not showing up. But now I understand I should have told you."

"I'm listening."

"For no apparent reason, he'd been acting like he was hypnotized at times, other times angry. He would focus solely on Camilla. Once, he stared at her cottage from the water while we were swimming off the beach from our cabana." My voice choked at the memory.

"She seemed perfectly normal when we first arrived, a sweet old lady who wanted to make new visitors feel at home in her rental. We settled in fine, but then things got weird. He was so happy to be here and relaxed at first. But it wasn't long before she diverted his attention by asking him to move things for her. And then I found the boxes in that rickety house, though I know you don't believe me."

I dropped my shoulders. "I admit it's bizarre. It doesn't make sense to me, either." I couldn't suppress my desperation. "Elam is gone. We came here to revive our marriage. He suffered a major heart attack a year ago." I winced at the clear vision of his painful expression just before he had clawed at his chest. "This trip was supposed to be good for him. For us. We've sold everything we had, business, home, car. This is our first stop on a life-changing trip." I lowered my head. Tears rolled down my cheeks.

Juan offered me a tissue. "I understand your circumstances. You will be notified if we get any new leads."

"Do you know Camilla well?" I dabbed at the corners of my lids with the tissue and tried to gain control of myself.

"Everyone knows her." He bit his lip and met the men's probing gazes. They each scurried to find something else to do. "This is my advice." He placed his enormous hands on my shoulders and bent over until his face was level with mine. "Stay away from her. It is the best for you. Leave Camilla alone."

Blood rushed from my limbs.

He let go of me. "Ride home or walk?" The conversation ended.

I sulked away without a reply, officially on my own.

****

Camilla's cottage sat undisturbed when I walked by. No point in going there.

I thought about Officer Juan's suggestion of infidelity, an easy way for him to ignore the ghastly experiences before Elam's

THE DECEPTOR'S CALL

disappearance. Elam was not the prowling kind. Infidelity was improbable. No one could convince me otherwise. He'd been faithful to our marriage during the thirty years we'd spent together. I knew he carried secret regret and pain associated with the loss of his would-be family. The memory of my secret minutes with her all those years ago crept in. I fought it back and re-focused. His recent mental state was disturbing. The hypnotic compulsion he'd displayed on more than one occasion was of grave concern.

    I recalled each cab driver's reactions and adamant refusal to drive us out to Camilla's rental without explanation. Convinced Juan's order for me to "stay away" from Camilla carried meaning he was reticent to share, I racked my brain for any conceivable explanation for the vision of the crates. The abandoned cottage had been empty when the officers were there. I had to accept it. My desperation to find Elam made me see things that existed only in my mind.

    Lack of sleep and nourishment added to the growing tension in my head and neck as if a vice grip clamped tight on my skull. Saliva filled my mouth at the thought of food. But in order to keep up my strength, I threw together a half sandwich and forced it down. The tension eased and my stamina improved.

    The sour aroma turned out to be my armpits. Nervous about there being a repeat of the hot water episode, I sponge bathed in the bathroom sink. The nozzles worked appropriately this time. I kept my ears peeled, wishing for Elam's heavy steps to enter the cottage and his voice calling my name. The futile effort only served to deepen my melancholy.

    Ed and Shauna needed to be informed of the situation with their father. My last attempt to email them had failed. Chancing the hotspot was reconnected, I grabbed my iPad and dropped onto the edge of the bed. I did not want to frighten the kids, but too much time had passed since I'd written to them.

BARBARA MICHELLE

As the device powered up, Frank tore into a round of bloodcurdling barks. I jumped off the bed. The iPad slipped from my hands. I prayed to the ceiling. "Please let it be Elam." I ran to the screen door. Frank watched in a rigid stance at the top of the deck stairs, smutty black hair between his shoulders on end like a Mohawk.

"Frank." I shouted. The barks lowered to a warning growl at the empty sandy street. Disappointed, I went back to the bedroom and my iPad. The mobile hotspot still not working, I typed the update I dreaded sharing. If by some miracle the connection returned later, the draft would be ready to send.

Five minutes later, Frank whimpered. I placed the iPad on the bed and returned to the screen door. Maybe I'd missed something before. I stepped out to the deck and found the mutt crouched and shivering behind the wooden chair, his short tail tucked between his powerful legs. Alarmed by the sight of his cowering posture, I scanned the edge of mangroves around the cottage and the street. The sun shone directly overhead. Nothing appeared out of sorts.

"What's wrong?" I asked as I patted his head. "Come." He didn't budge. "Frank, come on." He left the spot and stopped at my side. There had to be a reason for his reaction. I descended the steps to investigate further, Frank following me. We sloshed through ankle deep brackish water in the front yard then investigated the back yard and along the beach. "No one's here, Frank."

I'd grown to appreciate his company and come to respect his instincts. Something had spooked him, but I refused to fall apart and go running back to the village for help since the chief did not believe me. We returned to the cottage.

Deflated, I collapsed onto the couch, the fabric damp from the oppressive humidity. As I took in the small space, I thought back to the day Elam informed me he'd booked the place. The remote location put us at an extreme disadvantage. We wanted peaceful

THE DECEPTOR'S CALL

surroundings, but within walking distance to entertainment and amenities. Though I hadn't been happy about the abrupt one-sided decision to change from St. Thomas to Palm Isle, I was convinced privacy was important to 'rekindle' our relationship and improve Elam's sleep quality. Stress, I thought, would be nonexistent, restoring his happiness and good health was my main objective.

The sun sank to a cloudless evening then into nightfall as depression set in. Stiff and cramped, I rose and flipped on the overhead light. I filled a glass with water at the kitchen sink. Frogs croaked in the front yard pond. Gentle waves lapped on the beach. I longed for Elam and the positive force he emanated.

Despair made way for reflection and often suppressed remembrances. The room dissolved as old memories of my father came alive. My deceased mother had often boasted to friends and other family members of my discipline and good disposition as a child and teenager. "A bother to no one." She never knew of my tortured endurance of his abusive treatment toward me while she worked long hours as a cashier and stocking down at the neighborhood grocery store.

On several occasions during our years together Elam mentioned I was "dyed-in-the-wool dependable" through the difficulties of building the business. He said he never worried about the children under my guidance.

My tears stung. "I'm so sorry, Elam." I wailed to nothing but the ocean and nighttime frogs. "I swear if I could go back in time, I'd take it all back." *Could my heart break any more?*

The grind of a truck's engine brought me back to the present. I'd lost confidence in my instincts and was sure my ears played tricks. Besides golf carts, I had never seen any vehicles on the island. The grating engine grew closer and more real as it slowed and revved in the many deep sandy ruts.

I wiped my eyes and pulled back the curtain. The front pond shimmered. The empty road shone silver under the moon. The engine groaned closer. Frank snarled at my side. Double cones of white light stabbed the sand then bounced and narrowed as a 1930s truck-style hearse appeared. Wording on the side made visible in the dark by a green luminescence as if from a glow stick. I squinted and read the lettering as the truck dipped and swayed in the maze of sandy ruts.

Palm Isle Caskets
Death Lives

A series of gongs caused me to turn my head to the back wall in the cabana. The pendulum swung hard and fast under the antique clock and nearly tossed it off the wall. Each gong thrummed louder inside my head and chest. I covered my ears with my hands to block the resounding tempo. The eerie green light bounced up and down until the old hearse disappeared beyond the mangroves.

"Frank?" I opened the door with shaking hands. The pendulum slowed to its regular rhythm. The dog raced in and headed beneath the kitchen table where he wedged his bulk into a tight ball. His spooked reaction convinced me he'd seen the truck. It was not just my wild imagination.

The idea of giving up the solitary wait for Elam crept into my mind. I had to calm myself. Maybe it would be wiser to return to our hometown, get an apartment near Shauna in her dorm. There seemed to be nothing else. I had no idea which way to turn on the island.

A sharp strike of lightning buzzed through the room. Stars sprinkled the cloudless sky outside the window. Seconds passed. Thunder clapped. The reverberation shook my bones as it made its way through the flooring, the few wall ornaments misaligned. The overhead light flickered. The room went black.

THE DECEPTOR'S CALL

"Frank?" My call for the dog came from a natural desire for companionship. I remembered a flashlight in a kitchen drawer and made my way blindly to the counter. I searched through the junk drawer by feel until I touched one and pulled it out. I pressed the button. Nothing happened. Wind outside picked up. Another stab of lightning bathed the room white for a mere second then left me blind in the thick gloom. Heavy waves crashed on the beach in back of the cottage. I tried the flashlight again. Nothing. Strong winds gusted through the windows and screen door, worrying my hair. A living room lamp crashed off the side table onto the wooden floor.

My voice shook. "Frank, get over here." He did not respond.

Wind-hurled coconuts bashed the tin roof as if Paraiso were under attack. I dropped onto the couch and wrapped my arms tightly around my knees tucked under my chin. A third bolt of lightning speared intense white light into a distinct, yet indiscernible shape. The next sword of hot lightning blasted to the center of the room in the unmistakable curves of a woman's silhouette.

Wafts of sulfur fumes burned my nostrils in the blinding and disorienting blackness that followed. I jumped off the couch, frightened beyond a scream and no idea where to go.

A new storm raged outside Paraiso. Soft, unintelligible whispers floated through the open window frames. I shrank back and wrapped my arms around my waist. The whispers grew louder as I tried to decipher them. They increased to a decibel of roaring voices in a stadium.

"This is only a nightmare." I could not hear my own voice.

The ever-growing voices altered to a high-pitched howl and drifted out the back windows and out to sea. My pulse hammered inside my head in the silent darkness. I lowered my hands from my waist. Frank whined from beneath the table.

Low whispers returned then formed into consonants and vowels. "Sandy."

BARBARA MICHELLE

Involuntary cries of panic escaped my throat. I fell back to the corner of the couch and balled up; knees to chin. Frank's dark bulk lay still under the table.

"Sandy." The whisper hissed.

"This is not real."

"Sandy."

Frazzled nerves forced my acceptance of an intruder. "Who are you?" I yelled. My words caught in a sob. I blinked in the darkness.

"Jealous-s-sy." The word passed as a wind gust by my ears.

I curled tighter into the couch.

"Death," the whisperer hissed.

I sprang from the couch. "Whoever . . . whatever you are, get out." My teeth chattered. I rubbed my hands up and down my arms.

Lightbulbs in the kitchen blinked on. The overhead living room fan spun on high. My heart rate matched its speed. The kitchen light flickered off, the swish of ceiling fan paddles slowed to a stop. The pendulum ticked off seconds in the darkened stillness.

Intense white light flashed outside the back windows. The silhouette flashed once, bright as a star, a small bundle held to her chest. I cowered as dizzying spots flashed in my vision, decorating the black night. Shivers swept through me in the silence, my face and tank top drenched in cold sweat.

The fragment of my mind capable of rational thinking sought a reasonable explanation for the illusion. Perhaps an electrical problem with the old wiring of the house?

But something would not let me go. Old insecurities I'd spent a lifetime pushing back mounted in the dark. My father's belief I would never measure up wrapped me like a dismal fog.

The overhead kitchen fixture threw a searing blast of light. I blinked. Across the room Frank trembled under the kitchen table. He poked his massive head out and whined to me. The sight of his reaction increased my heart palpitations.

THE DECEPTOR'S CALL

Totally alone and with no desire to stay in the cottage, I had nowhere else to go until morning. I curled into my protective crouch, afraid to move.

A faint notion niggled at me then strengthened to a hunger unwilling to subside until satisfied. It displaced all other thoughts. As if I possessed no will of my own, my legs carried me down the steps and through the watery yard. Frank remained crouched, trembling under the kitchen table, watching me go.

I followed the unknown pull into the darkened boondocks as if by an alien force. I marched on without choice, stretching my arms forward in the dark.

CHAPTER TEN

Storm clouds slid steadily away from the moon. Wet sand stuck between my toes. The whispering sensation swirled around me and in my head, guiding me along the soft pathway beyond the sign covered over by grasses, no more than a nighttime shadow.

Starlight bathed the abandoned cottage resting on its three stone bases. The door's rusted hinges drowsed open. My heart's pounding had not eased since the night's frightening activity at Paraiso. Blood pulsed in my ears. Not knowing why, I wanted to be inside the dark structure. Under its spell, the unseen force sent me in. The curtains pulled aside, haunting moonbeam sifted in.

Sudden bright yellow light invaded the small interior from a bare ceiling bulb. I squeezed my lids tight against the onslaught of the overhead light until they ached. Fearful of what waited, I slowly opened them.

My body recoiled from the sight. A shriek stuck in my throat.

Five neat rows of wooden crates stacked against the wall. The same letters labeled on each one. *ELAM STEELE*. I shook my head and slammed my lids shut again. "This. Is. Not. Real." I opened my eyes. The stacks remained. Wobbly kneed, my controlled feet dragged me across the worn floorboards to the crates. I mentally railed against the force holding me hostage. My hands came out empty when I desperately felt for my phone and its camera. I wanted to run out the door, across the sea, and never ever think of Palm Isle again.

Wood grated against wood as the center box slid forward from its stack, stopping at the brink before toppling to the ground. Something tightened around my ankles holding me in place. The force pressed my head closer to peer over the edge of the open top. Shock seized my throat.

THE DECEPTOR'S CALL

I looked down on a hairy, muscular right leg, severed at mid-thigh; the knee and ankle bent to fit within the confines of the crate walls. I clutched my throat. "No," I wailed. The crate slid back.

A second box slid out from the left stack and stopped before it tipped over. Two large hands lay on the bottom, the left resting peacefully over the right. Dried crimson streaked the clean, severed wrist edges. A shiny glint flashed from the third finger. Small diamonds centered in the wide gold wedding band I'd chosen long ago captivated me, their brilliance mocking. The crate scraped back into place against the wall.

"God, no. No. No." I tensed my arm muscles to cover my teary face. The force refused.

Compelled to endure the presentation of a third crate, the force stopped me from turning my head away. "Please, no more." I pleaded with an invisible being and curled my hands into my chest. "I don't want to see anymore." My screams ricocheted between the shabby walls.

The crate tipped forward from its position. The smooth skin had been severed at the neck edges where it once connected to shoulders. Black curly hair, wisps of grey at the temples, covered the scalp of the human head. A five o'clock shadow tinted the cheeks and chin. Thick black eyebrows arched over Elam's wild stare directed at me. His lips tilted up into an insane grin.

"Elam," I screamed in crazed sobs. I jumped back as the pressure released my ankles and head. I ran to the open door. It slammed shut in my face. The rusted metal lock engaged. I jerked the handle hard with both hands. It refused to release. I pounded on its thick island mahogany. "Let me out," I shrieked as I pulled on the locked back door handle. Intent on climbing out, I dashed to a window. Black iron crossbars covered the open frames. The mysterious bars shielded each window.

Trapped, I spun to the center of the shadowed room. "What do you want from me?"

"You, Sandy," answered the familiar whisper that I heard in Paraiso.

"Why would you take Elam?"

"You caused his death."

I searched the room for a person. "Who are you?"

"You betrayed his trust. Jealousy. Greed."

"I love him."

"The comfort you have with your children will be lost."

My blood curdled. "Leave them out of whatever this is."

"Elam will be returned."

Relief mixed into my fear of the unknown.

"You will be removed from their lives, as the unborn baby was taken from his. You will walk alone."

I yelled into the room, "My family needs me. Why won't you show me who you are?"

"The time has come," whispered the voice. "You will repay debts."

A baby cried outside.

"No," I shrieked. "I was so young." My pleas were aimed at the invisible being.

The crying baby made me buckle down on the dusty floor. Queasiness wrenched my stomach. The painful onslaught of repressed memories appeared as bright visions. "I would never do something so foolish now," I cried as I shook my head.

The clear chorus of town voices chattered on the sidewalk as the reel of memory spun in my mind. *She stood close, as if right in front of me in the dirty cottage. His fiancée. Startling moss-colored eyes held me captive. She tipped her head up and grinned. Long red tresses cascaded down the front of her eggshell blue dress. Unable to resist, I scrutinized the whole of the girl. Elam softened at the mere mention of her name.*

THE DECEPTOR'S CALL

I had not meant for things to go so far. My plan was only to see for myself the girl who owned the heart of the young man who owned mine. Her striking square face, and his dedication to her, was too much. Elam had been meant for me. We were soulmates. The close friendship we'd developed had proven it. There would be no room for distractions. No time for split allegiances. I would work every day to prove to him I was worthy and devoted.

Snatched from the memory, the stacks shimmied against the wall. I jumped to my feet. Each crate slid out in succession, one after another, slamming back against the wall. The sound quickly morphed into staccato slides and bangs. My face tear-streaked, I backed away and bumped into the locked front door.

The yellow overhead bulb blackened. The raucous banging stopped. Silence buzzed in my ears. A spinning sensation filled my head before I lost my balance.

****

Eyes closed, a level of clarity dawned in my head. Frank's sharp nails clicked across the floor before his wet tongue made contact on my arm. My lids fluttered. My vision cleared. The living room ceiling fan came into focus in a dim light. From Paraiso's couch, I glanced outside to an orange dawn. I sat up and rubbed the kink in my neck created by my head's awkward angle on the sofa arm. Floral-scented daylight and sweet tropical bird trills filled my senses. The nightmare was over. I was in Paraiso, waiting for Elam's return. I sat up and hugged the small couch pillow. The hard floor under my feet anchored me in reality. No crate stacks covered the wall. No bars on the windows trapping me. Soft waves lapping on our little beach soothed my senses.

I patted Frank's head, grateful for his company. I climbed off the couch and stretched my stiffened joints. Bending my tender neck, I got a good look at the source of pain in my lower limbs. Light-blue bruises wrapped around both of my ankles. *Could I have done this to myself while dreaming?* The dog sniffed the edges of the living room then searched the kitchen. He followed his nose out of sight and into the bedroom.

As I made coffee at the counter, it hit me how my body and mind treasured the normalcy of the task. I was renewed and completely rested with more energy than I'd had in years. It was strange considering the horrible situation I was in. The frightening events of my nightmare played over in my head. The longer Elam was missing, the more my physical and mental capabilities had become overwrought.

I added a splash of cream to my coffee. Heavy footsteps on the front steps shook the kitchen floor. Creamer sloshed out as I slammed the container on the counter and crossed to the living room.

I gasped at the extraordinary vision; my hopes answered. Happy tears blurred my vision at the sight of my husband. The pilings shimmied beneath his weight as he climbed the steps. As if he were returning from a short stroll, a smile lit his face. I was torn between happy he was back and angry he'd put me through such worry and turmoil.

Frank joined me at the window. He recognized Elam with an eruption of welcoming barks and powerful high bounces on his massive front legs.

"Hi Frank," he called out. My spirits lifted with the musical ring of his laughter. He clapped his hands at the excited dog jumping up and down on his front legs while poking his head through the window. Dressed in the clothes I had last seen him, he appeared unrumpled.

"Elam," I cried to him through jubilant sobs. "You're back." We met at the front door. "I've been sick with worry." I reached for the

THE DECEPTOR'S CALL

screen door latch at the same time he twisted it from the outside. He pushed the door open wide. I hopped aside to miss being hit.

"I'm back," Elam called into the center of the room. The door bounced into place.

"Thank goodness." I stepped close and reached to pull him to me. "I've never been so happy to see your face."

"Hello?" He passed me and moved to the bedroom door. He leaned in. "Anybody home?"

"Elam. I'm here." I walked over and stopped in front of him, placing my hands on his upper arms. "Here." I side-stepped out of his way to prevent being knocked down as he crossed the threshold into the bedroom. Alarms gonged in my head.

"Hello." He surveyed the room. "I'm home."

"Elam, I'm right here. Stop kidding around." He stuck his head inside the bathroom. I followed him back to the bedroom door toward the living room. A strong breeze blasted through the cottage, disturbing the thick curls on his head. Bright morning sunlight blazed inside.

Distress replaced my delight. "What happened to you? Did you hit your head?" The nightmare still fresh in my mind, I scanned his neck and wrists. The skin was smooth and pink without visible signs of trauma.

Keeping an even voice, I attempted once more to talk to him. "Elam." My heart sank when he did not respond to me. *Were his hearing and sight affected during his absence?* He walked by me and into the kitchen. He opened the refrigerator door and pulled out a small bottle of orange juice, opened the top, and guzzled it as if he were parched.

Light footsteps tapped on the stairs outside. I raced to the door in hopes it was Officer Juan. I was knocked aside and stumbled as Elam charged in front of me. He threw open the door and rushed to the deck railing.

"There you are," Elam called down. "I was disappointed when I got here and you were gone."

"What?" I stepped out to the deck. By the time I reached the railing, the subject of his search stepped up onto the deck with a smile to melt a thousand hearts. I recognized the fresh, rosy-cheeked face immediately.

Tightness clenched my throat and chest, making it difficult to breathe. I fought the buckling that threatened my knees and legs. I staggered back one step and threw both arms out to the sides to stabilize my balance.

A gold, heart-shaped charm dangled at her neck, the charm I'd seen the old woman pull from Donut Lady's metal pail. The same charm she had worn on the day everything changed.

My husband gathered the striking girl in the eggshell blue dress into his arms. His face lowered into her long glossy red waves and nuzzled her neck. "Cam. God, I missed you," he murmured.

She pushed him away with a kittenish grin and threw her head back. "I've hardly been gone any time."

Wanting to lash out, I was rendered speechless.

His whole face sparkled. He drank her in like a starved man. "Why do I feel like it's been a lifetime?"

"You're hopeless." She giggled like a schoolgirl. "But I love you anyway."

A desperate croak escaped my lips as I hyperventilated. "Elam. Stop. I'm here. I'm right here." I gripped the handrail for support and forced my feet to move, one at a time. "Elam, please. Look at me."

The girl's presence possessed his attention. I reached out to pull his shoulder back at the same time he retreated to allow the redhead access into our cottage. Cam's dainty sandaled feet practically floated across the threshold. Sweet floral perfume bloomed in the air.

Elam closed the door and took her hand. I slipped in after them. He pulled her to the couch. Her lithe body landed in his lap.

THE DECEPTOR'S CALL

"Dammit, Elam. Stop this." I approached the girl. "Get out." I reached to knock her off my husband. As I touched her, no solid muscle or bone resisted me. My hand sank through her shoulder. She did not flinch or face me. My presence unknown, I witnessed my beloved husband's attraction to the young ghoulish girl. *Was I delusional?*

"Where's the baby?" he asked.

Arctic waves rushed through my limbs.

She pushed herself off his lap. "How can you ask such a question?"

He tensed. "What do you mean?"

"Elam, you know where the baby is." Huge tears spilled over her lower lids.

Concern crossed his face. He stood to join her. "No. I don't. Is he all right?"

"What's wrong with you? Our baby is dead." She backed away from him as if he were contagious. "How could you forget?"

His face lost all color as he struggled to come to terms with the news.

"Elam, I'm so sorry," I wailed, unheard. "It was never my intention. I didn't know."

"What are you talking about?" His voice rose an octave. "I'm sorry. Please, tell me."

"What's happened to you?" she cried.

"I'm telling the truth." He jerked his arms frantically. "I don't know." His face reddened as if he might explode. "Just tell me. Stop crying and tell me."

She wiped her tears with a delicate finger then set her shoulders. "He was knocked out of my arms by some crazy woman. She forced me out into the street. I tripped and when he fell out of my arms, a delivery truck was coming down the road."

"Oh my God," Elam exclaimed as his whole body shook. He buried his hands in his hair.

"Wait. She's lying," I yelled. "She was pregnant." I placed both fists to my temples then shoved them back down in frustration. "I didn't know."

Her chin trembled. "Elam, how can you forget?"

He lowered his hands. "I. . .can't explain."

Cam clutched his hands and pulled him to sit by her on the couch. She cupped his dismal face in her hands. "Elam, obviously your memory has blocked everything to protect you. A way for you to cope and move on."

I marveled at the instant change in her demeanor.

"You were wrecked when you found out, as much as I was. It was so horrible. I apologize for my reaction." She kissed his wet cheek. "Our entire world was ripped apart. But we're still together." She smoothed the hair at his forehead. "And I won't ever leave your side."

His body drooped as if drained of energy, lost. It was agonizing to see him relive the knowledge as new, a result of my anger and jealousy. "Elam," I whispered.

"I love you, Elam Steele," she said. "We have to go on living, as we have been. His spirit is always with us. A part of us, of our love."

"Have we moved on?" He was like a child in need of direction, in need of assurance.

Cam peeled her delicate nineteen-year-old hands from his lined, middle-aged face and laid them in her lap. "Yes, Elam. We've been working on a new baby for the past few months. I can't believe you could forget how hard we've tried."

"If I have to relive his death, how can I possibly love another child?"

"You will. We both will. The act of trying has helped ease some of my pain. The doctors did offer a bit of optimism considering the damage I sustained by the truck." She planted a light kiss on his cheek. "They said it's not out of the question."

Misery consumed me. I pinched the back of my hand to force myself to wake up.

"As devastating as it was to lose him, so violently, so senselessly, I still want to be the mother of your child, Elam. It means everything to me. We'll never forget him. We'll remember him every year on his birthday and the anniversary of his murder."

Any minute I would wake up from another nightmare and the knife-slitting pain in my soul would be gone.

"His brother, or sister, will be told about him. He is as much a part of us now as when we held him in our arms." Darkness fell over her perfect features. "Before *she* destroyed him."

I backed into the faded overstuffed chair and fell in. The weight of the past, the distorted version of the truth, stole my energy and left me little to fight back with. "Cam," as he called her, had been in front of the delivery truck.

"Who was it?" His voice filled the room with rage. "Who killed my son?"

"Elam," I begged. "You didn't tell me she was pregnant. I never meant to harm them. The baby was never born." I grappled with the weak point. "I gave you another son, and a daughter. We have a wonderful life together." My pleas were ignored. "You have to remember."

"Shush." Cam pulled him to her. "Don't hold onto the anger. We've found forgiveness. She's a stranger who disappeared into the crowd on the sidewalk. Several men chased after her, but she was gone. Even if they found who was responsible, it wouldn't have brought our baby boy back to us."

I sank deeper into self-loathing with her twisted tale.

She kissed his head then released him. "Please, let's focus on conceiving another one. On our relationship."

I couldn't move as Cam stood and clasped his hand. He joined her and melted into her arms. She led him into our bedroom and left the door open. The mysterious nonentity held me in the chair as I endured my husband's cries of ecstasy and climax blended with her moans. I begged for the nightmare to end. Pungent animal smell of their sex filled my nostrils. Stomach acid burned my throat, gagging me.

"I would never have wanted you to go through it all alone." His tender words spilled through the open door. "And I'm sorry I don't remember."

"Soon we'll get the news of a second chance," she purred. "I'll be so incredibly happy."

"I love you, more than life itself," he said.

"My Elam."

"This is not happening." Anger poured from me. "It is only another nightmare."

Satiated breaths of slumber filled the cottage. I listened as the invisible strength held me hostage in the chair. Frank snored outside the front door.

****

Forced to remain in the living room chair and listen to them sleep, I inspected my hand. Ugly purple bruises had formed on the back from my pinches, the ankle bruises remained. I was not asleep. It was time to face things as they were. I considered the possibilities. I'd somehow gotten lost in an alternate dimensional plane, moved in a different level of reality. No matter how much my mind wanted to wrap itself around the situation and make sense of it all, the more ludicrous it seemed.

Fully conscious and alive, an altered version of the past had unraveled before me. As if watching a horror movie, consequences of my past choices played themselves out.

THE DECEPTOR'S CALL

Yet, I was *in* the surreal actions without being seen or heard, unable to correct her lies. I had no control over the direction of anything said or believed. Another three possibilities occurred to me; I'd either experienced a mental breakdown, suffered a stroke, or been given a neuro-altering drug. The longer I considered the plausible explanations, none of them fit.

The only thing I knew for sure, it was up to me to find a resolution and bring my family back together. I accepted the truth without understanding.

Elam and I had traveled point-blank into a dimension of hell on earth.

****

Quiet amplified the next torturous hour as the chair held me prisoner. I recalled Cam's false account of the horrible day thirty-two years before. She had not survived. I remembered my nausea as the truck skidded to avoid her. She'd stumbled from the sidewalk. Wide curved black marks and fresh blood stained the faded gray asphalt. Her long hair fanned out like a halo of flames. Her pelvic area squashed under the driver's side front tire, both legs lay hidden by the wheel below the truck's undercarriage. Horrified and severely shaken, I'd faded back into the crowd, a changed person, one who would reap what she sowed. The newspaper article the following day revealed new information to me. A police press conference two days later reported the accident was a result of the young girl's depression. A suicide. And the murder of a child.

I lost twenty pounds over the following months. My grades had dropped so low I was placed on academic probation. But I forced myself to rally and bring them up. I was a solid shoulder for the distraught Elam to lean on. My father, wherever his soul rested, would see I was, after all, valuable and worth something.

An overwhelming need to hear the voices of my grown children brought me back to the present. I had to free myself from Palm Isle and return to my hometown. Homesickness added to the jumble of emotions currently tangled inside me.

Movement from inside the bedroom brought my heart rate back up. I needed to make my presence known. "Elam? Can you hear me?"

I heard floorboards creak across the wooden floor.

"Elam, please hear me." I had to continue the effort to make a connection with him.

Cam appeared in the doorway, hair disheveled and dressed in the robe I'd purchased specifically for the trip.

"I'll kill you," I screamed.

She crossed the living room in leggy strides, passing me for the kitchen. My hatred for her soared. Her fingers smoothed the tangles from her long glorious hair. It pained me to see the love-rumpled condition serving to enhance her natural beauty.

Cam retrieved a glass from the cabinet as if the cottage was familiar. She filled it with water from the tap and took long sips before placing it on the counter. She walked to the back deck and took a deep breath as the breeze played in her hair, the loose edges of my robe fluttering at her cleavage. If only I could free myself and put an end to this torture by choking the life from her tender bare neck. Physical violence would have been less painful for me than the visual and emotional blows.

Elam's rhythmic breaths played as background music to my insanity.

The redhead returned to the kitchen. As she walked past me, the hem of my robe blew open revealing her lean thighs. The gleam in her sea green stare and flawless beauty stirred my old jealousy buried decades before. I was determined to push them aside and stay in control of myself as I sought a way to freedom.

THE DECEPTOR'S CALL

The girl leaned back on the counter facing away from the kitchen. Elam, his curls rumpled, entered the room. She cast a smile on him as he stopped short.

"You're beautiful," he said.

My heart tightened at the words he'd never said to me.

Cam sauntered into his embrace then pulled back to arm's length. "I'm so happy right now." She stretched her body suggestively for better display. "Are you hungry?"

"I've definitely worked up an appetite."

She tapped the tip of his nose with her finger. "You're one special man, Elam." She pulled his face into hers and locked him into a long passionate kiss.

"Goddammit," I yelled as my rage boiled to a sob. "How can this be happening?"

Cam broke the long kiss and slid her arms around his neck until they were cheek to cheek. My heart hammered on the verge of stopping. She zeroed in on my swollen, tearstained face. Her gaze fixed tight on me. The corners of her lips pulled up into a sexy smirk.

"You see me." I fought against the invisible restraint.

Seized by her grin directed at me, she touched the tip of her tongue to the base of Elam's neck. She worked it up to his ear, gently sucking the lobe in between her pale lips.

"I'll kill you!" I fought to rise from the torture chair. "I swear I will." White hot anger seared through my veins.

"You turn me on, baby." Elam said, his voice rough and guttural.

Cam pulled out of his arms. She took his hands, led him to the small table, and directed him into one of the chairs. "I'm going to make you a breakfast fit for a king. Then we're going to spend the day on the beach."

"Anything you want. I'm yours." He remained transfixed on her as bacon and eggs sizzled in a pan.

"What. Is. Going. On?" I said between clenched teeth. I twisted in the seat hoping to find the slightest weakness in the force holding me in place.

Elam's dreamy, euphoric state lingered sickeningly on Cam. She plated the food then set it on the table in front of him. She filled a glass with orange juice and set it by the plate.

Fury twisted inside me as I was forced to watch her play house with my husband. "Why are you doing this?" I shrieked. "Revenge? You're dead."

With her hand on his shoulder, "I'll get ready while you enjoy your breakfast." Cam left for the bedroom.

Elam chewed, blissfully unaware, in his dream state.

"Elam, honey? It's me, Sandy."

He wiped his mouth with his napkin.

"I'm ready." Cam leaned against the doorframe, dressed in my new, black stringed bikini. One hand on her hip, she displayed her slim curves for my husband.

"Oh, my God. This is ridiculous." I squirmed and pressed my shoulders against the insidious force to let me go. "Get. Out."

He raised his head to her voice then placed the forkful of eggs on the plate. "How did I get so damn lucky?" He leaned back in his chair. "Come here."

Triumph set in her smile. She sauntered up to him.

"That swimsuit is coming off you right now," he said, his voice thick with lust.

The girl tossed her head back and cackled with witchy glee.

Someone in the room released a devastated whimper. I realized it came from me.

Cam stopped short of his reach. "You can do whatever you like once we get where we're going. Now get dressed to go swimming."

"Yes Ma'am. Whatever you say." Elam departed for the bedroom.

THE DECEPTOR'S CALL

As soon as he was out of sight, Cam crossed her arms and grinned at me. My blood curdled at the splintery, aged voice of elderly Camilla. "You killed us. You killed Elam's sweet, innocent baby."

"It was an accident. You're a monster...a ghost. You're not real."

"I'm completely real," croaked the voice from her full, pouty lips. "You thought you had it all under control. Everything you wanted. But it's time to repay life's debts. And it's only just begun, Sandy."

"I tried to stop you from falling. And I had no idea of your pregnancy. You must already know that."

"You hurt Elam in so many ways. Not only did you kill the family he planned to spend his life with, you caused his heart attack when he caught you burning pictures of me. Of us. You wanted to erase my existence."

"What else can I do?" I yelled. "I've done everything to make it up to him. It's the sole reason for being here on this weird island. It was his ambition to sell everything we'd worked so hard to build. Not mine. I'm trying to make him happy."

"He loved me. He was excited when I told him about the pregnancy. We would have been a sweet little family. But you were selfish, so jealous, you were willing to kill his dreams and cover it up. Never once, while you raised your own children, did you consider giving yourself up to him or the authorities. You're a liar."

I had slumped in the chair with the truth of her words. "I did not mean for you to stumble. What can I do to change this?"

"You cannot change the past. This is your prison. Your sentence has already begun." Camilla stepped from the counter then leaned back against it, arms crossed beneath her bulging breasts. "You'll find out what hell really is. Not some place under the ground where little red horned devils with pitchforks wait to burn you up." Her wicked smile flashed evil, pure and raw. "You can't imagine this kind of inferno."

"What does that mean? Who are you?"

Camilla pushed off the counter's edge and snickered at me as she slinked into the bedroom to join my husband.

"Wait, tell me one thing. Where did you come from?" The captive force vanished. Unsure, I wiggled my feet. Pain lingered on my ankles. A freed prisoner, I staggered after her on stiffened joints.

I entered to find the bedroom empty, the bedcovers pristine and undisturbed.

"Elam, where are you?" My fear heightened, alone in our cottage. The refrigerator motor buzzed. Frank shuffled and repositioned himself on the front deck.

As much as I wanted to believe I had experienced another torturous daytime nightmare, my stiffened muscles ached from the reality of the constant restraint.

I recalled the chief's strange reaction when Camilla's name and our cottage address came up. *Was he withholding something?* With no other alternative and nothing more to lose, I tromped back into the village for one final attempt to get help from Chief Officer Juan.

****

He sighed long and loud.

My words rolled out in an impatient rush. "I'm telling you," I pointed my finger in Officer Juan's face. "Elam came home. But he couldn't see or hear me. And the young redhead was there. When he left us alone in the room, she threatened me." With a huff, I lowered my hand.

He gazed beyond the window toward the blue green shimmer of ocean.

My jaw clenched. "You know something. Why won't you tell me?"

THE DECEPTOR'S CALL

His attention pulled back to me. "Camilla is an old lady. Her lands cover ancient burial grounds. Our ancestors spoke of demons, bad things happening there."

Both panels of the Dutch door were closed for privacy from activity and personnel on the other side. His voice low, he said, "I'm sorry, Sandy. You've have bad luck. I hoped my prediction of his actions with a woman, after drinks, were true." He hesitated. "Contact your family. Go home."

I held out both hands. "How can I go home? I have to do whatever is necessary to help Elam." I couldn't bring myself to talk about the contents of the crates. That would have given Juan the perfect out. Dead. Case closed.

"Things are unexplainable here. I am afraid I cannot help you." He offered his hand for a final friendly shake. I refused it. He lowered his hand back to his side. "I wish you strength. You will need it." He opened the door and held it open for me. "I have to protect my village. You must leave."

I left the tiny precinct for the lively vibe of the village, the world's loneliest woman.

CHAPTER ELEVEN

Pedestrians, bicyclists, and overloaded golf carts whizzed by as I dawdled in the streets at a loss of what my next step might be. Paying little care to my surroundings, I stumbled over a suitcase.

"Watch it, lady." The man in pink plaid shorts jerked the telescopic handle of his roller luggage. "This place is crazy." He ambled on.

"You have no idea," I said to his back.

I had to make contact with our kids. Ed was traveling for his job assignment. Shauna might be available at her dorm. I hated to tell them about their father, but it was important for them to at least know there was a problem. A lot of details would have to be withheld. It was all too frightening and confusing to put into words.

Frank greeted me when I reluctantly returned to Paraiso. Disappointed at his relaxed movements as if nothing untoward had happened in my absence, I passed my hand over his back on the way inside the empty cottage.

Hidden in a locked compartment of the bedroom closet, I checked on our stashed cash and passports. After one more shot at my dead cellphone, I pocketed several coins then headed out for the journey to the edge of the village, the ribbon of rural island road stretching out before me.

****

Halfway there, a trundling sound broke the calm from an undetectable distance away through the jungle as metal gears grew louder and closer. My heart galloped a warning.

The roar of a monster engine cut through the birdcall. I spun toward the noise. I stared into the grill of a truck barreling toward me. Behind the windshield, a man's eyes bulged, his mouth peeled

THE DECEPTOR'S CALL

back in terror as he fought the steering wheel. Black smoke billowed, filling my nostrils with the fishy smell of spent brake fluid. The tires locked and skidded over the center of the sandy road. I stood rigid and unable to move.

The truck skated close, the driver blocked from my view by the high-top edge of the grill. I clenched my jaw and slammed my eyes shut.

But the inevitable impact did not happen. I eased my lids open. The road lay vacant and undisturbed under the sun's glare. I rubbed my eyes and searched again. Only my sandals had tracked the sand.

A high-pitched squeal in the air broke my thoughts of our children. My senses sharpened, I stopped mid-step. The second sounded like an infant's squeal. A third echoed in the trees. Silence returned. I continued on. The fourth cry ripped through the forest. I searched the trees for the source. Branches rustled nearby. A white cockatoo with a high, yellow crest hopped from the branch of a grape leaf tree then settled its wing feathers. The baby's cry erupted louder, desperate.

Maternal instinct overrode all other senses. I stepped to the side of the road and searched inside the twisted forestry. From the wild canopy lining the opposite side of the road, the cry came again, increasing in intensity. I raced toward it, zigzagging across the road to follow the moving cries. The disjointed wails multiplied from both sides of the trees and creeping vines, opposite ends of the road, and overhead. The seconds between each wail from all directions shrank until it shrieked in one thunderous rage.

"Where are you?" I yelled. Sweat ran down my face and soaked my shirt. An undeniable, anxious need to find the baby and hold it close, protect it from danger, overwhelmed all sense of reality. "Baby." Crazed from separation of the baby and maternal paranoia, my body shuddered and I ground my teeth. The cries changed to madness, frantic sounds of need for protection. Close to losing consciousness, colors whirled in front of my eyes, spinning faster and faster.

My small, menopausal breasts reacted as a nursing mother's. They grew heavy and weighted with the need to provide nourishment. The longer the cries went on, the more burdened my body became. My back and shoulders tightened to support the new heaviness. Black spots appeared and replaced the colors in my vision. Dizziness threatened to overwhelm me. I held out my arms to each side to steady my balance. Sickness rolled in the pit of my stomach.

Pressure increased inside my foreign, swollen breasts. The built-in, sweat soaked bra of my tank top tightened like a belt with the weight and size of my flesh expanding on my chest. The single booming wail of the baby reverberated in my head. As if I had given birth to the infant myself, my newly engorged and painful breasts were so tight I feared any second they might split open and explode like grenades. Creamy white sprouted on the fabric as it oozed from the area of my engorged nipples. The white liquid spread wider, covering the whole of my chest. To free myself of the cloth cage, I reached down to wrench the shirt up but it had stretched to the maximum and would not budge.

I screamed and jumped backward. But I could not separate myself from what had to be monsters inside my chest. The fluid volume increased until it flowed as if from a gas tank. Milk pumped out fast and hard, jarring me. The baby screamed continuously as the creamy liquid changed to pink, then scarlet. A whiff of metal hit my nostrils, kicking in my gag reflex. I managed to stay upright and conscious as my body spewed the waterfall of bloody milk.

The pond at my feet rose high, enclosing me inside an invisible cylinder three feet in diameter. The level of alien fluid rose over my shoes then steadily up to my knees. As if my feet were concreted to the ground, it was impossible for me to escape the rising level of sticky fluid that escalated with the strengthening baby wails. It covered my thighs, then up until my hips disappeared below the mounting red/pink fluid. I reached my hands to either side and touched an invisible wall, smooth and solid.

As bloody breast milk covered my ribs, the weight pressed and restricted my breathing. My chest was hidden and tight beneath the rising liquid. I panted small breaths, unable to cry for help. Red fluid boiled from the continuous pumping action from my breasts. My heart hammered inside my constricted chest. My inner ears throbbed. I feared both eardrums would burst.

The pounding of my fists on either side of the invisible wall weakened. I would surely drown in my own fluid. Black spots swirled before me then widened until no light penetrated. Liquid engulfed my neck and chin as if a monster were swallowing me whole. Death would relieve my suffering. My terror eased. I relaxed, accepting the end.

A streak of sunlight pierced through the solid black of my vision. I flinched my head away from the torturous glare.

My dusty shoes were visible as if my mind had tricked me. I heaved in great gulps of air. My shirt and jog bra were dry and comfortable. Slight pain throbbed in my breast, but no residual swelling. A bird's menacing laugh filled the humid, still air. The cockatoo held firm to the tree branch. I stood alone, unharmed, but physically and mentally drained.

Movement ahead drew my attention. Farther up the road, Camilla, wrinkled and stooped, watched me from the roadside edging coconut and mangrove trees. Her mouth twisted into a stoic glare. The old woman backed out of sight, the thick underbrush and tree trunks virtually bowed in her presence.

Terrified but determined, I plodded toward where the old woman had been. No trace of her existed beneath the dark limbs and leaves, no visible footprints. I took off at top speed.

BARBARA MICHELLE

****

A public pay phone, set inside a purple booth, stood at the edge of a small playground near a worn school building. Hands shaking, the required coins clinked as I dropped them into the slot and lifted the receiver. An operator answered in Spanish.

"No *Española*," I shouted into the mouthpiece. I tapped a nervous beat on the side of my thigh with the fingertips of my free hand.

"What assistance?" she asked in broken English.

"I need to be connected to my daughter in the United States." I bit back the urge to shout again.

"Your name, please. And the number to connect."

"My name is Sandy Steele." I relayed Shauna's cell number. I waited, exasperated by the antiquated phone service.

"Please hold."

I marched in place to release anxiety.

A few seconds passed. A deafening white noise static fizzled through the phone line. My ear perked at Shauna's harmonic voice. "Mom? Are you there? Mom?"

"Yes," My throat constricted. I choked back tears. "Yes, honey, I'm here." For both our sakes, I kept my composure. "It's good to hear your voice."

"Hello? Mom? Hello?"

"Yes. I'm here. Can you hear me? Shauna?"

Static crackled over the line. "Yes. I can hear you now."

"Darling, I'm afraid we'll lose the connection so I'm going to get right to the point." My constricted throat choked on the words. "Your father..."

"Wait." She paused. "Who is this?"

"Shauna, what do you mean?" My words spewed in a rush. "I'm trying to tell you about your father. Something's happened."

THE DECEPTOR'S CALL

The static increased to full white noise, cementing the distance between us.

"What about my father?" Her tone edged with cold suspicion.

"I'm sorry to tell you," I yelled over the growing static. "Dad is missing." Emotion welled up with the last word.

"Whoever you are, you don't know what the hell you're talking about." A short silence followed. "What are you after something? Money?"

"No. It's Mom. Did you hear what I said?" My heart pounded in my chest, "Your father is missing." My desperation topped at an all-time high. "This island is frightening." I gripped the dirty purple receiver like a lifeline. The static increased. "Hello? Shauna? Are you still there?"

"Do not contact me again."

"What is going on?" I screamed into the phone.

"My father is dead, you bitch. He's been dead for months."

"No. No, your father is not dead, Shauna. Listen to me, it's Mom." Tears flowed free as I choked through the words. "Please listen. I'm scared."

Static scratched louder. I pulled the earpiece an inch away from my head.

"Go to hell." The static line clicked then went dead. A second click and a dial tone filled its place. I pulled the receiver from my ear and stared at it.

"Nooo." I banged the retro handset against the phone. Stopping before it cracked, I shoved my hand deep in my pocket for more coins. The pocket was empty. I screamed a loud sob of disbelief and confusion.

Two little girls in school uniforms stared at me, their hands clasped together, fear etched on their faces. They hurriedly traversed the park to the opposite side, mesmerized by the emotional wreck of a stranger. The receiver fell from my grip. I staggered away from the dangling metal cord in a shell-shocked daze.

I drifted out of the park zombie-like, a breathing existence without purpose. I slogged on for an hour or more. Desolate. Confused. My own daughter didn't recognize my voice.

Back toward the cottage, I ambled forward in a stupor. Birds cackled at me. Cautious and physically drained, I followed the street, defenseless against the evil trailing me like a shark to blood.

Elam's face remained in the forefront of my mind. Lucidity broke through, and I regained my focus. He needed me. There had to be a way to get to him and force him to see me.

I thought back to the morning I woke up to find out Elam had cancelled all our travel plans and rebooked our stay here. Normally, he would have consulted me, and we would have decided together. Of course, I would have agreed, and stifled my anger regarding the nonrefundable charges. But he had spent many hours planning, excited about what he thought was the perfect travel year. The overnight sudden change, and his aggressive manner toward me, had been out of character. "It speaks to me," he'd said the morning by our globe.

Another world existed on Palm Isle.

I trudged on to find protection and companionship from the only living being that had shown friendship.

****

I followed the road around the curve until I saw Frank asleep on the deck. His ugly face and snout lay on his paws overhanging the edge of the planks.

My heart raced in fear of what had happened inside the cottage. Frank's unruffled presence helped to quell the fear. I crossed Paraiso's newly dried front yard littered with tree branches and withered coconut skins, their ends protruded like kissing lips.

THE DECEPTOR'S CALL

The planks squeaked as I climbed the stairs to join my guard dog. I had to take time to think and form a plan. The pull to make another attempt to connect with Shauna was strong. There had to be a way.

Frank greeted me with a wagging tail. His wet tongue dripped as I reached the top of the stairs. My heart swelled at his wanting to be by my side. Afraid but determined, I opened the screened door, pursed my lips, and followed him inside.

The peaceful cottage appeared as a haven, free of chaos and ghosts. The refrigerator motor hummed. My shoulder muscles relaxed at the rhythmic ticks of the clock's pendulum. I filled an empty bowl with water and placed it on the floor for the drooling dog. When he finished lapping it up, he yawned, licked his lips then dropped into a pile by the sofa. I lay on the couch exhausted, frightened of what had occurred in the tangle of jungle and on the phone. Nebulous ideas of what my next move should be tumbled over in my mind until I fell into a deep sleep.

CHAPTER TWELVE

Mauve twilight filtered inside the cottage. I pushed myself up to sit on the lumpy couch and stretched. I set my shoes on the living room floor without disturbing Frank, who was wrapped in a ball, sound asleep. I plodded through the darkening room, my body ragged as if I'd crossed a marathon finish line. Energy low and chest sore, I examined the light purple bruises on my breasts.

A sad haze clung to me with my accepted new normal of insanity. The things I'd witnessed and experienced shouldn't be real yet were undeniable.

Holding my breath in dread of what might be waiting, I flicked on the lights. The low bulb threw a deceitful warmth and comfort throughout the small living space and kitchen. I blew out a relieved sigh and moved into the bedroom. The bed cover and pillows remained neat and undisturbed, and no evidence of Elam or the ghost in the cottage. Shauna's bizarre reaction to me during our brief phone conversation replayed in my mind. Heart aching, I entered the bathroom.

Physical longing for my children pulsed in my every nerve, strengthening my emotional connection with each passing moment. There had to be a way to communicate. Phoning again was the only option. My cell phone and iPad dead, I would have to make Shauna hear me and understand she had me on the line. The island's aged phone system had to be the problem. The static must have distorted my voice since she thought I was a stranger.

Avoiding my last fearful experience in the shower, I twisted the sink handles and let the water run until it was comfortably warm then shed my sweat-stained clothes. I retrieved a wash cloth and sponge bathed. I bent over and let the hard pressure from the tap massage the tension from my soaked scalp and neck.

THE DECEPTOR'S CALL

I envisioned the power to reverse time, to return to college. If only I could erase the secret bus trip to get a glimpse of Elam's fiancée and the negative impact it caused. I should have retraced my steps to the bus stop. She shone like a star among the crowd on the sidewalk. Unaware of the pregnancy, the product of Elam's love for her did nothing to detract her beauty, but rather enhanced her vulnerability in my memory. Elam had devoted his life to her, to their child. He'd planned to graduate and create a perfect life with them. I would have been nothing but a memory, a good friend mentioned in rare conversations about the past. I recalled our meeting.

I stopped beside her at the edge of the sidewalk. She didn't notice me as she brushed loose strands of hair from her face, light floral scent wafting in my space. Overpowering envy surged through me.

"Cam?"

She searched my face, "Yes?" Her hands rose to her belly and rubbed protective circles, a movement I paid no mind to. The newspaper article revealed the reason for that detail the following day. "Have we met?"

I stepped closer to her. "Elam knows me."

She tipped her head to the side, perfectly arched brows raised as surprise spread across her lovely face. Her skin glowed like delicate porcelain in the sun. Freckles lightly dusted her cheeks.

"He's in love with me," I said. The lie spilled unplanned, unprovoked.

She straightened her neck, her brows snapped together. "Who are you?"

"It's over between you." My words tumbled out without forethought. "He wants to marry me." My purpose for the visit to his hometown was only to see her, not talk to her.

The hot water cooled, and the memory faded. It did no good for me to relive things from so long ago. "You can't change the past, Sandy," I coached myself out loud. "Deal with the present."

BARBARA MICHELLE

Sponge bath complete, I dressed in clean shorts and tank top and went into the kitchen. A sickle moon hung beyond the open window. I intended to wait out the night for first light before trying to make a second contact with Shauna. I had to leave the island. Staying to help find my husband had proven futile. Without help from the police and no friendly connections, there was nothing left for me to do. The island, a living presence, did not want me.

I decided to pack up and take a water taxi back to the mainland then a car taxi to the airport. Without available Wi-Fi or working cell phone, I would have to reserve the first available seat on a flight to the U.S. Once I arrived at the airport, I would wait there until its departure.

My train of thought was interrupted. I held still and listened to garbled voices outside in the night air. At first, "Cam" was the only word I understood.

"Yes," said a feminine voice. "She was beautiful. And she loved that boy. She could hardly wait to get married."

"But did you know she was pregnant?" The question was posed by a masculine voice.

"Everyone knew."

Drawn by the conversation, I eased from the kitchen to the back deck and leaned on the railing. I listened, waiting to hear Frank rouse from his slumberous pile by the couch. Light glittered through branches and leaves lining the side yard, the same place I'd seen the picnic table days before. Branches widened without aide, allowing me to clearly make the illuminated faces of the couple I'd been lured to before by the donut lady. The mysterious source of light glowed from within the dark. They were seated at the same picnic table at the end of the pathway through the trees. The path had led me too far for me to see their faces and understand the clarity of their words.

I stretched out over the railing in order to hear them better, the voices muffled, as if my ear pressed against the end of a tube.

THE DECEPTOR'S CALL

"Of course, everyone knew," she said. "She never tried to hide it."

Everyone knew, except me.

"The baby was not his, poor boy. Elam was a smart, handsome young man. I knew he'd be a success at whatever he chose to do with his life."

"What do you mean, 'the baby wasn't Elam's'? She told everyone in town about it. Why would she do that if it weren't his?"

With an innate desire to get closer, I tiptoed down the deck and shuffled through the side yard to the slight opening of trees at the path. My hesitation to proceed lasted a split second before I followed the path, stopping just before the opening on the other end. As if they'd never left, the couple wore the same clothing and seated as the day before.

He said, "She practically made it a public announcement." A rogue wave crashed loud on the surf, "But beauty is powerful. And she was in love with his popularity, as were all the girls."

They turned in my direction. I inched farther into the darkness.

"Come out and join us, Sandy," she said.

Blood whooshed in my ears. I held still.

"There's no point in hiding."

My feet refused my demands to run. I crouched low to the ground but kept them in view.

The man patted age-spotted hands on the space beside him. "Come sit by me. There's no need to be frightened."

Curiosity won out. I rose and crept out into the open glow.

"Fine, if you want to stand," the woman said, her limp gray hair bouncing over the boxy jacket shoulder pads.

"The mother," the man said, "she wasn't as honorable as anyone believed her to be."

"I . . . don't understand," I said.

"Cam and me." He coughed. "We managed to keep our little relationship a secret."

BARBARA MICHELLE

The woman leaned across the table, a savage glint in her eye. "Tell her."

I cocked my head back in reaction to the cold remark.

"She simply got pregnant. We both knew it was mine, but I wasn't interested in playing house. I still had wild oats to sow." He shook his thinning wisps of gray hair, half of it had been combed to one side and stiff as if coated with hair spray. "I've regretted it every day since. I should have reached out to the little one. I could have saved him an awful ending. And now," he smiled, and spread his arms wide, "I'm here to spend eternity in paradise."

My stomach tightened. His thin skin paled. It must have been the peculiar glow of light. I peered deeper. His complexion had a sick whitish tone, the woman's skin tone equally ashen.

"Elam caught you burning pictures of her," he said. "Pictures of her during her pregnancy."

I inched back from them. "How do you know that?"

"I'm living my punishment. But you," he pointed at me. "You're the reason for so much pain. You'll never experience enough pain to equal killing an innocent child."

Self-hate and fresh regret returned. I raced away on the path for the safety of the cottage. Their evil howls of laughter bellowed in the distance. I banged up the steps, slammed, and locked the back door.

His position unchanged, Frank snored peacefully in the living room.

Breaths labored, I struggled with shaking hands to stuff our passports and cash into my pockets. I nabbed an extra change of clothes and zipped them into my backpack. I slung the pack over my shoulders and headed out the front. If I had to swim, I would find a way off the island.

I crossed the front yard and stole a backward glance, hoping to see Frank one last time. Something must have been wrong for him not to awaken during my last ordeal. My heart heavy for the

THE DECEPTOR'S CALL

companion I'd found in the dog, I left him and Paraiso for the village, my way lit by the waxing moon. I paced my running with fast walking, the backpack bouncing on my back. *Where had the couple come from? Did they even exist?*

Once in the village, I met with the vigorous energy of late-night lovers, arms draped each other, party goers singing off-key as if it were mid-afternoon. I approached the water taxi terminal, doors closed and padlocked. A purple phone booth stood near the terminal. I'd noticed it when we'd first arrived on the island. I would try to phone Shauna. My last painful call to Shauna seemed like an entire lifetime ago. She had to learn the truth and that I would find a way back to her.

I dug out the coins, loaded each one into the slot in the payphone's belly. I nervously pressed Shauna's number. Potential obstacles played out in my mind. The operator might end the call too soon, Shauna still would not recognize me, or the phone might not make the connection at all.

The receiver pressed hard against my ear, I listened to successive clicks.

"Operator."

"I have to connect with my daughter in the U.S." I forced myself not to yell. "Please make sure this goes through."

Painfully long series of clicks intermixed with short dial tones, finally changing to rings. Hope leaped in my heart. The backpack grew heavy on my shoulders.

The rings ended. "Hello?"

"Shauna. It's Mom." The words spewed forth before she cut me off. "Your father. There's trouble here. I'm coming home. Do you understand me?"

"Do. Not. Call. This. Number. Again."

"Don't hang up," I begged. "You have to hear me out."

A click. A dial tone.

"Agh." I beat the receiver against the phone. I threw it back against the base when it broke in my hand.

No point in trying another call. She would probably refuse to answer. I trudged to the padlocked terminal.

The island's beauty repulsed me, the brightly colored foliage repressive and suffocating. I'd developed a loathing for the whole place. I wanted my husband back safe and sound. I wanted us together.

Ropes secured empty tender boats to metal cleats. A passenger boat bobbed alongside the dock, ready for the morning rush of passengers. I waited for the terminal to open and hoped for an available seat on the first water taxi scheduled back to the mainland. From there, I would take a taxi or public bus ride across town to the airport. I could then purchase a plane ticket to our home town. When I'd finally arrive by taxi at Shauna's campus and her dorm, she would realize her mistake. Together, we could figure out a way to find her father. We would contact Ed. The situation had become too dangerous for me to continue to try on my own. We would work together as a family.

Too upset to sit on the bench, I paced the dock by the blue clapboard building, prepared to wait until morning.

CHAPTER THIRTEEN

A spotlight illuminated my nervous back and forth pacing as I waited for the water taxi terminal to open. I detected movement in my periphery. Raucous merriment cut through the darkness beyond the wash of light. I stopped and squinted into the darkness. Assaulted by a searing flare of sunlight, I crushed my eyelids together until the burning subsided.

Cam sashayed from the sea onto a narrow beach, water dripping off my black bikini. But that couldn't be. No beach existed beside the terminal.

The redhead faced back to the water. "I told you I could swim faster."

Elam, salty hair and swim trunks plastered to his thighs, emerged from clear water to the sand. I had purchased his swimwear specifically for the trip.

His focus glued to her, he said, "Okay, okay. You beat me." He gathered her in his arms. "I'm starving. Let's get back." My heart surged as he scanned the area and settled on me. I smiled and raised my hand. In his fragile state, I didn't want to frighten him. His gaze passed over me like I wasn't even there. I gritted my teeth as he reached around to the tiny knot in the center of her back. After a tug at the tie, he crushed himself to her supple body.

She placed her hands on his shoulders and pushed him away. "You bad boy."

Fresh hate blazed in me with her sing song voice.

"You have to wait."

"You're torturing me," said Elam. "Not even a peek?"

She giggled and sashayed across the beach. He caught up and took her hand as they strolled on.

My miserable heart crushed, Cam sneered at me over her shoulder. The nerves in my back shivered. The wick of sunlight blew out. Caught off guard, I stared into the onyx night, exposed and vulnerable.

The wind's speed increased. Unintelligible whispers hissed around me then formed into words. "Elam," they whispered, "needs you." I dreaded whatever she had in store for me. But I had to stay with Elam. I did not wait for more.

Terrified of the cottage, I accepted there was no choice, no time to contemplate my next move. I had to be there with him. Instincts kicked into high gear. Sprinting from the terminal, I caught up with the couple just as they were crossing into our cottage's screen door. I bounded up the steps to the deck and let myself in.

As if she belonged in my place, young Camilla faced the stove, a spatula in her hand. An open carton rested on the counter beside broken eggshells. She stirred something in the cold pan. Tied at the waist, my robe draped above, exposing her heaving cleavage. Frank snoozed by the couch.

Wrapped in a towel from his waist to his muscled thighs, Elam reposed in a chair at the table, his facial features relaxed in a smile. I was confused by the obvious lapse of time between their entering the cottage and the calm aftermath countered by Frank's seeming lack of movement in my absence.

Her back to Elam, Cam placed the runny eggs on a plate. While following her every movement, he sipped from a glass of OJ.

She turned from the stove. "You worked so hard to have Elam for yourself, didn't you, Sandy?"

Elam's puppy-eyed expression stayed fixated on her.

A tiny glass tube filled with yellow fluid appeared from nowhere in the girl's right hand. She held it out in my direction. Under the harsh ceiling light, the liquid glinted gold inside the vial. "Lucky you," she said. "You've got a front row seat."

THE DECEPTOR'S CALL

"What are you doing?" The now familiar, invisible force pressed down on my shoulders holding me immobile by the door. "Why are you here, dammit?"

Cam refocused on the plate and tipped the vial. The contents dripped onto the raw eggs. The barren tube dropped to the counter and rolled away, smashing on the floor. Elam's reverent gaze remained on her, unflinching with the breaking glass. She grasped the plate and stepped to him. She lifted the fork from the napkin and postured in front of him. "Open wide," she said in a syrupy tone. "Momma's going to feed her little boy."

"Stop," I yelled. "Stop."

He clasped his large hands on her narrow hips and pulled her close until she lingered above him. He reached up and widened the robe, her cleavage bulged.

"Yes, Ma'am." As ordered, he opened his mouth.

"No, Elam." I pushed against the invisible restrains. "Don't eat the eggs."

Cam placed a forkful of gelatinous, yellow goop between his trusting lips. His mouth clamped over the fork prongs. She backed the empty fork out of his mouth. He chewed the uncooked food, a smile stretching across his lips, his gaze held on her.

The invisible manacle held tight. The pressure intensified.

She tipped another forkful of eggs into his mouth. Pleasure beamed in his grin as he chewed as if it were the best thing he'd ever tasted.

"Elam, she's poisoning you." I jerked against the restraints.

Camilla chortled at me as he swallowed a third forkful of eggs.

I nearly wrenched my bones from their sockets. "No, Elam. She's going to kill you."

My warnings unnoticed, he said. "You're the best thing to ever happen to me, Cam."

"Yes," she tapped his nose. "I am."

"Dammit, Elam, listen to me."

"I'm so in love with you, Cam." Elam stared at her, practically swooning.

She looked at me, curling her upper lip. "Isn't this fun?"

His blissful expression plummeted, lips parted, brow pinched. Wild-eyed, his cheeks and forehead purpled. He dropped his gaze from her face to the eggs, then back to her. His lips swelled. He gripped his abdomen with crossed arms and leaned forward. His chest heaved to pull in more oxygen.

"Elam," I yelled.

Frothing at the mouth, his whole body lurched in a series of spasmodic jerks. A final giant seizure sent him sprawling to the wooden floor, his head hitting with a thud.

Frank snoozed peacefully by the sofa.

Elam's facial muscles tightened into a grimace. His body contracted and contorted violently. He flipped over on his back like a fish out of water. His swollen tongue protruded from his lips. His jaw snapped shut, his tongue caught between his teeth like a finger in a doorjamb. After a deep-throated gurgle, blood trickled down the sides of his face.

"Elam...oh, God." I pressed my shoulders hard against my sly captor. The pressure released me at once, the momentum toppling me forward like a rag doll. I scrambled back to my feet and rushed to him. Crouched by his side, I held his face in both my hands.

"Here comes the best part. The big finale." Cam said. "An experienced murderer such as yourself, Sandy, will appreciate this."

The skin over his cheeks and forehead heated and bubbled as if he was being cooked from the inside.

I jerked my hands from his face. "You witch!"

The bubbling maxed to a fast boil.

"Make it stop." I pressed my fists against my ears.

THE DECEPTOR'S CALL

The boiling ceased as if a cauldron had gone cold. His skin, reddened and misshapen, sank away from the supporting bone. The toneless tissue sagged. Blistered welts rendered his handsome features distorted, monstrous. Tears leaked from the outer corners of his lids to his hairline as he stared at me.

The extent of the damage pained me. I averted my eyes before I realized what I'd done. My lips pursed, I beheld his revolting face. "What have you done to him?"

She peered down to his fresh ugliness like a cat over a bowl of milk.

"Why? Why would you hurt him like this?"

"You were always such a gullible young man." Cam's complexion brightened, dewy and pale, like a torch glowing inside her skull, the dermal layers nearly translucent. Small patches of her cheeks and forehead swelled like goose eggs. The glowing beam faded from under her skin. The swollen areas multiplied until her face was covered. Her jowls drooped and settled into creases, shadows lay under bone crevices. The lids hooded. She morphed until I stared up into the elderly face of Camilla. The enviable long red tresses shortened; the vibrant color replaced by wiry strands from her gray roots.

Her wrinkled lips parted. "You no longer exist, Sandy."

"Now, your precious Elam is returned to you." Her tone was harsh and roughened with age. Her lithe figure bent forward and shrank into the timeworn, twisted spine. Her sagging frame trudged across the floor and out the front door. I stared after her as the screen door bounced shut.

Biting my lip and clutching at the neck of my shirt, I took in the sight of Elam. I'd worked so hard to keep him with me. He lay before me, innocent and damaged beyond recognition. His bottom lip drooped to his chin, the lower row of teeth and gums exposed. The skin of his masculine nose had wilted to the shape of bone and cartilage underneath. His mottled cheeks dampened by unending tears. I remembered his pain decades before as a result of my callousness.

My heart burned at the sight of him. "Are you in pain?" I swallowed hard.

His barely perceptible nod was enough.

"Can you speak?"

Elam's stared at me as if I were his lifeline. The distorted lips twitched as a grunt escaped. He sighed with resignation after two more attempts to speak. Tension eased from his body. Frustration remained in his glassy eyes.

This man of strength and confidence I'd loved so fiercely had been reduced to something physically vile.

I wanted to believe my mind played tricks on me, but I had learned there were no limits in this new existence. The walls around us rippled. I bent over Elam as a protective shield. Within seconds, the whole cottage evaporated around us. The ocean lapped gently against the boat hulls. We were back at the boat terminal.

I pushed back my emotions of grief and pain. Determination to find help surged. We were reunited. I would not desert him.

Orange-purple dawn split the inky black night. I had to get him off the island. But first he needed medical attention. A few blocks walk would get us to the tiny medical clinic Elam had pointed out soon after our arrival to Palm Isle.

"We need to get you some help. The medical office isn't far from here. Can you move your legs?"

He bent his knees an inch at a time.

"Try your feet." He flexed both ankles and wiggled his toes. "Do you think you can walk?"

His wheezy breaths through the exposed lower teeth caught my attention. Skin had closed over his left nostril. The lower lip drooped as a grotesque and nonfunctional tissue flap.

THE DECEPTOR'S CALL

"Elam, you'll need to sit up. I can help."

His upper shoulders and torso stiffened. A painful moan passed through what had become no more than a mouth hole. I pulled on his upper arm with both hands until he was upright. His head drooped. He drew in long gasps from the effort.

"Take a minute to rest then we'll have to get you up on your feet." I wished I could alleviate his pain.

Less confident than I let on, I worried about his condition and labored breathing. Elam's manly frame outweighed me by at least eighty pounds. If he were able to stand, I wasn't sure he'd have the strength to walk far on his own.

Five minutes passed. "Okay, let's see if we can get you up." His placid face showed no expression. He stared at me with what I understood was fear. "Elam, we have to try. The sun has barely come up so there's no one else around to help."

A thin line of saliva slid from the corner of his formless mouth. I forced a neutral expression. He could not be allowed to see the pain in my heart. I reached up and wiped it with the pad of my thumb, a lump knotted in the back of my throat. I wiped the saliva on the sandy pier out of his sight.

I placed myself in front of him and bent in a ready position. "Let's see what you can do." Guilt accompanied my determination to push him after the trauma he'd experienced. But I was terrified Camilla would appear before I could work out a way to get him to the clinic. Considering the early morning hour, I hoped at least one person was on staff.

Elam hesitated, then uncurled his legs in stages and worked himself over to one side. Pressing the ground with both hands, he used his strength to move to an awkward, half stand. With an extra pull from me at his side, he came to a full upright position. Labored breaths blew through his uncovered bottom teeth, his energy drained by the effort.

I pressed his hand. "Stand here and catch your breath." I twisted to shift my backpack on my tensed back and scanned the area for someone to help while on constant surveillance for another surprise appearance from Camilla. I hated being vulnerable out in the open. She had no limits. I longed for cover.

Nearby, someone whistled and rattled keys. My heartrate picked up as my sense of direction was thrown off. I searched the colorful storefronts and homes close to us, some open shacks. Rays split the early morning and slanted across the roofs and docked boats. Long shadows from trees and buildings crossed the sandy streets and alleyways.

A man emerged from a corner of a building and rounded the corner whistling low under his breath and twirling keys on a chain between his fingers. I noted his roughened bare feet.

Elam's shoulders and body slouched.

"Excuse me." I waved until the whistler spotted us. I bottled the raving lunatic boiling inside me.

The key twirling slowed. He stopped and stared first at me, then at Elam.

"I'm sorry, but my husband is not well." I offered a pleading smile. "Would you mind giving us a hand?"

He hesitated then walked over to us. "You need help?"

His cologne tickled my nose.

"Your man is weak."

"We need to get to the medical clinic but I'm afraid I don't have enough strength to support him that far."

He waved me to the side, stepped close to Elam, and reached under his arm. "Lean on me." He placed Elam's arm around the back of his neck. "He can rest inside. I own the taxi. Where are you staying?"

"In a rental out of the village." I refused to tell him which cottage after the negative reactions we'd previously received.

THE DECEPTOR'S CALL

"The doctor is my friend. She lives close by. I will run to her house and bring her here."

I resisted the urge to hug the stranger. "You're very kind. Thank you."

I followed as they shuffled together to the entrance, step by slow step. He supported Elam easily with one arm as his free hand worked a key into the padlock until it clicked. After pushing the large metal door with his foot, he assisted Elam inside the waiting room and eased him down to the center of a long line of benches bolted to the concrete floor.

Our savior took off at a run. "How can I ever repay his kindness?" My words echoed in the large open room. I place my arm around Elam slumped on the bench beside me. "They'll be here in a few minutes, Elam. He will get you taken care of."

Fifteen silent minutes later, the taxi owner rounded the corner at a jog shaking his head. He stopped in front of us." The doctor has fallen ill. She is too weak to walk. She cannot leave her home."

I broke out in a sweat. "There has to be someone. Isn't there another physician on the island? I'll pay double their fee to help him."

"She's the only one."

"Doesn't she have a nurse or an assistant?"

"Her son assists her. He is suffering the same sudden illness and is weaker than his mother. We have no other medical person on the island."

My mouth went dry. "This is unbelievable," I said as I pushed away from Elam and forced air from my throat. "What the hell is up with this place?"

He lands a concerned look on Elam's distorted facial features. "Someone will be able to help on the mainland. The first boat for the city leaves in thirty minutes.

He walked into the glass-enclosed office to a nineteen fifties style cash register and pressed keys to accept my payment. I pocketed our boarding tickets and returned to my seat by Elam.

As he weakened, Elam listed to the side. I tugged on his shoulder and let him lean against me. I brooded over finding help for my husband and the long trip ahead. I was on constant watch for the appearance of a gray or red-haired Camilla.

The owner stepped out from the pay booth and moved toward us. "Time to go."

No other passengers had entered the terminal.

"Isn't it too early?"

"It is not unusual for there to be just a few customers at this early hour."

"Let's go, Elam," I whispered. His drooping eyelids opened at the touch of the owner, ready to assist him.

"I will help." He gently helped Elam up. They shuffled together until he helped Elam into the boat and placed him on a seat in the corner.

Emotion overwhelmed me. I touched his arm, "I can't thank you enough for your kindness." I settled in by my husband.

The owner smiled assuredly at me and stepped to the helm. The engine roared to life, and he maneuvered the boat into the open turquoise blue waters.

My thoughts moved forward to the upcoming transfer of Elam. The next leg of the journey would be long and difficult.

Something had to go our way. The compassion shown by the water taxi owner revived my hope for a successful trip. Freedom and medical assistance were on our horizon.

Drool oozed from Elam's lip. I wiped it away.

CHAPTER FOURTEEN

We skimmed over the calm, crystal surface. I relaxed under the hypnotic hum of the water taxi's engine and stared mindlessly at the boat's long shadow on the sea floor, cast between the sun and the water's clarity. Distant soft-needled pine and coconut trees covered numerous small islands scattered out to the horizon. White seagulls and dark frigates soared in close and matched our speed before arching up and away. Each left a heartsick memory of the thrill I experienced seeing the great sea birds on our first arrival to the area. Elam drifted off to sleep, and I closed my eyes.

I dreamed of the halcyon days with my elementary school aged children. *Ed, the protective older brother, always kept one eye out for his little sister. Shauna telling us of the latest chapter book she'd finished and which one she planned to delve into next. We walked in a joyful circle with joined hands, the children repeatedly sang Ring Around the Rosie, Elam and I linked our hands between each one. Genuine satisfaction with the life we lived and pride for them both shone in his broad smile. After many rounds of the song, I spun out of control. Ed pulled hard on our hands, and we all fell to a jarring impact on the floor.*

The abrupt slowing of the boat's motor jostled me awake. The water taxi no longer slid and bounced in open water. Instead, we arced toward land. Trees bent over the water's edge, visible from our short distance as we rumbled nearer. No main harbor bustled in sight. No buildings or vendors lined up ready to make an aggressive bid for our business. People did not wait in line on a wide concrete dock in wait for passage off the mainland. The sun had climbed higher from when we'd left Palm Isle. The harbor docks should have been bustling in the late breakfast hour.

I bolted upright. The captain whistled the same tune under his breath as he had on Palm Isle.

"This isn't the mainland terminal. Where are we?"

"I have been redirected for a delivery." He tossed me a sideways glance. "Will be quick."

"Is this normal? Adding stops on the way to the terminal?"

He nodded and smiled pleasantly. "It happens. No problem."

Frustration mounted at finding us wasting time. We desperately needed to get out of the country. I longed for the security of being with my children and the strength of the family circle. Left with no choice, I leaned back in a huff. The taxi's schedule was out of my control. Besides, the captain had been helpful with Elam.

I shrugged and smiled at Elam, staring at me. "Don't worry." I said. "Everything's going to work out."

The captain steered the boat along the broad curves of the land. The tip of a tiny weathered dock came into view. As we pulled around a bend, the motor stirred bubbles in the water. No taxi employee waited to assist us. The area devoid of people, we rode in closer. The roughened and twisted end of the dock seemed familiar.

I stepped cautiously to the right side and peered over the edge to the clear deep-sea bottom. We rounded the last long curve of land, the full length of the dock visible. Birds trilled from inside the condensed woods. We motored between floating coconuts as we neared the dock.

I spotted a small decrepit building set back in the woods edge. My knees weakened. A sour tang filled my mouth. I gripped the side of the boat. "We're back at Palm Isle."

The abandoned cottage, tilted from its corners resting on the three stones, jeered at me from its position between the dock and the long path through the tall grasses.

Prepared to unleash my wrath, I swung my gaze toward the captain. Whispery movements of air circled me. He stared ahead. His brow smoothed, he did not blink against the stark damaging rays of the sun full on his face. Before I'd fallen asleep, his cheeks and forehead had bunched in the absence of sunglasses.

Elam sat up, his damaged face unreadable as he watched the little house. His knuckles whitened in the tight grip of his hands on the bench.

"Elam?" Blood rushed in my ears. "You know this place?"

His body tensed as we neared the dock and closer toward the dilapidated building.

The captain piloted the taxi right up to the dock, his head forward in the direction the boat headed. As if controlled by a puppeteer, he did not turn and rely on his vision for the intricate process of a smooth docking. His hands automatically worked the steering wheel and motor controls.

"No," I yelled. "Don't stop here. This place is dangerous." I stepped to his side and reached for the wheel to change course back out to sea though I had zero boating experience. I had no idea which direction the mainland was in relation to the island but we couldn't stay at the dock.

Without looking at me, the captain raised his hand and pushed my chest. Faltering backward, my leg hit the nearest bench and I stumbled to the deck floor. I pulled myself to my feet. "Hey, listen to me," I yelled. "Pay attention." He did not flinch as he steered the boat perfectly parallel to the dock.

Water sloshed gently against the fiberglass hull. Exotic birds called out.

"Can't you hear me?"

The captain stepped to me like a robot, undeterred by the sway of the boat. I backed up and reached the far side. He stopped directly in front of me and reached his hands under my armpits. "No," I yelled.

Swinging my arms to hamper his strength was useless. He suspended me over his head as if he held a baby. My limbs writhing in the air, he carried me to the opposite side and tossed me like a pebble.

I sailed through the air, landing hard on my side. My head bounced off of the splintered worn planks. I pushed myself to sit, shook off the dazed fog in my head, then clambered back up.

The invisible force returned on my shoulders and held me in place. I screamed and pressed to wriggle out from under the strength of my unknown captor.

The captain approached Elam sitting on the bench. He carried Elam and pitched him over as easy as a child's ball. My husband landed with a groan at my feet.

"Elam." The shoulder pressure disappeared, and I crouched. "Are you all right?"

The engine sputtered and boiled underneath the water's surface. The captain revved the engine, shooting a spray of water. The fiberglass taxi grumbled away from the dock and raced out to sea.

"Come back." My shouted yells through my cupped hands dissolved in the humid air. I stomped my feet. "Dammit." Anger squelched my last drop of hope. *How would I ever get us off the island?*

I regarded Elam's sprawled body and regrouped my thoughts. He still needed me to lead him from danger.

"Elam, get up. You have no choice, now. I can't carry you."

He twisted himself awkwardly to sit up and set his distorted face on me.

"We have to get ourselves to safety. You'll have to walk."

With my assistance, he worked his limbs and joints warily until he held himself up. My heart ached for him, but I had to stay strong. Across the grassy yard, the building rested undisturbed, the fabric unmoving in the window. My skin prickled with the feeling of being watched.

"What do I do now?" Without knowing what or whom I was dealing with, there was no way to judge the best direction to take. Trusting my intuition was all I had left.

THE DECEPTOR'S CALL

Elam's hand was cool and heavy in mine. Grateful for the daylight, I said, "Let's go." We hobbled together. He leaned on me as we made our way toward the path. Internally frustrated by our slow pace, I refrained from urging him to go faster.

Sharp metal creaked from the direction of the little cottage. The hinges squeaked as the front door yawned open. Little hairs crawled at the nape of my neck as I eyed the darkened interior. Elam moved at his sluggish maximum speed.

The salty wind picked up. Ghoulish hisses woven in the air current swirled around us and whispered in my ear. "Inside."

I tugged unsuccessfully on his arm to hasten our steps for the protection of the jungle forest. We trudged on, gaining little distance between us and the cottage.

In a split second we no longer stood outside. We were in the center of the dim cottage. I dug my fingers into the flesh of Elam's upper arm, his weight leaning on me. Dust danced in the ray of light slicing across the wooden floor from the open door. Old hinges screeched as the door banged shut. Light filtered through the red curtains. We faced the stack of crates covering the wall, each labeled with his name. I screamed over Elam's moan.

Shrill baby cries ripped the silence from every direction. My disorientation returned as it had during the previous experience of baby wails on my way to Paraiso. The temperature dropped at least thirty degrees. Shivering, I braced myself against Elam until we were almost one body.

Cam appeared in front of us, red hair cascading like blood dripped on a white gown waving in a breeze, her face obscured by the dimly lit interior. No draft touched my skin.

"You're here to stay, Sandy, loathed by those who loved and trusted you," Her aged voice reedy thin, as she continued, "Did you not believe what you've been told?"

My whole body shivered in the cottage's windless chill.

"Elam, Love, your splendor is destroyed. Who would have you now?"

He fixed his drooped stare on her.

"Now Sandy, it's time." A box, centered in the middle stack, slid forward.

Facing away, I bit my bottom lip.

"You cannot avoid your fate."

Shauna's voice, small and as if at a distance, sounded from inside the crate. "Mom? Are you there? Mom?"

"Shauna?" I glared at the white gowned apparition. "What have you done to her?"

"She's waiting for you."

Unable to resist the desperation in my daughter's voice, I left Elam's side to peer over the edge of the tilted crate. As if through a microscope lens, Shauna stood as a miniature inside her dollhouse-sized living room. I observed her pacing from one end of the tiny room to the other.

Shauna searched the box's perimeter surrounding her. "Mom? Where are you?"

"I'm here Shauna." My voice came out choked. "Are you all right? What's happened to you?"

Her miniature head tilted back to see my face, a giant towering over the box edge. "Mom, why? Why did you do it?"

"What are you talking about?" I grabbed the sides of her crate.

In a flat voice, she said, "You killed his fiancée, then you burned her pictures."

"Shauna," I cried, "We're in trouble here."

"How could you? You killed my father." The flame of her anger singed my soul. "How could you take him away from me? He loved you. He loved all of us."

"No, Shauna. Your father is right here with me." I pointed to him. His knees buckling, I started toward him.

THE DECEPTOR'S CALL

"Elam won't help you, Sandy."

"Elam?" I urged, ignoring Camilla. "She needs to see you. I'll help you get closer."

"He's been reduced to nothing," said the red haired, faceless figure.

"Why are you doing this?" I slammed my fist against my thighs. "Why are you hurting my family? They've done nothing to you."

Shauna's tiny voice broke through from inside the crate. "I hate you," she howled, her words sharp as a blade. "My brother hates you."

"Please, Shauna, I'm begging you. Don't say that. I'm telling you the truth. Your father is here with me."

The crate scraped back out of my hands and into place against the wall.

"Shauna." I shouted but she was already gone.

The gowned figure cackled from the corner of the room. I returned to Elam's side.

Wood scraped against wood as a second box eerily moved forward.

I held still, terrified of what waited inside. The invisible force pulled me away from Elam. My feet tangled, I stumbled. A pressure forced my head to a downward angle. A shiny silver metal pistol with a pearl covered handle lay inside.

"My gift to you, Sandy."

"I want nothing from you."

"You'll find it valuable. There will come a time."

"What does that mean, damn you?" My hands tightened into fists.

"I worked hard to get what I deserved. You took him then snuffed me and the baby out as if we were nothing more than yesterday's trash."

"I didn't go there to hurt you. I wanted to see you."

"You didn't show up on the sidewalk as a friend." A distinct sound of breaking glass filled the room. Her red hair and white gown slowly fissured without separating. The wraith suddenly disintegrated into millions of crystal fragments. The tiny pieces hung in the air, then vanished.

I returned to Elam just as his legs lost strength. His tall body crumpled to the floor, landing with a thud. I grabbed his arm. "We have to get out of here."

It occurred to me that time had fractured. Days and nights had no meaning. I navigated two intersecting dimensions. The reliable rotation of the sun and moon marked one; a chaotic pulse marked the other. Danger lurked at every turn. One event proved more absurd and inconceivable than the next, whirling into a kaleidoscope of evil.

My terror and anger coupled with Elam's weakness. I'd let him down, and we were in trouble. Doom had replaced the space in my mind where a slim light of possibility had burned. All of my efforts had failed. We still needed help if there were any chance of escape.

A knock on the door jolted my nerves. As his strength lessened, Elam's head and shoulders tilted forward. The door jiggled at the lock with a second round of harder whacks.

The open room, filled with nothing but stacked crates, offered no place to hide.

"Sandy, come out." The baritone voice boomed through the door.

Useless to pretend we weren't there, I said, "Chief Juan?" A tiny flame of belief glimmered inside me.

"Yes, open up."

I held my trembling hands tight to the knob.

"We made another search for your husband."

Relief swept over me when the lock turned over on its own. I snatched the door open and threw my hands over my brows to shield my eyes from the sunlight. I resisted the urge to hug him. "I'm so glad to see you." A painful knot formed in my throat.

He searched over my shoulder to Elam's folded form on the floor. "You found him."

"Yes, but he's been through a lot." I appreciated the officer not flinching at Elam's grotesque appearance. "How did you find us?" Before I could explain about the crates, he walked by me and approached my husband.

"I can carry him." He handled the dead weight with the strength of an ox. Elam released painful groans as the chief hoisted him from the ground to his shoulders.

Instinct steered me to the open crate. Nerves zinging, I reached in and wrapped my palm around the cold pearl handle of the pistol. I stared at the foreign object. I slipped it into the band of my shorts, my long-waisted tank top covering the bulk.

I repeated the unanswered question. "How did you know where to find me?" My steps doubled to keep up as we neared the parked golf cart.

The chief helped Elam sit on the second-row bench then perched himself at the steering wheel.

I settled in beside Elam. "Where are we going?"

He twisted the key in the ignition and pressed the gas pedal. We drove over the open yard and onto the path to the sandy island road. I received no reply.

"Answer me," I demanded. "Where are you taking us?" I rested my hand, ready, on the gun's handle poking from my shorts. Juan's amber gaze reflected back to me in the small rearview mirror. Then the chief's focus returned ahead as the cart bounced over the ruts formed in the soft road.

"Speak to me, dammit." I slapped the back of his seat.

He drove on in silence.

I leaned in close to his ear for a test. "Hey," I yelled.

The man's face registered no change.

The opening of palm trees to our cottage lay ahead. My heart slammed inside my chest as we neared it. "Do not take us back to that cottage. I won't go there," I yelled, slapping my hands against the seat once more. He met my demand with silence. "We will not stay here." He drove on. Elam remained still. As we neared the opening, I contemplated jumping off the fast- moving golf cart with the intent to lead Elam away from the rental property. But there was no way to get Elam off besides pulling him off with me. My hand brushed the handgun. I was repulsed by its existence, yet the slight sense of protection it gave was undeniable.

The cart approached the opening in the trees. Weathered and worn Paraiso loomed over the yard's rain collected pond, secrets lurking inside. The golf cart slowed down. I grasped Juan's shoulder. "You can't stop here."

The curtain in the window blew out as Frank sprang out, landing on the deck. "Frank!" He bounded down the steps barking, water splashed as he raced toward us. "Stop the cart." Juan did not turn toward the snarling dog but the cart's speed reduced to a crawl. Frank raced to the edge of the yard and crossed into the road straight toward Juan, seemingly unaware in the front seat. While Frank gnashed his teeth at him, a deeper sensation of fear moved through me. I realized it was the dog's fear mixed with fierce protectiveness of me.

Frank's muscular legs bent preparing to lunge up at his target, saliva drooling from his mouth. He sprang upward and his powerful jaws opened, aiming for Juan's left arm. His teeth positioned to sink into the chief's flesh at full speed, his massive head slammed into solid air with a thud as if he hit a glass wall. His body lurched backward and he landed on his side.

I exploded from my seat to reach him, Elam leaned slightly. The golf cart halted its movement. I reached Frank and crouched down to him laying my hands on his dazed head. His eyes set on me then stared far away. "No," I wept as I sensed his life essence leaving him. Reaching my arms around the massive neck, I hugged my loyal friend, wishing I would feel him lick the side of my face just one more time.

Remembering my husband, I returned beside him on the seat, Juan remained silent and motionless behind the wheel. Sorrow and confusion consumed me. The cart lurched forward and I stared at my lost friend until we followed the sharp turn, the trees blocking him from sight.

I kicked the back of the front seat and sobbed uncontrollably, distraught over the death of my friend. I walloped the back of the chief's head with my fists. "Why?" The cart puttered forward on the road and rounded the corner, past Camilla's dilapidated cottage. The front door open, two pair of blue and red child's swimming trunks waved from a clothesline across the front yard. I recognized the older woman, arms stretched up to remove the clothes, a metal pail balanced on her head. A laundry basket rested at her feet.

Juan passed by the donut lady without looking her way. He drove blank-faced with the continued beatings I wailed on the back of his head.

Leaving the bewitched woodland, the cart rolled us into the village's frustrating laid-back atmosphere. Elam and I followed a journey through a hellish paradise.

CHAPTER FIFTEEN

The one-sided fight with the chief's head proved helpful only in unleashing my tangled ball of emotions. Energy drained, I sank back into the seat depleted and miserable, gaining no satisfaction from the officer's disheveled black hair.

"Help us," I yowled from the speeding cart. "Please help, we're in danger."

Villagers moved as if deaf to my pleas. I pounded a fist on the back of the seat ahead.

I refused to dwell on the appalling vibrant colors. Pressing my lips into a frown at the joyful tourists, I envisioned kicking over the reggae band's steel drum in the palapa bar. I never again wanted to lay eyes on the island. Abuzz with too much movement, too much activity, businesses and shops lured potential customers in with their open doors.

I yelled out a warning to the unsuspecting tourists. "Get off the island before it's too late."

Every glance my way by the locals now seemed suspicious, as if they withheld secrets.

Bicycles whizzed past, tempting me to extend my foot from the cart to knock one over so I could hop on for a quick getaway. Clad in pressed uniforms, groups of children lined up and entered their faded, yellow concrete school building. Village life pulsed in a lively regular rhythm while Elam and I suffered alone.

We swept past the village center then came to an abrupt stop, jerking us forward and back. I grabbed Elam's ragdoll body, leaned toward the outside edge. His weakness worsened as the minutes ticked by.

The cemetery spread out in front of us. Bordered by the black iron fence, the haphazard rows of colorful burial vaults and rebar above the expanse of the sandy carpet were littered with fallen

THE DECEPTOR'S CALL

coconuts. The once enchanting, multicolored cemetery now chilled me to the bone.

Four men brandishing shovels bent over a site in the back. They stabbed their spades into the surface, deeper than the existing tall concrete crypts. Alternating turns, they hefted the soft soil out. The discard pile grew high.

What are we doing here?

The officer slid out of his seat and approached Elam.

"Don't touch him." I pulled hard on my husband's arm. He slipped from my grip and was hoisted over Juan's head. The officer's deadpan expression resembled that of the water taxi driver.

Doom beyond death lay over the colored vaults. Elam bounced on Juan's shoulders in rhythm to the chief's steps as he strode toward the working men. I followed on leaden feet.

"Why did you bring us here?" Juan did not respond. I moved faster and stepped in front of him, blocking his passage. Elam's watery eyes were barely open making it difficult to determine his level of consciousness or whether he was even still alive.

The chief showed no concern for my post-like stance.

"Stop," I screamed, placing my hand on his broad chest.

He released his hand supporting Elam's legs and pushed me aside as if swatting a fly. I lost my balance and landed across a page of a giant concrete Bible secured on a blue vault. My palm scraped across the roughened surface. The pearl gun caught between the high edge of the vault and my hip, causing a sharp pain. I pushed myself off the crypt and dashed to catch up with the chief. They headed straight for the sweat-soaked men and their open grave.

Unaware of our approach, the gravediggers continued their work in silence. The chief halted at the dirt pile's edge. The men jabbed their metal spades into the earth, tossing the dirt onto the growing mound. One pair of pineapple patterned shorts stood out on one figure among the working men. His braid hung over one shoulder as he worked the shovel in the bowels of the plot.

"Dave," I cried.

He toiled alongside the others without noticing my desperate cry.

A roughly hewn stone slab loomed at the head of the newly dug plot, the narrow stone angled out of the sand. I leaned closer. "No," I whimpered, as I made out the spelling of the worn words. The roughened letters spelled the name of the intended occupant, *ELAM STEELE*.

Eyes open, Elam draped across the chief's shoulders like a human shawl. The four laborers slogged on in silent focus.

The pain at my hip partially allayed, I knew the gun resting there could either be a hindering piece of metal or give me a level of control in this untenable situation.

I stepped to Elam's flaccid head and snapped my fingers in front of his face, confident the men took no notice of me. "Elam."

He raised his head and directed his attention to me through wet, misshapen lids.

"You can hear me?" His lips twitched in confirmation. His expressionless face held no hope.

I analyzed all potential scenarios. The grave had reached approximately ten by five feet long and four feet in depth. The men glistened with sweat like suntan oil. Working on autopilot, they exchanged no words or glances.

The soft swish of dirt heaping onto the pile ceased. Dave and the other diggers stepped back, spreading out on either side of the rectangular hole, their spiritless expressions facing the chief approaching the edge.

"Elam, kick your legs." I placed my hands on his feet and gave a slight shove to drive my point.

THE DECEPTOR'S CALL

He grunted as he tried to bend his weakened knees with no effect on his captor's superhuman grip. In a single quick movement, Juan removed his hand from Elam's ankles and placed it on his thigh, the other stayed on the shoulder. He raised Elam over his head as if he were a barbell.

Camilla emerged from behind the largest Jesus sculpture next to a pink vault. Her mouth curved in a malicious smile. She wobbled on her bad hip to the edge of the grave and stopped beside the headstone meant for my husband. Her white dress swathed over the sagging flesh of her torso. The chief stared at Camilla and, like a soldier at attention, waited for further instruction.

The constant slow stream of passersby on the street surrounding the graveyard drew my attention. They meandered completely unaware of the grisly scene taking place inside the iron fence.

"You can't have Elam," I said.

"I don't want him. Not yet." The lines in her lips smoothed as they quirked up. "He'll stay here for safe keeping, until I decide I'm ready for him." Her gaze passed lovingly over the decorated home for the dead beneath the canopy of Caribbean beauty. She spread her arms wide. "They are untroubled now. They wait their turn for the call to serve." She dropped her blue-veined hands to her sides. "Elam will soon join them."

"What do you mean, *to serve*?"

"Palm Isle holds those meant to serve."

I bristled at the burn of her fevered stare.

"You will drift. There will be no rest."

"You've caused enough pain." My teeth chattered in the oppressive island heat. "Elam has done nothing to hurt you."

My husband remained suspended in the chief's solid grip over his head. Camilla nodded to Juan. He bent his knees and positioned himself for a throw. Even though my strength was a fraction of his, I had to stop him. I stepped a few feet away and crouched low.

I charged and smashed into the officer's meaty thighs. He lost his balance, sending all three of us careening into a heap on the ground.

Elam's painful grunt filled me with regret. I scrambled to my feet. The officer pushed himself halfway up, his previously clean shirt now smudged sandy beige. He blinked several times, glanced around as if confused, then directly up to me. He scrutinized the sight of Camilla and the small army of gravediggers.

His brow and lips pinched as if he finally recognized her for the first time. Camilla stood over the grave like an old queen. He jumped up, bent over and slid his arms underneath the weakened man, and manhandled Elam skillfully across his shoulders. "Go," he yelled as he trotted toward the cart. I dove into the back. He tossed Elam on the bench beside me. Juan leaped into the driver's seat.

"It's no use, Sandy," Camilla called from the gravesite. Her eerie cackles faded as the golf cart shot away.

"What the hell happened to you? Where are we going?" I held Elam with one hand, the other held tight to the hold bar as the cart jostled us at top speed.

"You must leave," he said. "We have to get you off the island. You are not safe."

"We WERE headed off the island. But something happened to the water taxi captain. He brought us back when I accidentally fell asleep."

"She will not be denied. She gets inside our minds and controls our actions." He drove on, the cart tilting at turns. I feared for our lives as the cart edged close to pedestrians and bicyclists. We left the village to a remote promontory on a part of the island I'd never seen. "I can get you out."

"But how did you break free?" I asked, holding onto the cart's roof edge with one hand to steady myself and Elam's arm with the other.

He cut another sharp turn. Elam's head lolled to the side.

THE DECEPTOR'S CALL

"If you don't slow down, you're going to throw us out."

"My will became stronger." He whirled the cart over a hole and we bounced in our seats. "Camilla uses the locals. She forces us to do things."

"How? What do you mean 'she forces you'?"

"We try to avoid her. Islanders know if she wants you, you may never be seen again."

Eventually, he skidded the wheels to an angled stop in front of an open hangar. The short airstrip stretched parallel to the seashore. Weeds shot up through crevices in the faded asphalt.

"I had no idea there was an airport on Palm Isle."

"It is empty most of the time."

The chief dashed from the cart and jogged around to Elam. With his lips peeled back and a groan, he carried him inside the hangar.

We advanced to a small counter where a bronze-skinned woman seated at the desk put her copy of Salem's Lot on the desk. She coolly surveyed our motley group. She reached inside a drawer and retrieved a set of keys on a ring, placing them in the chief's open palm.

"Follow me." He lumbered outside. I followed him around the side of the building to a twin-engine plane held in place by yellow blocks wedged in front of each wheel. He opened the passenger side door. "Get in the back."

"Seriously? You're a pilot? You can fly this thing?"

"I use it for emergencies only. Hurry. Get in."

The compact cockpit included two narrow bucket seats in the back. Using a roll bar inside the small doorframe and a stepladder beneath the door, I pulled myself inside. I climbed into the back and settled in. My mind reeled at the situation we were in as I clicked the safety belt into place.

The officer practically dumped Elam into the small bucket seat beside me. He closed the passenger side door and disappeared. He entered the plane with the yellow wooden blocks in hand and stowed them in a compartment near his seat. He strapped himself in the pilot's seat behind a dashboard with enough gadgets to operate a flying saucer. We were crammed inside the tight space like clowns in a car.

I reached across Elam, strapped the safety belt across his waist, and leaned him gently against me. Juan slipped the key into the ignition, manipulated buttons on the instrument panel, and the motor roared to life. Propellers on the front of each wing spun into grey transparent hazes.

We slowly rolled to the tarmac then gained ground speed on the straightaway toward the end of land. My stomach dropped when the ground gave way to air and the nose tipped up. Brilliant blue sky and puffy clouds filled the wide windshield. Inertia pulled my head snug against the back of the seat. The whining engines reverberated inside my head as we soared through the clouds before leveling off.

The chief placed headphones over his ears. Catching me in the rearview mirror, he pointed to his headphones. I found a pair hanging from a hook in a corner of the ceiling and slipped them on.

He fiddled with the dials on the control panel. "Good back there?" His voice came through the embedded mic system.

"What's happening?"

He stole a quick glance at me over his shoulder.

Elam slumped against me.

"I need answers."

"You are not safe there. None of us are."

I glimpsed out the window before returning my gaze to the back of his head. "Then why do you stay?" I leaned forward.

He caught my stare in his rearview mirror.

I squinted at his reflection. "You can obviously leave whenever you want," I said, not bothering to keep the sarcasm from my voice. With squeezed fists, my fingernails bit into my palms.

THE DECEPTOR'S CALL

"My people need me. We are strongest together." He shook his head. "No more questions. You must trust me."

I raised my voice. "Our life has been torn to pieces." I jabbed my fist into the back of his seat. "So, don't tell me I have to trust anyone. Why is this happening? The island is haunted. I've figured that much out."

Juan jutted his chin toward the windshield, discussion over.

I sighed and sat back to think. A fold of green lush mountains located on the far end of the island materialized in the distance. Bright coral reefs visible below the surface disappeared as we glided away.

Two hours passed. The ocean below changed from crystal blue to dark blue-green.

The chief broke the silence. "Florida."

White narrow beaches lay as margins between the land and the ocean. I wanted to cry with relief to finally see our home country. I replayed visions of our emotional reunion when Shauna would finally see me and her dad in the flesh. I'd be able to explain everything we'd suffered and leave it all as a bad memory.

I slid my hand to the band of my shorts, the metal handgun warm against my skin. There had been no need for it. I planned to dump it after deplaning.

We flew over a full sea port appearing miniature from my window. Luxury cruise ships lined end to end at a large terminal dock. Glass skyscraper hotels soared over white beaches. Palm trees lined perfect manicured rows, contrasting the wild tropical beauty of Palm Isle.

I tingled in relief. "I wondered if I would ever see my country again. We still have a long way to get home. But I thank you for bringing us, Juan."

He nodded.

From our height, our destination below resembled a child's play model. The sprawling airport's asphalt runways zigzagged like a puzzle. Jets parked at terminals. Cars and buses followed strips of highway running in every direction. Trains chugged on tiny tracks. Clusters of houses and apartment buildings with minuscule blue pools dotted the flat landscape.

The chief's voice popped in my headphones over the buzz of engines. "We land soon." The plane banked wide around the city as we descended closer to ground. The Atlantic Ocean stretched into blue-green infinity. I ached to stand on the solid ground of my country, to get to our hometown and Shauna. Never leave again.

The small plane bounced inside air pockets and currents as the ground reached up to us. I braced for a harsh landing. The nose gradually lowered then pulled up as the landing gear was released and the rubber wheels lowered. We bumped on the ground then skidded. Elam's head struck my shoulder. I doubted he could endure much more. The plane smoothed out on the runway.

A voice broke through on the radio from the air tower, directing Chief Juan into the rotation of pulsating airport traffic. Commercial jets and trailers, heavily laden with baggage, zoomed by. As instructed, he eased the small aircraft to a stop a few yards from an empty terminal gate. Several vehicles materialized, topped with flashing lights.

"We wait for air traffic control." the chief said.

I touched Elam's shoulder. "We're going to have to get off the plane as soon as we get the go ahead. How are you feeling?" I received a thumb's up answer though he remained slumped against the window. My heart lifted amid familiar comings and goings of an urban airport.

A mob of blue emergency lights flashed in the distance. I surveyed the area for a wreck or disturbance to see where they were headed. Regular busy jet traffic, official vehicles, and the baggage

THE DECEPTOR'S CALL

carts zigzagged on the blacktop. Nothing out of the ordinary. I returned my attention to my husband and took his hand in mine.

"I'll get you to a hospital and then, as soon as you are released, we get flights to see Shauna." He gave a slight nod. His skin had settled to a reddened waxy sheen. We were finally done with Palm Isle.

I leaned forward to the chief still wearing his headphones. "How long will it take them?"

He stared at the flashing lights and didn't answer.

I tapped his shoulder and raised my voice. "Are we going to get off the plane?"

He shook his head. "A bit longer. Still waiting for the tower's okay."

I reclined back in my seat.

The flashing lights brightened as they converged in our direction. They were not emergency vehicles as I'd assumed. Five black and white police cars closed in and fanned out until they surrounded our plane, sirens silent.

His attention on the police cars, Juan removed his earphones and sunglasses. He placed them on the empty seat beside him.

"Oh, no," I groaned. My heart dropped to my stomach. "What now?"

"I was not notified of a problem," he said.

I stared out the window. "None of them are getting out. What could be going on?" The cockpit's soundlessness roared in my head as the stuffy air staled. Sweat beaded on my upper lip and forehead. The inside of my shirt dampened and stuck to my skin. As the plane idled, claustrophobic panic boiled in my head. "I've got to get out of this plane." My breaths deepened. "Please at least crack the window open and let fresh air in."

The chief eyed something out the window. "I believe we can open the doors soon." I followed his gaze. I released my safety belt.

Two men, dressed in black knit collared shirts and ball caps, climbed on the small metal steps outside the cabin doors. Harsh, unflinching stares and handguns zeroed in on me through the windows. My heart pounded inside my chest. The odor of acrid sweat filled the sour air inside the cockpit as we each held perfectly still.

What the hell is happening?

The men outside held us hostage for what seemed an eternity. Were they waiting for instruction from someone inside one of the cars or the terminal? My sweaty skin pricked at the staredown between them and me.

"Mrs. Steele," said the officer on my side, his voice muffled and low through the glass. I read his lips. "Put your hands up. You're under arrest."

"Me?" I swallowed hard. "But I've done nothing wrong," I shrank into the leather seats and wrapped my arms around my waist.

"You're being charged with the murders of Cam Wyatt, her child, and your husband, Elam Steele."

I was sure I'd been transported inside an episode of The Twilight Zone. "I had no idea Cam was pregnant. She was hit by an oncoming vehicle when she accidentally fell into the street," I yelled as I slid myself to the edge of my seat. "And," I pointed to Elam, "my husband is not dead. He's right here. You can see he needs medical attention right now, for God's sake. He's been poisoned."

"Ma'am, put your hands up. We can do this the hard way or the easy way. It's up to you."

"Who do you think this man is?" *What would it take to make them understand?* "He's Elam Steele. I can prove it. I've got his passport."

"We can get him to a hospital as soon as you give yourself up."

"This can't be happening." I slammed my fists down on the seat. "Juan, help me," I pleaded. "Explain this to them."

THE DECEPTOR'S CALL

Our eyes locked in the rearview mirror. He changed his focus to the policeman. "I am the Police Chief of Palm Isle," Juan called out. "She is telling the truth. This man is Elam Steele."

The gun aimed on me, the officer answered, "I respect your position, Sir, but I've never heard of Palm Isle. And she is a wanted fugitive." Then to me, "Ma'am, I'm going to open the door and you will step out." He released his left hand from the gun and lowered it to the plane's door handle. His right hand held the gun, a finger on the slide. A third identically dressed and armed officer appeared in the window, his gun pointed at the chief. Electric currents zinged through my limbs in anticipation of violence ahead.

I cast into the recesses of my mind for a way out of another problem I was totally unprepared to handle. An idea sprang like water from a fountain. Old Camilla's words floated back to me. 'It's your gift. You will find it valuable.'

I inched my left hand away from the seat up to the waist band of my shorts. *Please let this thing be empty.* In one quick movement, I wrapped my fingers around the pearl handle and pulled the pistol out. Sliding my right arm around Elam's neck, I drew him against me, the barrel pressed into his temple. My entire body trembled as I freed my right hand from him and fumbled around until my fingers touched the metal of his seatbelt and unbuckled it. I studied one officer, then the other who had spoken. "Both of you put the guns down, or I'll shoot him."

The chief hesitated. He raised his hands above his head where I could see them.

Emotion for Elam swarmed me. He hadn't reacted to my threat and the pistol at his temple. The officers did not move. Juan remained facing the cockpit window.

"Take your hand off the door handle. Keep it slow." I had to get us out of the aircraft. I would not be held prisoner.

I pulled the barrel back an inch from Elam's temple. He flinched. I willed him to understand before snatching him to me a second time, the barrel back on his temple.

"Drop the weapons on the ground or I swear I'll blow his head clean off his shoulders." The muscles of my face trembled.

They released their guns, one at a time, and placed them on the tarmac below. The hustle and bustle of the Miami airport runways had ceased.

"Step off. We're coming out." I shook so hard I feared the gun might slip from my hand. Inexperienced with firearms, I pushed ahead.

With the barrel firmly on Elam's temple, I opened his door. "Everyone on the left side. Now."

"Mrs. Steele," said the second officer. "There's no need for anyone to get hurt. Please, let him go."

"Do the right thing and turn yourself in," the officer on the chief's side said.

"No talking. All of you step down from the ladders with your hands up." I recalled lines from a movie. "Stay away from your vehicles. Lay face down with your arms spread wide."

The officers shocked me by following my instructions.

"Elam, I need you to let Juan carry you again," I murmured.

"I will not get off this plane," said the chief defiantly, his hands up.

"You have to help us," I said through clenched teeth.

"I have helped all I can." He did not meet my gaze.

I rammed the tip of my free forefinger into his muscled side as if it were my gun on him. The real gun remained on Elam's temple out of Juan's sight. "You're the only one strong enough to get Elam out. Now, open your door. Get out and come around to Elam's side or this pistol will tear every muscle in your abdomen to shreds." My breaths

THE DECEPTOR'S CALL

came short and fast, my hands shook. "No quick moves." *Would he see through my façade?*

I exhaled as he opened his door and slid down to the tarmac. Hands in the air, he rounded the plane to Elam's door and opened it. The officers had not budged. Juan reached in and hoisted Elam onto his shoulders and waited. I kept the gun aimed on the chief as I slid over Elam's empty seat and climbed out. I expected the whole ordeal to unravel any second since the men outnumbered and outsized me. The officers on the ground observed my every move.

I had to orchestrate my next steps carefully. One mistake could cost Elam his life. Elam needed to be treated in a hospital. Shauna had to see her dad was alive. Our family needed to heal.

I pressed the tip of the gun into the chief's back. "Walk to that closest police car."

When we neared the closest car, Juan stopped. "Stay right there," I said and took one step closer to the official vehicle. Keys dangled on a ring from the ignition. Faith dared return to me. A vision of Shauna's relieved face when she would finally see us formed clearly in my mind. "Place him in the back then take the wheel."

Juan did as ordered. I settled in behind the driver's seat with the gun buried in his hair. The group of black clad police officers remained on the ground.

"Get us out of here."

He shifted the gear, revved the engine, and sped off. The plane and the officers dwindled in size as the tires squealed on the asphalt. I kept watch through the back window but cars pursued us. He steered the patrol car to an empty tarmac, around bends and away from the strip of the main runway, until we stopped.

"This tarmac was busy. Where is everybody?"

Juan offered no answer. I read a sign ahead of us on an unguarded iron gate, *Official Vehicles Only*.

"Check the gateway," I said. "Don't even think of running. You won't make it."

The chief got out, stealing a glance back at me. I wrapped the pistol's pearl handle with both hands and held my quivering chin high. Sweat poured from my forehead. He approached the gate and pressed the door. My nerves buzzed with the electric control of the gate swinging on its hinges. He opened it all the way. "Get in," I called. He returned to the driver's seat. I checked the area as we whizzed through.

Elam moaned beside me, perspiration rolling off his wrecked face. The reddened waxy flesh appeared more swollen, interrupted by misshapen eye sockets and one open nostril. His teeth bulged asymmetrically.

"Hurry," I demanded as I tapped a nervous rhythm with my sandals on the floorboard. "Get us to a hospital."

Juan sped on the highway surrounded by convenience and souvenir stores welcoming newcomers to purge their wallets. I spotted an H on an official green sign directing motorists to the nearest hospital. "Up ahead. Turn there." He followed the hospital signs for the next two miles. "Turn right."

He pulled up to the doors of an aged block-design hospital building. An *Emergency* sign marked the entrance. Two ladies in hospital scrubs chatted by bushes off to the side, cigarettes between their fingers. We crawled to a stop. He shifted the gear to park.

"Get Elam inside." I pointed. "There's a wheelchair."

He retrieved the unused wheelchair by the entrance door and pushed it to Elam's side of the police car. The chief jostled my husband up and settled him awkwardly into the wheelchair. I followed him, the gun back in the waistband of my shorts. Positioned behind Juan, I slipped the pistol back out and pressed it into his side, my hand concealed between us.

THE DECEPTOR'S CALL

The chief led the way inside. I was certain we looked suspicious. Few staff members and patients were present in the emergency area.

A woman in blue scrubs and a gray streaked ponytail approached us. "Can I help you?" Her name tag indicated she was the head ER nurse.

I stuck close to the chief's arm and jabbed the barrel harder into his side. He coughed. "This man needs medical attention," he answered in his soft island accent.

She glanced at his name tag then Elam's torso slumped in the wheelchair. She scrutinized me first then the chief. Bending closer to Elam, she took in his ruined appearance; an unprofessional pinch of her lips exposing her revulsion. She quickly recovered and straightened, meeting Juan's eye. "He'll have to check in at triage. The waiting area is right over there."

I followed her pointing finger to a small room where empty chairs lined walls. "This man needs attention now."

The supervisor set her shoulders. "I can see that, but proper paperwork must be completed before treatment. Hospital rules."

"I don't give a damn about your rules." I set my shoulders to match hers. Every muscle in my body tensed. "Take him to an exam room. Right now."

"I'm sorry, but he has to go through the system, same as all our patients. Triage first. Then I'm afraid he will have to wait until . . ."

My teeth clenched. "Take him back."

"But we have to follow protocol."

I backed the gun a few inches away from the chief.

She glanced down at the weapon in my hand. After a stilled pause she said, "Follow me."

I sighed in relief as our odd trio ambled and rolled behind her ample backside to an empty hallway consisting of curtains pulled closed to form private examination rooms. Someone whimpered inside one of the makeshift rooms.

A tall man, mid-sixties, in green scrubs with a matching surgical cap walked the hall toward us. He nodded a greeting to the nurse. She stepped directly in his path, nearly tripping him. He arched his eyebrows at her bold interruption.

"Excuse me, Doctor." She cocked her chin toward Elam.

The doctor curled his lips and tilted his head back an inch.

I was shocked they weren't tripping over themselves to help Elam.

"He needs attention," The nurse said.

"Incredible." The doctor gawked at my husband as if he were a scientific study.

"Umm, Doctor?" She cleared her throat. "Could you please take a look at him?"

He grimaced as if she'd suggested he scrub the bathroom toilets. "My shift is over." He maneuvered around us and strode down the hall.

"No one else is available right now," she said to me.

A small sign on the wall up ahead read *EMERGENCY SURGERY* with an arrow leading the way.

"Take him there." I pointed to the sign.

"The room has already been prepped for another procedure. That patient will be taken in soon. There's only one surgeon on duty right now. I'll send him right to you as soon as the case is finished."

"No." I changed the gun barrel's aim away from the chief and toward her. "My husband will be taken in now."

She half cried; half yelped. "But the room is set up for an abdominal exploratory procedure. The instruments are inappropriate for..." the skin around her eyes bunched as she looked down on Elam, "for his particular case."

"Chief," I said without breaking eye contact with her, "push Elam into that operating room right now."

THE DECEPTOR'S CALL

"No," she said to Juan. "You're not properly scrubbed and covered." She held her hands out. "He'll contaminate the sterile room."

I moved until we almost touched noses. I pushed the barrel into her ample abdomen. "Then you'd better make sure he doesn't."

CHAPTER SIXTEEN

The cadence of the heart monitor's beeping pierced the tension clouding the room. My untied paper gown, tossed at me by the head nurse before I entered the operating room, hung loose from my shoulders. I waved the gun in the direction of the closed door of the cold, sterile operating room. "Get out," I spat. Three nurses in pea-green, sterile gowns and matching hair covers huddled together, their clean latex gloved hands held up. They had entered the room as assistants. Green aliens in a horror film came to mind. Covered by clear masks and visors, their eyes darted back and forth as they considered my pistol and the distance to the door.

"I said, get out. Now. Before I change my mind."

An assistant nurse closest to the door made eye contact with her coworkers. She slipped the door open and disappeared. The others followed, one at a time. The door finally clicked to a close, leaving three of us alone. I assumed authorities had already been alerted. My fatigued body shook. I aimed the weapon back at the surgeon beside the gurney standing in the center of the room.

Previously prepped and rolled in by the head nurse, my unconscious husband lay on the gurney, a sterile green sheet draped over his body and head, a hole exposed his face. A needle, inserted and taped to the crook of his arm during her preparation, was attached to a fluid bag hanging from a pole near his head. A nearby monitor beeped incessantly.

Bright red blood dripped from the scalpel in the surgeon's hand onto the sterile drape sheet covering Elam. Fear flashed in the surgeon's eyes as he flicked his stare my way.

"Finish, dammit." I waved the metal tip of my weapon at him then backed against the wall for support and to prevent someone creeping up on me. He returned to Elam's face and continued his work in silence. In spite of the required cool temperature,

THE DECEPTOR'S CALL

perspiration prickled inside my shirt underneath my half-donned gown. Acid burned the back of my throat from the overpowering metallic smell of blood.

I kept an eye on a metal trash can lined with a plastic bag. It had been only twenty minutes since Juan left us outside the operating room. I hoped he'd slipped out of the hospital unharmed and free. Thoughts of him gave way to small tremors in my abdomen. Full waves of nausea intensified. I could hold off no longer.

The smell of blood coupled with stress bubbled and cramped my insides. I lifted the loose mask from my mouth and vomited. The contents of my stomach gushed into the trash can. I couldn't remember the last time I'd eaten. I wiped my mouth with the front of my loose paper gown and quickly turned away, humiliated. I replaced the mask over my mouth and nose. The surgeon watched me but resumed working when I caught his stare. Constant beeps from the electronic monitoring systems played in the background.

Landing in another place, out of my element, caused mounting misery and worry for Elam.

"How much longer?"

He peeked at me through his plastic visor. "I'm suturing him up now. But it takes time to bring him out from the anesthesia. I'll have to watch him." The doctor resumed the procedure. With overwhelming anxiety, the absence of an anesthesiologist had not occurred to me. Jumbled thoughts bounced in my head with the excruciating wait. The heart rate monitor pounded monotonous tones.

Elam had suffered too much. Finding a safe place for us to stay while he recovered was imperative. And I needed to get flights back to our hometown and connect with our daughter. She had to see us in person. Then she would see her dad was alive. I had to get our family back together.

The surgeon raised his head and focused on the tip of the gun barrel. "Your husband suffered extensive nerve damage." Light glinted off the steel surgical clamp and needle he used to sew Elam's face. "He'll need a lot of rest. His recovery will be long and painful."

Unable to plan ahead, I grappled with unformed ideas of getting us somewhere to hide out during his recovery. Needing more confidence, I clung to the fact that we'd made it at least this far.

My appreciation for the surgeon's work could not be shared for fear of losing control of the situation. The high probability of police barging into the room at any moment stayed with me. I envisioned them waiting outside the room to swarm me at the surgery's completion.

"There will be a lot of sutures. Maybe a half hour since I'm working alone." He operated silently for another five minutes. "I'll need to monitor him closely for at least an hour after I'm done here. He'll need care while the anesthesia wears off."

I weighed the options. I had to make a decision of the next move. If I wasn't handcuffed by police when we left for recovery, I would stay by Elam's side. I could slip away and use a phone to book a hotel room.

Thirty minutes passed. The surgeon cut the final suture and removed the blood-soaked paper drape over Elam, letting it drop to the floor. He worked the anesthesia monitors by Elam's head. The gun still trained on the surgeon, I marched to Elam's side and peered down at his gauze wrapped face.

"Elam?" The surgeon spoke softly. "You're all right, now. The surgery is finished. You're doing fine." He straightened. "I have to move him to the recovery room."

"It has to be you," I said. "And only you."

"I'll stay with him." He hung the IV bag on a pole attached to the corner of the gurney. "Besides we're in this together, him and me." He maneuvered the gurney to the door. I assisted by guiding the foot of the stretcher with my free hand, the gun still aimed at the surgeon's head. "Open the door," he said. "We'll ease him out,"

I released my hand from the foot of the stretcher and grasped the doorknob. The monitor's monotonous tones changed to frenzied beeping. The bright pulsating line on the screen bounced in erratic points.

"Wait." The surgeon wrested Elam's flimsy hospital gown up to his chin.

"What's happening?" I dropped my hand from the knob.

The erratic lines on the monitor flattened.

"We have to move him back into the operating room. Now!" He tipped his chin up. "Push that big red button there on the wall." With the operating table back inside, he pumped Elam's chest with his hands, arms straight, like I'd seen on television.

I located the red button and pressed my fist hard against it. Nothing happened. "Now what?" I cried.

"This is a code blue," he panted between chest presses. "Anesthesia and the code team should have been here by now. They're probably too scared of you. And that fucking pistol." The surgeon knitted his brows above his mask, his eyes shot a resentful glare on me. "Run out there and get help!"

I threw open the door, thinking only of Elam's safety. "Help," I yelled. "Help, please." My pleas echoed down the hallway. No medical employees sprinted to my aide. No patients or family members loitered about. "Help. Please. Someone." I glanced quickly back in the room, my heart pounding, barely able to breathe for fear of losing Elam, again. The surgeon worked frantically on Elam's chest. My shouts for the head nurse I'd threatened went unanswered.

Desperate and still wielding the gun, I ran down the hall back in the direction we'd first come. "Someone, please help." I passed through the empty surgical area and back into the emergency department. I raced between the ER partitioned rooms, every privacy curtain pulled back, every stretcher empty. I slowed my sprints to a walk, gasping as the hallway opened up. "Where is everyone?" My words reverberated in the expansive, cold space of the empty waiting area and triage check-in desk.

The panicked surgeon screamed down the hallway. "Hurry, dammit."

I would have welcomed the irony of police surrounding me and helping Elam.

"Is anybody here?" Blood rushed in my ears. "Help." My voice ricocheted within the walls.

No assistance materialized. I abandoned the mission to get experienced aid. The surgeon had only me. Darting back to the operating room, I threw open the door. The pistol dangled at my side.

The surgeon stood in the center of the room next to the gurney. As if splashed from a bucket, shiny crimson covered his paper gown. He leered at me through a blood-splattered visor. The scalpel loose in his right hand, red drips splattered on the floor. His left arm dangled straight at his side, his fingers splayed out in a tight grip buried inside a bloody dark mass of black and gray curls of my husband's severed head. Elam's lips pleaded silently to me. Horrific crisscrossed suture lines patterned his face like pick-up sticks.

He raised my husband's decapitated head toward me. "The surgery was successful." His words muffled by the blood-soaked mask. "Your husband recovered faster than expected."

The floor shifted underneath me. I stumbled backward with the sensation of floating as if in outer space. The surgeon, and Elam's head, moved in a slow spin, gaining speed with each rotation. My weapon clanged to the floor. The spinning slowed. My brain ordered my feet to move. I reached for the door and pulled until it swung back and banged against the wall.

The surgeon's voice stopped me. "You can have him back now."

THE DECEPTOR'S CALL

The bloody scalpel slipped from his fingers and clinked on the linoleum. The deranged doctor untied his mask and visor, Elam's scalp still gripped in his other hand. He let the mask drop. Elam stood in the surgeon's blood-soaked gown, his dazzling college-aged smile planted on me.

My knees weakened. "My god," I whispered. The chill, surgical temperature dropped another twenty degrees. Shivering, my breath clouded.

His glowing pallor suddenly diminished to lackluster and drawn, the skin above his cheekbones smudged gray. No evidence of injury from Camilla's poison, or the macabre surgery existed. "Welcome to hell, my love."

Shuddering at his vile grin, I backed away. "How is this possible?"

He followed, step-by-step. He tipped his head back and let loose wicked laughter, matching the frigid temperature of the operating room. I winced as his fingers sank into the flesh of my upper arm, preventing me from bolting.

"You can't leave now, Sandy." His voice produced no clouds of vapor, as mine did, in the cold room. "There's so much you have to see."

I tried to wrench out of his tight hold. "This is a nightmare, you're not real." His fingers burrowed deeper.

"I'm as real as you are." His tone was scathing. "You were warned of your altered existence. You no longer hold earthly considerations."

"What are you saying?'

The severed head fell from his fingers, landing with a sickening thud. It rolled to a stop, the mangled face resting on an ear.

"Camilla has called on me. She's shown me the truth. The truth of what you've hidden from me. You took the love of my life, my son, my heart."

"No." My voice quivered. I clutched my arms around my stomach as my legs trembled. "I swear, she fell."

"Yes, she fell. She fell after you stepped close. You forced her to lose her balance. It was easy with the baby inside her, changing her center of gravity." He did not raise his voice. "She took me back to the day. I've seen how you stole her pictures from my secret box the day you burned them." He shook his head, his features drawn downward in a grimace. "I trusted you. You were my best friend. You manipulated our relationship and made sure I married you instead of her."

I stepped back and bumped into the wall, the door to freedom on my right. Low wails echoed within the operating room walls.

Elam tipped his ear toward the ceiling. "Listen."

Prickles crawled under my skin. "Someone, help me," I yelled.

He dug his fingers deeper into the flesh of my arms. "Listen, Sandy." The baby cries grew stronger, more desperate. "The sound of my boy. I loved him. I wanted to finish school. Earn my degree so I could make a good life for them. I wanted to be a good father to him." He jerked my arm toward him, pulling me in. "But you took it all away from me." His spittle spattered my top lip. "You stole my whole life."

I swiped the saliva off on my shoulder. "Elam, it was an accident." I reached for his arm to make him listen. "Cam's pregnancy wasn't showing so I had no way to know. You didn't tell me. And he wasn't your son, she tricked you."

He knocked my hands away. "But she loved me. She loves me now. We are finally the family we should have been all those years ago."

The high pitched wails amplified. The door moved beside me, stirring Elam's anger. His resentment melted to rapt attention at the subject in the doorway. Camilla's flaming hair cascaded over her shoulders, the simple eggshell-blue shift fitted over her slim figure, light sparkled off the gold heart charm dangling at the notch of her sternum. She tipped her face, glowing in maternal awe, to the angelic baby cradled in her arms. Elam released my arm as if he'd forgotten his hatred.

Growing up, our children reveled in their father's attentions and support. But I'd known his grief for Camilla and their unborn child possessed the majority of his heart. The birth of Ed and Shauna failed to replace those losses. They had made no difference in his secret, painful devotion to the baby another man had fathered.

Elam, middle-aged and appearing as if he's hovering on death's door, and Cam, unchanged from the youthful age of her demise, formed a loving circle around the tiny creature. The baby's gray smudged skin was identical to that of Elam's.

A stranger invading an intimate moment between family members, I shrank back from the ghastly happy couple. I wanted the closeness of my own adult children, my living flesh and blood, born out of love with the man I had cherished for decades.

The family lost in their triangle of bliss and deathly reunion gave me an opportunity to slip away unnoticed. He'd made his choice, I chose the living. With light steps, I eased behind his back, through the door, and out into the desolate hallway. I tore away and left the operating room.

"Did you really think I'd let you go?"

I spun about face. "Elam."

"I will leave you to be with your first family. It's obvious that they're the most important to you."

"No. You will not see my children without me at your side. We're bonded ...forever."

Heavy iron clamps locked around my wrists. A scream ripped from my throat like a glass shard.

"You went to extremes to have me." He held his wrist up, bound with an identical iron clamp. Thick steely links of chain jangled between us. Camilla and her bundled baby led the way.

He tugged me along. I caught my balance and tread wearily. "Where are we going? You can't do this," I demanded. The edge of the clamp bit into my skin.

As he strode ahead, the iron links pulled tight, jerking my wrists. I stumbled then caught myself and reluctantly fell in line, a prisoner of the man to whom I'd devoted my life.

CHAPTER SEVENTEEN

We clanked through the empty emergency room hallway past the chairs, desks, and monitors; the building spiritless as a forgotten relic. The open curtains of the treatment rooms exposed gossamer spider webs woven over time, strung between outdated electronic equipment, corners, counters, and rusted stretcher legs. A thick layer of dust blanketed all surfaces. Empty medicine cabinets hung limply on the walls, shattered glass on the counter and floor. A black rat scurrying across a counter stopped and stared as we passed by. Chairs lay on their sides in random patterns.

Our morose line clattered around a gurney angled in the center of the hall. I recognized the clunky monitor equipment from a past decade. It was identical to the equipment the surgeon had used with Elam.

My thoughts returned to the surgeon in the blood-stained paper gown. I searched Elam's face. The skin was the same ash gray with deep sunken eye sockets. "What happened to you?"

"The same as you, Sandy. We're all the same."

I clutched at my chest. "How are we the same?"

He held his finger to his pouted lips in a shh gesture. "Quiet, you'll upset the baby."

Panic and frustration bubbled inside me. I suppressed the scream threatening to rip free from my throat. The chain continued to pull the metal clasp on my wrist, link clinking against the link with each step.

I snuck a peek back at the hospital building as we exited. Sharp pointed glass fragments left in the windows like fractured teeth from thrown rocks. Other windows covered by plank boards. Weeds covered the parking lot.

My chest tightened beneath the expanse of stars in a brilliant cluster. I feared suffocation when the quilt of stars dropped to my face. The still brightness evolved to a slow rotation, and then gradually picked up speed. My legs weakened. The chain tightened as I fell. Loneliness borne of isolation formed my premonition of something unwanted and undesirable yet to see. To learn.

The suffocating starlight blanket levitated like a magic carpet. It vanished, leaving me in a total darkness like I'd never experienced before. Taking in a deep breath, my chest expanded. A wave of nausea rolled over me then disappeared.

Darkness dissolved into spinning mixed colors as my vision broke through the blackness. The kaleidoscope of colors settled in the form of a room. Freed from the iron clamp and chains, I stood alone in a living room of an unfamiliar home. Fluffed pillows were propped on the loveseat and sofa. Flames sizzled inside a cozy stone fireplace, pictures set on the mantle above. I inched closer and inspected the young family in the frames; a woman and two young boys approximately seven and nine. One man, possibly late twenties, posed alone in another. Recognition came to me as I studied the faces I knew intimately. "Shauna." I gasped. "Ed."

I faced the room's center. Metal pots clanged in another room. The scent of roasting beef wafted in, filling my nostrils. My mouth watered. Wooden drawers slid open and closed. A timer buzzed. Metal hinges of an oven door scraped open then slammed closed.

"Boys, dinner's ready." Her voice from the kitchen caused my burning hot tears to break free. Aching to hold my daughter, I wanted to join her in the kitchen. My feet were held in place as if by concrete. I opened my mouth to call out to her.

"Coming, Mom." A child's voice from upstairs distracted my intention. The living room ceiling thudded and bumped from the pattering of feet.

I held my breath. The picture on the mantle of Shauna and the young boys shimmered at me, snagging my attention. Footsteps clambered down a staircase out of my view. An undeniable connection pulled on my soul. Without seeing their faces, I knew them intuitively.

Understanding dawned upon me. I'd been transported forward in time.

My futuristic grandsons exclaimed their delight of dinnertime.

"Did you boys get your homework finished?"

"Yes ma'am," one chimed. "Sort of," said the other.

"Did you guys put it in your book bags to turn in tomorrow?"

"Sure did," said one. "Yep," said the other. "When're we going to Dad's house?"

After a slight pause, she said, "Maybe the weekend after next."

"Maybe?" they answered simultaneously.

"He might be going out of town. He says he'll call you one day next week. Sit down and I'll make your plates."

Silverware chinked against plates. Chairs scraped on the floor. A desire to join them filled me with an overwhelming sense of homesickness. "Shauna?" I called. She did not answer.

They ate in silence then the boys cleared the table as instructed. I listened to their invented game of the chore and constant banter. My heart yearned to see their faces.

My daughter entered the living room. My heart swelled. Her face, once fresh and glowing, now swollen and stressed, her middle bulged over the front and sides through a loose silk blouse.

"Shauna." I reached for her.

She crossed the center of the room, grazing my outstretched arms. She approached a cabinet in the corner and pulled an envelope from a drawer and counted the dollar bills inside. She replaced the envelope and closed the drawer, passing me on her way back to the kitchen with the bills clutched in her hand.

"Shauna," I repeated, my heartbreak unbearable.

"Here boys. Each of you give this money to your teachers for the field trip next month."

"Okay," they answered in unison.

I wanted so badly to know them, to learn their names.

The doorbell chimed. Startled, I nearly lost my balance even with my feet stuck to the floor. Shauna returned to the living room and glanced at the wall clock. Her knitted brows and the shake of her head indicated she was not expecting a visitor at the late hour. She peeped through the sidelight window then quickly opened the door and stepped back.

"Ed," I cried. My son stepped over the threshold. His smile glowed as he gathered his sister in an embrace, picking her up off the floor.

He set her down. "This is awesome," she said. "I had no idea you were in town."

"I just arrived." He dropped his duffel bag by the door. "There'd be no fun in me giving you a head's up." His typical chuckle at his own joke made me smile through my tears.

"Ed." I waved at him. "It's me, Mom."

Ed exhaled and viewed the whole room. "It's good to be back."

"Come in to the kitchen." Shauna tugged his arm. "I know two guys who'll be thrilled to see their favorite uncle."

Celebratory whoops and hollers burst through the house as Ed disappeared for the kitchen.

"Whoa, whoa." Ed chortled. "You guys are so big, you almost knocked me over."

"Uncle Ed." one boy shouted, "Are you staying with us?"

"Yeah, are you sleeping here, Uncle Ed?" added the other.

"Boys, boys." said Shauna, "Give Uncle Ed some space. I'm sure he's tired. Of course, he's staying. He's got to get you two in line."

My lonely spirit lifted into a smile at my family's happiness from the kitchen.

"If you guys don't mind, I'd like to stay for the next week."

"Awesome," they sang.

THE DECEPTOR'S CALL

"You can have my bed," said one boy.

"No, he can take my bed," cried the brother.

"I'll sleep on the couch. That way I can catch the first one of you who sneaks down the stairs in the middle of the night and snatches leftovers from the fridge."

The boys laughed along with Ed. Their happy adoring teases with their uncle made me love them beyond words.

No matter what happens to me, I'm happy to know they remained close and I have two loving grandsons.

"Okay boys, it's late. Go brush your teeth and get ready for bed. Morning comes quick."

"Mom, please," they sang. "We want to stay up with Uncle Ed."

"Tomorrow is Friday. You can stay up late with him for the whole weekend. Now off with you." she teased.

"Good night, Uncle Ed."

Their stomps up the stairs boomed in the living room, evidence of their reluctance to leave him.

Tortured by my unknown presence in the next room, I wiped at my moistened cheeks. I wanted more than anything to see the boys.

"Let's talk in the living room where it's more comfortable," said Shauna. "You can catch me up on your glamorous jet-setting life."

The siblings entered the living room and settled into opposite ends of the couch. Both had grayed slightly. Ed's athletic frame had not changed a bit.

"Shauna." His expression was grave. "I'm actually here on a mission."

"Sounds exciting."

"Well," he rubbed his hands together, "I've recently learned some disturbing news. I thought it was best to tell you in person rather than on the phone."

Her smile disappeared. "Do I want to know?"

"You have to hear this, Shauna."

"Mom, can we come down and give Uncle Ed another good night hug?"

"Of course." She smirked at Ed for the appreciated delay in bad news. "Come down." A competitive clamber downstairs ended with Uncle Ed at the bottom of a loud, couch pileup and all in hysteric fits.

My throat tightened with love. I beheld the sight of my elementary school-aged grandsons; dark-haired and apple-cheeked. Ed left his seat and hugged them in a loose chokehold. "It's good to see you two monsters." Each boy received a playful hair ruffle. "We'll have breakfast together then I'll walk you to school. How does that sound?" Cheers and high fives all around ended the fun. The boys scrambled up to bed.

All quiet upstairs, Shauna settled back in her seat on the couch. "What's the disturbing news? Let's get it over with."

Ed released a long sigh. "I was going to start at the beginning. But I'll cut right to the point." He exhaled through puffed cheeks. "It appears," he raked a hand through his hair, "Mom not only murdered our father..."

"That's not true, Ed," I cried. His words cut me to the quick. Though they could not hear me, I had to try to make them understand.

"No." Shauna stopped him, her palms facing him. "I know I do NOT want to hear this."

"I'm sorry I have to be the one to tell you, but you have to learn the truth. We've been living without the whole story. Secrets other people kept from us."

Shauna dropped her hands in defeat. "I was just beginning to come to terms with things as they were, Ed." She steeled her face against unwanted information.

THE DECEPTOR'S CALL

"Don't do this," I yelled. "I didn't murder your father." I swept my arms toward him. "I didn't murder anyone." My declaration fell on deaf ears as if I were alone in the room.

"It turns out Dad was engaged to a girl when he was in college. He'd dated her in high school. She'd gotten pregnant then, but he went on to college. They planned to be married after he graduated."

"Wait." Shauna breathed out with a gasp. She clenched her fists. "We have another sibling?"

Her pained expression cut me to the core.

"Well...we almost did," he continued. "Mom and Dad became good friends in college, which you already knew."

"Yes." Shauna white knuckled a pillow on her lap.

"Dad told her about his pregnant girlfriend back home. Mom secretly caught a bus to his hometown. He had no idea. She searched until she found the girl in town on the sidewalk. She shoved her into the street when she saw a bus coming. The girl was killed instantly."

My frustrated yowls fell like concrete.

"Oh, my God, Ed." Overcome by the news, Shauna rose from the sofa and paced circles near me. "You know this as fact?"

"She covered it up by getting on a bus back to campus. Dad didn't know she'd even gone. The coroner ruled her death a suicide. No one knew Mom had been there."

Shauna fell back onto the couch cushions. "I can't believe this."

"Mom found the pictures he'd kept of his fiancée. She hid this secret for years until he caught her burning the pictures years later. You were a senior in high school when it happened."

"No," she breathed.

"Yes. Dad's heart was broken when he realized what she'd done." His chin quivered in his pause, "The burning pictures were of his first family, taken early in her pregnancy." Ed stopped talking. With an angry jerk of his hands, he wiped his cheeks. "Mom then became overly nice at home. Remember we thought she was taking new meds to help with her menopause? But, no." He left his seat and walked a few paces away, his hands clenched in fists. With his back to Shauna he went on, "It turns out she was sucking up to Dad. She was doing whatever she could to keep him from leaving her."

He spun back toward his sister. "When he wanted to go on their crazy world travel trip, she told me she didn't really want to go. But she said she wanted him to live out his dream because he'd worked so hard all those years at the business." Ed returned and dropped back into his seat. "She told me his heart attack was the result of his work stress." He shook his head. "And I believed her. I would never have believed our mother was capable of doing anything remotely close to murder." He lowered his head into his hands.

"And then," Shauna added, "she killed him on the island." Her voice wavered. "Their first stop. He didn't even get to see more of the world. He wanted to see all the great sights so badly."

"But, Shauna, it's time you know how she did it. No more living with lies."

"Jesus, Ed. Why are you doing this to me?"

"I kept it from you because I wanted to protect you. You had moved into the dorm and were involved in your classes. I knew Dad would have wanted you to finish school. I did what I could to keep your stress level down so you could graduate. You had to stay focused. I'm sorry I didn't discuss things with you. At the time, your studies were most important."

Shauna melted back into the cushions as if she hoped they could shelter her from her brother's secret.

"He didn't tumble over the side of a boat like I told you. If you'd have known the truth, it could've been too hard for you to get through your classes. And I want you to understand lying to you hurt me. It hurt almost as bad as learning our mother was capable of something like this."

Shauna slammed both palms to her temples. "Get on with it."

THE DECEPTOR'S CALL

"The police officer who phoned me was head of the small police force on Palm Isle."

"Yes, I knew he reached out to you."

I was startled by his mention of the chief. He'd flown us to Florida. I had no idea where he'd gone. He'd been with us in the emergency room but not when we made it into surgery.

"There *was* a boat involved. But the problem really started when he and Mom had settled into their rental, the beach bungalow. You remember? The one he found online and was so excited about?"

"I remember."

"The police chief said his department received complaints from the landlord. She was an old lady living nearby. She reported hearing Mom ranting at Dad so loud her voice carried through the trees between the two bungalows. Once, the landlord asked Dad to help her move some furniture or boxes, or something. I forget what, exactly, but something too heavy for her. But, anyway, he agreed to give her a hand and Mom went nuts."

"What you're describing doesn't sound like Mom at all. It's like you're speaking of someone else."

My disbelief at Ed's information sent my stress shooting through the roof. I was on the verge of a breakdown.

"No. It's not like her. But, that's just it. The weird thing, none of it sounded like the mom we knew. It's like we're grieving someone else. A stranger."

"You still haven't told me what really happened." Shauna's hands trembled as she pushed hair back from her face.

"Apparently, Dad went to help the woman anyway."

"He always was the best person," said Shauna with a softened tone. "And why everyone in this whole town loved him. He would do anything for anyone."

"This is the hard part. He helped the woman out on several occasions. I can see Dad trying to help an elderly woman living alone.

He couldn't have turned her down even if he'd wanted to. She said he was the nicest man she'd ever met. Actually, the words he quoted from her, 'kindest and heartfelt man.'"

Shauna's tearful face crumpled. "She got that right."

Resigned to the fact they were not aware of my presence, I was forced to endure more.

"The woman claimed Mom threatened Dad if he went to help her one more time. The officer said Dad had befriended the old lady and was worried what Mom might do. The next night while he was asleep..." He stopped and took in the worry etched on his younger sister's face. "I'm so sorry, Shauna."

Shauna jumped up off her corner of the couch, her body tense. "This is horrible."

He stood and hugged her then helped her settle back down. "Mom used a cleaver from the kitchen. Dad was asleep."

My shoulders ached under the unrelenting tension.

Shauna shook her hands at him as if to ward off the words to follow.

"She hacked him to death." He stopped and dropped his face into his hands as if all energy had drained away.

Shauna clutched the edge of the couch cushion, her expression flat.

"They found him buried in a fresh gravesite at a local graveyard." He sniffed and wiped his wetted cheeks with the back of one hand. "There was a small cross marker with his name engraved on it."

"My, God," she whispered. "She planned it."

"The site where the marker was found was a grave dug earlier, intended for a local person whose burial was scheduled for the next day. They exhumed Dad's body. He wasn't even in a coffin." Ed slid closer to his sister and took her hands. He whispered the final blow as if afraid of the words themselves. "This is the part I recently learned. His dismembered body was buried in thirty individual parts stacked neatly in the ground."

Shauna's right eye ticked.

"I was told thirty wooden crates with Dad's name were strewn nearby, bloodstains inside each one."

She jerked her head back and her mouth dropped open.

"I wish you both could hear me." I fought to release myself from the paranormal force imprisoning me. "I'm here with you." I hoped for the slightest sign of recognition from her.

"How do you know any of this is actually true?" Shauna said in a whisper.

"I caught a redeye flight down there after the call. Since Dad had been murdered, the local government refused to release the body without one of us there to identify and claim him. I arranged to have him cremated there. And the same with Mom's body."

"You didn't tell me you had to take care of it."

"Like I said, you were so stressed with your classes and declaring a major. I decided to handle it for both of us."

"I don't know what to say, or what to think. And being clueless all these years."

"I'm sorry to keep you in the dark. You've always had so much else going on in your life." He protectively rubbed her shoulder then continued. "Mom buried him and hid out in an abandoned shack for two days. The police found her there and they took her into custody."

I witnessed the pain in Ed's grimace.

With a shake of her head, Shauna lowered her chin to her chest. "One last thing."

Shauna faced her brother holding her hands out. "I can't stand anymore."

"You have to hear me out, Shauna."

His Adam's apple jumped in his neck as he swallowed. "Mom hung herself in her jail cell on the island." His shoulders relaxed with the release of telling her.

He waited. Dead silence buzzed in my ears.

Shauna's posture contracted from him as if he were fire. "You told me she fell out of the boat. Where does the boat come into all of this mess?"

"Three elderly people were fishing on a small fiberglass boat a short distance from Mom and Dad's cottage. They said they heard screaming. They were staying at another of the landlady's rental cottages. All of the cottages were in a thick, remote jungle away from the main village."

"I thought you said it happened when Dad was asleep."

"Yes, it did. He was taking a nap, that's when they heard the screaming."

"Shauna, Ed, I'm here." I beat my hands on my thighs. "You can't believe any of it. It's all lies."

"Mom?" called a frightened voice from the top of the stairs. "Are you all right?"

Shauna raised her hands to either side of her head. She took a deep breath, lowered her hands and said calmly toward the ceiling, "Everything's fine, boys. I'll be up in a few minutes. Go back to bed."

Footsteps creaked above us.

"I have to settle him back in or he won't be able to go back to sleep." She dried her face with the back of her hand. "This is unbelievable. It's like I'm hearing gossip about another family. The kind of crap that's written in novels."

Ed hugged her then stepped back. "I'll stay here as long as you need me. I can help with the boys."

She left him and traipsed up to my grandsons.

My heart bled as Ed rested against the back of the couch, the corners of his mouth turned down in a frown. He pushed off the

THE DECEPTOR'S CALL

couch and approached the window with a heavy sigh. So much like his father, he ran his hands through his dark curls and peered out into the night through an opening between the curtain edges.

The weight from the pain he'd carried alone for the sake of his sister seared into me. I doubled over my shackled feet as his tortured expression raged inside me. Maternal instincts caused my heightened desire to touch him, to hold my son, until all the lies and negativity were wiped clean from inside him.

Without warning, the pressing sensation at my feet holding me apart from my family dissolved. I pulled my legs up one at a time as a test.

Approaching Ed, I reached out to comfort him. He needed his mother's love. As my hand touched his shoulder, it disappeared into his flesh and bone. Instinct caused me to jerk back. My heart raced deep in my chest and up to my throat as I remembered the same thing happened when Elam had returned to the cottage. An examination of my fingers showed no signs of change or discoloring. The nailbeds appeared pink. Pain throbbed as I pinched the skin on the back of my hand. I opened and closed my fingers in a fist without pain in my joints.

I tried to touch him again with the same result. I pulled back. He continued to stare out the window, unaware of my hand entering or leaving him.

Ed released the curtain. He returned to the sofa, unimpeded as he walked straight through me.

CHAPTER EIGHTEEN

My son's frown and slackened posture as he rested on the couch indicated his misery with having shared the information with Shauna and causing her more pain. I had screamed, cried, and spoken to them without a twitch of acknowledgement from either of my children. Any hope I was hallucinating and would forget dissolved. We, mother and son, so close, were kept apart by a veil of infinite distance and horror controlled by an unnatural entity. The separation from my family in this way and to hear the false twist of reality was cruel beyond my imagination.

The padding of her footsteps down the stairs preceded Shauna's melancholy appearance when she entered the room. "This is all so hard to digest." She crossed by me, our arms melding as one on her return to the couch. "This story about Mom is so outrageous." Fidgeting, she left her seat. "There's still something I can't ignore."

"What is it?" Ed asked.

"Mom was not strong enough to load multiple wooden crates into a grave. And how could she have carried the crates from the cottage anyway? You said their place was in a remote location, but the graveyard is close to the busier part of the village. Right?"

"Yes. Right."

"Okay." She jutted her hands out to her sides. "Did anyone explain how she did it?"

"Good, honey," I cried. "Now you see the story can't be true." I dared not breathe.

"That's where the small fishing boat comes in," he said.

"No." I paced the floor shaking my head. "There was no fishing boat."

"The chief officer told me she loaded the crates, one at a time, onto this little fiberglass boat from a dock near the abandoned cottage. That's all the information I've got. But she must have been

THE DECEPTOR'S CALL

familiar with the owner of the boat since she had to have had the key to turn the motor on."

Shauna slumped her shoulders. "I was hoping it couldn't be true. How could we have not known there was a hidden beast inside her?"

"You poor kids." I said. "We're all being tortured. I have to find a way to make you see the truth."

Both lost in their own thoughts, the room went silent.

A knock at the door shattered the somber mood. They shared a questioning exchange with raised brows.

"Were you expecting someone?" he asked. "At this time of night?"

"No." Concern edged Shauna's voice. "The only visitors we get are the neighborhood kids." She hesitated before moving to the door. Ed abandoned his seat. "I'm not up to dealing with anybody right now," she said reaching for the knob and pulled the door open. Her body stiffened as she looked out.

I tromped closer to see who had caused the shock stretched on her face. "No, it can't be. Will this hell never end?"

Gray-faced Elam smiled his charming greeting to his daughter. Young Camilla, the baby in her arms, lingered by his side.

Ed walked to Shauna's side to see the visitors outside the door. Chest out, he stepped in front of his sister. The baby reached out from his mother's embrace to Ed. Elam, middle-aged, stood before his eldest son. Camilla, younger than Shauna by more than a decade, held tight to her child.

Ed stepped back. I sensed his fear as he glowered suspiciously to the baby, so similar to his own baby pictures. "Who are you?"

"Son," Elam said, "I came for you."

"This is obviously some kind of sick joke. You need to leave." As he closed the door, Elam stopped the door with his quick hand.

"I'm here for my grown children to meet the family." The enchanting smile darkened, threatening. "And your mother is here, too."

"Shauna," Ed said, as he stared at the vision of their father, "go upstairs." She reacted to his firm tone by rounding on her heels and running for the stairs. Her steps thudded above us.

"You. Are. Not. My. Father."

"Yes, Son. I am. You wouldn't want to protect your sister if you didn't believe it." Elam shouldered past Ed to enter the living room, Camilla following in his wake. They stopped in the center of the room.

"Elam, why are you doing this?" I asked. "Leave them alone. I'm begging you."

"Get the hell out." Fear laced the confusion in Ed's tone.

"You're intrigued, Ed. You want to learn the many secrets about your mother." Elam peeled his lips back in a menacing grin, sending shivers down my spine. "She's been here all evening, listening to your discussions while you and Shauna had to relive the torture she brought upon our family."

"What are you talking about?" Ed was visibly shaken.

"Here." Elam pointed to me then stepped to my side. "She's right here."

Ed's pupils enlarged. He sucked in more oxygen. His pallor whitened. "Mom?" He breathed.

"Ed?" Shauna called from upstairs.

"Shauna," he said, "stay there."

"Ed," I said, my heart bursting, "I'm sorry, please believe me. This is all beyond my control. And none of what you've been told is true. I've no idea how this is happening. But we're in another dimension right now, an alternate reality."

"Get out," he shouted at me. "All of you."

THE DECEPTOR'S CALL

"Please, Ed. I'll tell you what's really happened to me and your fath..."

Ed angled his chin toward the stairs, never releasing me from his pulsating hateful glare. "Shauna," he called, "call the police."

"The police can't help you. Your mother will get the punishment she deserves for what she did to my family. For what she did to all of us."

"Stop this, Elam," I yelled, my fisted hands close by my sides. I faced my son. "You don't understand. I didn't kill them." I lowered my voice and lightly touched his arm.

"Shauna, call the cops. Now."

Soft patters sounded down the stairs. Rigid as a pole, Shauna stood by the living room entrance. "You're all supposed to be dead." The phone thudded on the stair.

"Cam, put the baby down," Elam said. Camilla placed the bundle on the floor.

Shauna's head tilted back at the same time her legs folded and she fell toward the floor like a discarded puppet. Camilla, relieved of the baby, caught Shauna mid-fall and laid her unconscious body gently on the floor.

"Shauna," I called and stepped close to her.

"Don't touch her," yelled Ed as he advanced on us. "Get the hell out." He shook Shauna's shoulders, trying to get her to wake up.

Elam smirked at me. I clenched my knuckles between my teeth, not knowing what to do to help, not wanting to upset Ed further.

"I hope you're happy, Sandy." Elam nodded to Camilla. "It's time."

"Leave Ed and Shauna out of this," I screamed. The strong force returned by pressing hard on my shoulders. It pushed into the back of my knees. I landed on my backside. "Elam, you have to stop this."

The unmoving baby lay near me, covered in dark dried blood. Its face intact, the back of its head had been smashed. A wide tire tread imprinted across the tiny flattened torso and one arm. A sprig of dark curls lay soft in the crushed head tissue. Screams ripped from my mouth as I slid away from the infant.

Camilla stretched a perfect venomous sneer at me. She edged around where Ed was crouched over Shauna. She pulled Shauna's unconscious body away from him with uncommon strength for her diminutive size. A flash of light reflected from Camilla's hands as they opened over Shauna's face. A long dagger replaced the light in her hands, the tip pointed straight down, inches from Shauna's awakening face. Blood spurted as it plunged. Her screams curdled deep in my soul.

"Shauna," I cried. The back of my throat torn to shreds with my screaming, I pulled against the paralyzing shackles. "Camilla, stop, you fucking monster."

Ed stared shell-shocked at the blade. The boys scampered down to the horrific shrieks and skirted the corner into the living room. Both came to a dead stop, stricken by the vision of their mother being sacrificed.

"Sandy," Elam shouted over the mayhem, "you thought you'd get away with manipulating me, removing the people who'd meant everything to me."

"How could you?" I shrieked between sobs. "Your own daughter?"

"Shauna will be with me forever. They'll all be with me, Sandy."

"You're a monster!" I continued to press against the force holding me down, powerless to protect my children and grandsons.

The knifepoint repeatedly pierced into my daughter's eyes. Lips frozen open, her primal screams hushed. Her teeth bared as crimson geysers spurted upward. Blood spattered out in the carpet, fanning out around her.

Camilla left the bloody corpse of my beautiful daughter on the floor. The pungent scent tasted like metal on my tongue. She

THE DECEPTOR'S CALL

approached Ed, his lips retracted and frozen in horror at witnessing his sister's murder, then glanced back at his phantom father. Elam gave her a nod. She rose one hand up in the air. Flames erupted from her fingertips. Her hands on fire, she bent over and held them to Ed's running shoes. My throaty screams dwindled in despair and revulsion of the scene. I was forced to watch the rubber soles melt then brighten as red-orange flames caught the canvas material and licked up the flesh of his calf.

He did not jerk or yell, as if held prisoner by the same evil that restrained me. "Ed!" Tears slid from the corners of his widened eyes as flames licked up to his shorts and shirt. Evil fingers of fire melted and consumed the whole of my son.

The boys, unmoving, watched from the corner.

My son's crouched body transformed into smoking blackened bone, his horrified facial expression the last to succumb. His soft body tissue disintegrated. The skeleton fell apart. The bones bounced and rolled away. Final curls of smoke rose from the black pile; skin, hair, internal organs burned to ash.

"Devils!" My shrieks worn to a rasp.

The flames from Cam's hand lowered to a simmer then died.

The force at my ankles and shoulders released its hold. I ran to embrace my shock-stricken grandsons. I reached for them. "Boys." My hands melted through their skin. "I'm your grandmother. I'm here with you.

Neither child flicked an eyelid.

"It's no use," Elam said. "You don't exist in their world. They think you died long ago."

I knew pleading with him would do no good. He meant to strip me of everyone I loved.

"But don't worry, my love. These boys will live. For now." He reached out his hand for her. Camilla stepped to his side.

****

Exhausted, I blinked repeatedly to remove the sand from my eyes. Dizziness filled my head and the sensation of falling took over.

The vertigo ended. I was no longer surrounded with the blood-spattered floor and walls of Shauna's living room.

Back on the dock, I gazed at the tilted abandoned shack, water lapping below me. Wind sailed through the sunlit glassless windows. Birds squawked and whistled from their hidden perches high in the coconut palms. They had formed the beautiful beginning backdrop of my darkest, nightmarish experiences.

I trembled uncontrollably under the humid blast of the sun. Strong intuition told me there was more to come. I knew I couldn't run away from whatever awaited me. The physical ache and need to see my grandsons was strong, though they'd not been aware of my existence. Elam had forced me to watch the executions of my children. But I had seen Shauna's boys.

I would find my way back to them, a light and new purpose of my desolate existence.

****

Irrefutably drawn to the ramshackle building, I'd become inured to the expectation of pain, its dilapidated condition fitting to my shredded heart. Wind rustled through palm leaves and penetrated the warped door. It occurred to me I placed my hand on the knob, no need to knock. Whatever waited inside was meant for me. I pushed the door open, the hinges creaking. Sunlight stabbed into the darkened, one room dwelling.

Within the shadowy interior, the wall directly ahead of me was covered with stacks of wooden crates. *SHAUNA* labeled on one stack, *ED* printed on another. Seeing my dead children's names on the crates cut deep into my soul. The two crates at the top of the stacks slid out simultaneously.

I covered my eyes with the heels of my hands. My defiance did nothing to stop the crates from inching forward. In spite of myself, I opened my eyes as they scraped to the edge and fell onto the wooden floor; the contents spilling and crashing in revolting bumps. My children's heads were detached at the neck. Their faces in perfect condition, expressions serene, as if Shauna's eyes had not been gouged out by a dagger and Ed had not been burned alive. Their heads were presented to me as if to let me observe them at peace. The horror I'd experienced left me feeling empty inside.

As I backed out from the shack, the door latched. By a mystical pull, my feet took me away from the water and cottage. I followed the familiar sandy path cut into the open field of high grass. In my dream state, I continued on, enclosed by wild jungle ending at the sandy main road.

I followed the twists of the road and wound through the dense forest to Paraiso, where Elam and I had once been happy. Before the old woman destroyed us.

My heart swelled with the sight of Frank as he barked a greeting and bounded down the steps from the deck. I reached to pat the grimy crown of his black head, thankful for a friend. To be acknowledged. His body stiffened.

His glare confused me. "Frank?" I sensed him search deep into my soul.

His black lips drew back, baring two rows of razor-sharp teeth. I jumped back from his bone-chilling bark.

"Frank. Easy, boy. It's me."

He stepped forward. His fur bristled on end along his broad back. His body trembled, tail straightened, positioning for attack. I stepped backward to the road, too frightened to yell out to him. He turned and bounded up to the deck where he dropped to the boards and stared down at me as if on guard against a stranger. I glared back until I rounded the corner.

Camilla's cottage appeared empty in the next jungle clearing. Children's jubilant conversation reached my ears from inside the old lady's cottage. Not wanting to give in to the desire, I passed quickly by at the destructive empty structure. Intending to keep my gaze forward on the road and ignore them, I stole a sidelong peek at the source of happy shouts and laughter in spite of myself.

My two grandsons raced down the stairs. I was terrified to find them on the dangerous bewitched island. The older one won the speed contest to the bottom, ending in the middle of the front yard. Two paddle boards and long paddles lay in the sand. Each boy wrestled with the awkward equipment but managed to drag them, by sheer stubborn will inherited from Shauna, until they disappeared to the back yard. I couldn't resist following.

They dragged their unwieldy burdens to the edge of the water on the small beach. I waited back a few feet. They lay on top of the boards then paddled hard a short distance off the beach before standing up on shaky legs. Both boys placed their single adult-sized paddles down into the sea's calm, mirror like surface. They worked until they gained some distance away from the beach.

"Come back," I yelled. "You're heading too far out."

With no regard for my shouting, they continued guiding the boards too long for them. Skillful paddle motions pulled them farther away from me until they were miniatures in the distance. They closed in on the opening to the channel, widened and curved on its far end into the small harbor. I flew out of the yard, chest burning, to get to the port docks and watch for them.

****

Emptied tender boats, waiting to transport the ship's passengers, lined the concrete dock of the fishing village. An imposing white,

THE DECEPTOR'S CALL

luxury cruise liner lazed at its mooring in the deeper water offshore. The recent influx of cruise tourists crowded and congested the harbor. Local fisherman had arrived with their fresh catch from an early morning workday at sea. Competing restaurant owners peered into the boats driven up onto the short beach, scrutinizing the best choices.

I made my way to the main dock and passed between the shorter docks, tender boats extending out on each side. I reached the end of the dock for the best view of the channel opening into the harbor area. The boys would paddle in from the short channel formed between the point of a beach on one side and a small island close by on the other. All boats and marine life passing through were visible from my vantage point. I scanned the marina in case they had beaten me there.

Locals milled around the dock. Tour guides and taxi drivers waited while more tender boats tied up and delivered their cruise ship passengers. Dive and snorkel excursion boats bobbed half-filled with customers eager for new sights and experiences. Drummers, dressed in colorful native costume, beat a welcome serenade.

The tilted sunken fishing trawler sat in the center of the harbor, abandoned, sad-looking. Its once white gleaming edges and screws now rusted.

Focused on finding the boys, I bumped into a couple holding hands. "Excuse me."

"Watch where you're going, lady," the woman yelled. "You almost knocked me off this dock." She and her partner shoved off toward the crowd of waiting vendors. I had made real physical contact with the woman as I bumped into her. The couple had acknowledged me. They knew I was there, in front of them.

My search over the channel and small beach resumed, concern growing the longer I waited.

BARBARA MICHELLE

The taller one in the lead, the two young boys paddled painstakingly slow from the narrow channel into the wider mouth of the harbor. Crystal blue canal water shimmered around them as they neared the docks. My love for them boiled over though they were unaware of my existence. Their voices bounced over the calm surface. I could not understand the words, but their friendly chatter gave me hope I might get to know them, and for them to know me. I sensed they had no recollection of their mother's, or their beloved Uncle Ed's unearthly demise.

"Boys." I waved my arms over my head. "Boys, over here."

Their conversation stopped. They stared at me across the water.

I chose a tactic to prevent their being afraid of me, a stranger. "I'll help you get up on the dock." Theirs stares unchanged, I continued. "Then I'll explain who I am."

They held the paddles still in the water and talked, their words out of earshot. My heart fell when they resumed their paddling and guided their boards away from the dock. They veered into a wide arc away from the pier and across the narrow channel closer to the island on the opposite side. The boards hugged the opposite bank until they passed it.

"Boys, this way." I waved my arms, frustrated with not knowing their names. "I'll explain."

They exchanged glances but did not answer me or follow my advice. I berated myself for frightening them. I resorted to discreetly watching and thinking of a way to keep them safe. We were, after all, family.

The ocean opened up a quarter mile out from the pier and to the right of the smaller island across the channel. I held my breath as my grandsons paddled the wide arc. Their choice had forced them too far out toward the open sea current. They muscled the paddles faster and steered back to the harbor's placid waters. The older boy pulled closer first. He beckoned his brother to safety, his shouts echoing

THE DECEPTOR'S CALL

across the water. The front tip of his younger brother's oversized board swung slowly right, and he paddled until they were together.

I pressed my palm to my chest in relief and left the pier. I neared the fishing boats. The boys crossed into the harbor toward the safety of moored sailboats and the *No Wake Zone*. To prevent appearing as a stalker to my grandsons, I blended in with the fish-selecting business of the restauranteurs.

As they reached the middle of the open area, my attention was drawn to a diving tour boat, empty of customers, slowly motoring in from around the point. The captain manning the vessel wore a towel wrapped around his head against the harsh sun.

The powerful engine revved high into an ear-splitting whine. The aft helm of the boat swerved erratically left, then right. Each turn pushed water cascading into large rolling wakes. The captain's face held in a rigid grimace as he struggled with the controls.

The waves hit the younger boy's board and tipped it. The boy fell off but immediately climbed back on, his paddle held in one hand. His older brother paddled closer to the anchored boats and looked around the area. "John, hurry up," he called to his little brother. He stopped paddling and kept his brother in his line of sight.

John knelt on his board. He pulled the paddle to his side and set the end into the water. One knee slipped, and the board tipped.

"Swim over," yelled the older boy, authoritative for his years. "You've got to get away from there." It was touching to hear his concern for the well-being of his brother.

"I can get back up." John attempted to climb onto the board.

"Dammit," The captain yelled over the roar of his boat growing more out of control. The engine began a cycle of speed followed by silence then erratic side to side turns.

"John, get out of there." I yelled and pointed. "The boat."

The older brother furiously paddled to John out in the center of the harbor. "John," he called. "Swim toward me. Forget the board."

John first viewed his brother. He then observed the herky-jerky movements of the tour boat behind him.

The captain yelled to John in the center of the open water lane. "Get out." He waved his arms frantically to my grandson. "Move out of the way."

John's brother continued to paddle swiftly to him. "Johnny, swim to shore," he called. "Swim to the beach."

The boat swerved closer, the sea water jostling frantically. John swam a few yards closer to shore, his board floating adrift.

Meanwhile, the older boy veered his board back in line with John's. The crazy stops and starts of the tour boat created larger and larger wakes. The highest wakes grew to a full wave crashing near his board. He worked the paddle to hold steady on the churning surface. Powerful ripples rolled. The fiberglass board tipped. He slid off and a wave rolled over his head. He emerged just as the boat soared above the surface.

Time and movements slowed as if I watched a film reel. The engine screamed at a high pitch. Everyone on the waterfront, beach, and pier turned toward it. The bow arced up toward the sky and rocketed twenty feet above the harbor's surface. Water gushed from the hull as it held suspended in the air. The crowd erupted in shouts of terror.

The captain jumped off the starboard side. His body hurled through the air then landed in a splash. In slow motion, the unmanned boat tilted to its side. The captain's limbs thrashed the water violently to get out of the way.

Time sped back up. Gravity pulled the boat as it dropped like an air bomb. On contact, sea water shot up and out in all directions. The captain's flailing movements ceased.

I kicked off my sandals. Water splashed up my calves as I ran into the shallow wake, between fishing vessels and an astonished crowd, to get as close to the boys as possible. They swam hard to pull themselves toward the beach. I thrust my way through stunned men and women packed knee deep in the water. I plunged into the water and swam with every ounce of energy and adrenaline left in me.

John swam an arc away from me as I approached.

"Get to shore, John," I said as I pushed beyond him. "I'll help your brother."

I stopped thirty yards from the older boy. He bobbed up from the high waves until I could see his face. He swam toward me. I pulled forward, my pace slowing by the oncoming wake's current. His head disappeared and reappeared between smaller wakes.

One revved-up roar of an engine tore through the air. A long shadow fell across the water, covering me and my oldest grandson. As he swam toward shore, outside racket fell away. Hissing noises sifted in my head. My skin chilled and bristled in the warm Caribbean current. In slow motion, the rogue, unmanned vessel ascended a second time from the water. Suspended fifty feet in the air, it rolled to the side. As if released from a giant crane, the massive boat hurtled downward and slapped on the rolling surface.

A chorus of screams pierced my ears. "Nooo," I yelled. The landing force sent water up in walls, droplets sprayed in a glittery rain of diamonds. The capsized boat recoiled from the deep and settled into an aimless float. All moored boats bobbed in a frenzy in the strong wakes; tied vessels slammed against the docks.

My eldest grandson no longer swam to safety.

CHAPTER NINETEEN

I swam frantically in search of the older brother until I reached the capsized boat. More distress piled on with each consecutive lap I made around. John's pained cries from the beach spurred me on. I inhaled deeply then torpedoed, open-eyed into the merciless burning salt of the sea. I pulled deeper and deeper with all my strength, blinking against the sting as I reached the deck of the upended hull. He could have been snagged in a rope or pinned under. With no sign of him, my heart pounded and my lungs demanded more air. I was forced to resurface.

Time being of the essence, I pulled in deep gulps of air, ready to resume my search. Something in my periphery appeared on the surface a few feet away. The unrecognizable shape bobbed gently with the current toward the pier.

I swam closer and grabbed the broken piece of the boy's paddle board. My heart wrenched at the sight of it in my hand. Releasing the board, I returned to the wrecked boat. My lungs were spent. Disheartened, I breeched the surface and swam away from the wreckage to attend to John.

The stoic-faced throng of tourists and locals went mute. *Why didn't anyone come to help?* I swam toward the crowd in search of John. The swarm of people slowly resumed where they left off and carried on as if a flip of a switch had turned off their emotions.

John wasn't on the beach, but I knew he wouldn't leave his brother. My feet bumped on the sand, and I left the water to search for him. A high-pitched shriek pierced the air.

"John." I ran toward him to the end of the concrete pier, pushing people aside. On the way I noted that no one reacted to his piercing cry. From the end of the pier, I took in the crowded waterfront. Nobody showed concern for the crying boy. We existed in our own bubble.

THE DECEPTOR'S CALL

He stared into the water. "John." My heart overrode any choice of keeping my distance. I placed my hands on his trembling shoulders to guide him back to a safer distance from the pier's edge. Keeping his sight on the water, he shoved out of my hands. I glanced over his head.

The unfathomable events bringing me to the present moment had not prepared me for the tragedies my grandsons had been forced to endure.

The bright red current billowed away from an odd-shaped object floating on the surface. My brain registered slowly what captured John's attention. At the end of the pier, my eldest grandson, whose name I had not learned, lay buoyed by the salt of the sea. His unfocused eyes stared at us. The top row of teeth exposed in a face permanently frozen in a stretched grimace. Both arms bobbed out to the sides on the gentle current rolls. His lower limbs did not follow. The boat had severed his pelvis clean through his hips.

John's teeth chattered in the humid heat as if he were locked inside a freezer.

"I'm so sorry."

Seconds passed without answer to my inadequate condolence. His wide eyes, blue lips shivering, met mine. In it, I saw a lifetime of innocence marred by witnessing such cruel tragedy. His pain-darkened eyes regarded me for the first time, deep and inquisitive. "Y-Y-You," he said through the chatter of teeth. "I know you."

"I'm your grandmother, John. I want to take care of you."

He stepped back from me to the end of the pier where half his brother's body floated below. "No."

"Please." I stepped toward him. He matched my backward step. "I'm here for you. We're the only ones left. We can get to know each other."

BARBARA MICHELLE

"I-I-I don't w-want to know you," he chattered. "I've s-seen your picture in the newspaper articles Mom kept in her closet."

Choking back grief, I said, "I can only imagine what you read. But the stories aren't true." I pleaded, feigning calm. "I can try to explain." I stumbled over words trying to find the right things to say, "I promise." As a sign of caring, I reached out to him.

John retreated another step, too close to the edge.

All the pain, hurt, and death my family had endured by whatever netherworld or devil had haunted us flowed fresh and sharp through me.

"I can't make this up to you. I can't change what you've been told about me or tell you why your brother had to leave. But," His ashen face stayed glued to me. "I'm so thankful to know you two existed."

The upper body drifted away from the pier and into the area of the anchored boats. Sadness stabbed my heart. "You boys did not deserve what's happened. He was so brave. And you were courageous to swim into the beach. I'll go out there now and bring him back. Then I'll find a way to put him to rest. For you, John."

"But you can't. You're dead," he said.

Ice gripped my spine.

"And besides, you k-killed my grandfather."

"No, I didn't, John." I fought back panic. "What you saw in the papers was wrong. Completely wrong. I loved him more than anything. He, your mom, and Uncle Ed were my entire world."

His blue eyes stared unblinking back at me.

"I'll take the biggest red snapper." The man responsible for the distraction bent over a little fishing boat driven halfway onto the beach. Choosing the catch of the day, he exchanged money with the fisherman standing inside the boat.

I scanned the area. Other fisherman negotiated prices. Cruise passengers filled tender boats at the dock. People strolled about. No one paid notice to a child's body floating in the harbor.

THE DECEPTOR'S CALL

I spun back to the shivering, frightened boy. "I'm going to bring him in now. And I want you to stay right here and wait for me. Then I'll get one of these men to help us find a place for him. Will you wait for me here?"

He continued to stare at me.

"John, will you stay here?"

The boy still did not answer. It pained me to leave him, but I couldn't let his brother be taken by the sea. The current caused the body to drift toward the moored boats. "I'm going now, John. I'll return for you when I've taken care of him."

I was caught in a terrible position, leaving my youngest grieving grandson alone on the pier in shock. Without his mother to hold and protect him, he had only me, the grandmother he believed to be dead. The grandmother he believed to be a murderer. I had the job of retrieving the mutilated body of the older boy, brave beyond his years. His attempt to save his brother from danger had been heroic. Shauna would have been so proud of her boys if she'd known.

I swam toward what was left of the body as it bobbled and bumped into the side of one of the moored sailboats. Given the horrific experience, there had to be a chance Shauna knew of the bravery of her boys, no matter how dreadful. Anything seemed possible then. I accepted and wanted the responsibility to keep John safe, though the core root was beyond my comprehension.

Without a concrete plan of how to handle the body, I neared the small bobbing torso. Tears blurred my vision at the wretched sight. I stretched my hand to what was left of him and touched a shoulder.

I reluctantly peered into his blood-drained face and beheld the pain of his youthful innocence, his jaw set in determination. A small wake from a passing sailboat washed gently over his body and face. His brown eyes abruptly broke their death stare and settled on me. I wanted to swim away but was unable to do more than dog paddle in place. The blue lips loosened from their determined death grimace. "You caused these problems, Grandmother."

"No," I yelled, swimming until I was back at the beach. I ran clumsily out of the shallow water. My soaked clothes, pasted on like an extra layer of skin, dripped a trail of water. I reached the pier where John shivered alone, close to the spot where he'd first seen the body.

I mustered calm. "John, we have to leave."

The angelic voice drove a knife deep into my soul. "Where is my brother?"

I searched for soft words. "He's gone, John." My own trembling hand took his smaller one. "Let's walk together."

I followed his eyes glued to where the sunken body had been. I swore to myself I'd never share with him what had happened in the water. It would remain my secret.

We walked the length of the pier together, grandmother and grandson, forlorn and lonely with only each other. No one paid attention to our sad journey. At the pier's end we stepped onto the concrete sidewalk running parallel the length of the short beach. The abandoned sunken trawler I'd seen when Elam and I first arrived, lay in the furthest edge of the harbor. I remembered the dark sorrow I'd experienced on our snorkeling trip there. Its tilted position reminded me of bad choices made, causing one to run aground.

I adored the precious child walking beside me. The sheen of his dark hair glinted in the sun. His shivers had subsided. I would find a way to get us off the island. With no backpack, money, or destination, the only possibility was to beg a ride on the ferry.

My gaze was drawn back to the rusted vessel. The people around us, fisherman, tourists, shop keepers, all moved as if on autopilot.

Little John walked beside me. I thought back to the boys coming out of Camilla's old cottage. They had taken a step back when they saw me, a stranger on the street.

THE DECEPTOR'S CALL

"Why did my brother have to die?"

"I have no answer." The question surprised me. My heart went out to him. "I don't understand it myself."

He walked in silence as if deep in thought. "Why did you come to us? You're dead."

The direct statement caused me to stop and face him. "Something has happened to change both our lives. Your grandfather, Elam, and I came here as tourists. It was great in the beginning, but things changed quickly. It wasn't so great anymore. Strange, horrible things happened I don't fully understand. I eventually ended up back here. Then, I saw you and your brother at the cottage."

He studied my face. "My dad left us. He didn't want to stay with us after he found out about Papa Elam and you. He said me and my brother would grow up to be bad people with that kind of blood in us."

Shauna's husband had left her and my grandsons. Because of me. Another knife to be driven into my soul.

I couldn't lose John. I had to keep him close. He was a gift; he was all I had. "I'm sorry he said that. From what I've seen, you, your brother, as well as your mother, are heroes. Each of you in your own way, and your Uncle Ed, too."

He gazed off in the distance as if considering my words. I waited. He looked deep into my eyes. "You think I'm a hero?"

I smiled down to him. "Yes, John. You're strong. And full of love for your family. Your father made a mistake. He's the one missing out. You're pretty special. And from what I seen, your brother was, too."

One side of his lips pulled up in a saddened smile.

"John, I'd like for you to stay with me. Everyone we know, and love, had to leave us. But I'm so lucky to have you. And I hope you'll give me the chance to prove myself to you. And to be a real grandmother. Do you think you'd like to try?"

He tumbled my idea over in his head. I pleaded silently for his agreement.

"Maybe. But only for today."

I wanted to wrap him close and hold him tight, but I didn't want to frighten him further. "Understood, just for today. Thank you." A moment passed and I asked the question burning inside. "Would you share your brave brother's name with me?"

He stared down at the ground. I feared I'd lost him.

"Elam." His voice was barely audible. "His name is Elam."

My heart swelled into my throat. "Elam."

We walked on. I assessed our surroundings. People passed us by, oblivious of our presence. A gentle breeze caressed my face. My mind searched for a way to get us safely off the island.

The refreshing draft snapped to a cold gale. Goosebumps raised on my arms. The wind whipped a sad moan then grew into stronger howls. I let go of John's hand and pulled him close for protection.

The cold howls stopped abruptly, leaving moist Caribbean air on my skin as if my mind had played a trick.

Fishermen continued their job of cleaning the day's catch on wooden benches erected in the sand beneath the shade of the massive palm fronds. I faced the sea and the rusted ship tilted in the marina's center. Three windows had been broken out on the upper deck above the shimmering surface. My search grazed the open windows and single porthole before scanning out to sea. Then a shadow pulled at me to return my gaze to the ship's windows.

Thinking I noticed a movement, I focused on the vessel. The windows peeked above the surface. Water licked and roiled inches below the bottom of the windowsills, the ship stuck in its watery grave as sailboats and tenders cruised around it.

A darkened shadow moved. I clasped John's small hand. Through the round porthole, a saddened face peered out at me like a forgotten prisoner. More faces formed, one after the other. The faces multiplied

THE DECEPTOR'S CALL

until there was no room left. They bulged out beyond the circular window and then filled the next one. I tightened my grip on John's hand and pulled him protectively closer to my side. More faces appeared, stuffed and angled within the confined space like fitted pieces.

Concerned for my grandson, I realized he held his stoic face ahead, unaware of the shocking vision. The rusted portholes pressed with the multitude of desperate faces.

Blank eyes from those windows rested on me, I could not distinguish one from the other. All at once, each face pulled back into individual expressions of sorrow and longing, as if I could release them from captivity.

One by one, I recognized the crowd crammed in the small spaces. "Oh, my god." I knew each unique face well. Like balloons being inflated, their faces expanded forward and bulged against the pane in succession before retracting in.

Officer Juan's face came forward then retreated as it made room for young Camilla's baby, followed by Elam's grieving expression. Shauna appeared, angry and lost. A wail escaped me as I reached my hand out toward the abandoned ship of souls. Ed. Brave, adventurous Ed. His longing expression begged for me to rescue him. The frightened face of my oldest and brave grandson expanded, his mouth stretching until I could virtually hear his sobs.

The fear in John's face spurred me to action. Leaving him, I bounded through the shallow beach and headed for the deep blue, intent on freeing his lost brother in the vessel window. An understanding of acceptance washed over me. I stopped wading into the water and glanced over my shoulder at John.

"John," I yelled as I scanned the beach, the pier, and the smaller docks. A caged parrot squawked from the sidewalk over the busy chatter and calls of vendors. Normal business carried on. He was nowhere in sight.

I returned my gaze to the abandoned boat imprisoning my family. The many faces stopped their competition for my attention. One called to me in silent despair. Little John's fresh desperate face bulged then withdrew.

My strength faltered as my ankles and knees wobbled underneath the waist-high salty sea. He, the last person left to me, was ripped away. All hope of our escape vanished.

Maternal love and a need to relieve their suffering in the darkness of an iron prison propelled me forward. I gained a sharpened awareness and my energy returned. Adrenaline surged to push my muscles through the harbor between the bobbing sailboats tethered to the invisible sea floor.

I swam until I closed in on the boat once more, squashed faces staring at me. Hopeless moans grew to an agitated song of the damned. I feared I might sink under the weight of their despair.

I grasped the rusted lock at the bottom of the hatches near the portholes. Brown rust had eaten through the latch. The lock would not budge. The moans burrowed deep in me as I worked and pulled on the stubborn metal. Giving up on the hatch, I swam level to the corroded windows. Their facial expressions changed to hopeful, their moaning stopped. My determination to free them bolstered.

As I reached Little John's anxious face, black iron bars appeared at the edges of both portholes. They snaked and weaved into crossbars, preventing his escape, separating me farther.

"How?" I inspected my uninjured hands. "This can't be happening." I gripped the bars and pulled, both feet flat on the side of the boat for leverage. My muscles strained uselessly against the bars.

I swam away from the windows to the other side angled through the surface. A small window frame, rusted and partly submerged, offered them a way out. I placed my hands on either side.

THE DECEPTOR'S CALL

Dark shifting startled me from inside the cavernous interior. A black blurry shape breached the inside surface. My heart pounded as Frank's snout protruded inches from my face. My hands slipped as black iron bars suddenly snaked over the open window. A rope tightened around his muscular neck. Mouth open wide, a grotesque display of his sharp teeth caused me to push back. I thrashed my arms under the water as I took in the sight of the trapped dog that had proven his friendship and loyalty, the whites of his eyes bulged as he stared back at me. "Frank."

Determined to find a way, I swam around to the back of the boat in hopes of locating another opening but found none. I plunged below and searched, the saltwater stinging my eyes. I returned to the surface, gasped for breath, and let my tears fall and wash away the burn.

A shadow passed over me and arced across the water. I shielded my face from direct sunlight. Wide-winged frigate birds circled and screeched above. They descended from the air and landed, some on the boat, some to float on the surface. Their squawks warned me away.

Strength flagging, I skirted around the boat, one hand holding onto the edges to help me stay afloat. Reaching the aft end, bars covered all visible windows. I pulled myself back to the front and the familiar moaning faces.

The screeches increased. Two frigates swooped down toward me. In midair, their long necks stretched, their beaks pointed downward. As they neared me, they sank their sharp hooked claws into the top of my scalp. My body too heavy for their size, they lifted me halfway out of the water as they flew. I thrashed my limbs below the frigates, my legs dragged through the sea. I screamed to the crowd, unaware, carrying on in the tiny harbor.

They dragged my body, partially submerged, through the water to the beach. I swung my arms to knock them away, but my strength was gone. The painful, tight grip of the frigates' claws in my scalp relaxed and my body scraped across the beach. Dazed, I watched the birds as they soared back and land on the boat. Warm blood dripped down my scalp.

Physically spent and all hope drained, I wanted to drown in the immense volume of moans from the damned. Hundreds of frigate guards trailed down to the trawler from the sky like a storm cloud. The harbor buzzed in usual fashion.

No one witnessed the devilish crisis.

CHAPTER TWENTY

The desperation of the imprisoned dead, past and future, lingered with me. The harbor and beach activity hummed near the beach where I slumped. Hundreds of birds of prey stood guard, flapping their powerful wings over the watery bar-covered prison, separating me from them. Staring back at the pitiable faces, lost and innocent, I pictured the rest of my life.

The boat covered by sleek feathered guards, understanding suddenly emerged in my brain as if the unseen force opened a written book in front of me. My entrapped loved ones paid the price for my past choices. Their souls would live an eternity of torture by unresolved need. Souls to never find peace. Never to find their final respite. My catalytic role led to their eternal demise. I had played too close with the evil spirit. Having my grandsons pulled away, a destiny I could not have imagined, had been a final act of vengeance. My life no longer held any meaning or purpose.

Physically weakened and unsteady, I lay down on the sand and rested my head in my hands. The pivotal scenes from the past rolled in my mind, directed by the outside force. Elam's horrified expression dawned clear, the day I'd found Cam's pictures and burned them, removing her forever from our lives. It hurt to know he had kept her pregnancy hidden. The grief in his exclamation of her name as her picture had drifted up in flames, confirmed what I'd already known; he had never stopped loving her.

Fresh aching stabs needled their way into each level of my backbone until it reached my ankles. Both hips throbbed. I assumed it was brought on by being dropped onto the beach by the sorcerous frigates. The pain worked its way slowly. I could not tear my gaze from the wretched souls across the water. As the agony settled into me, I surmised the changes in my body were meant to be permanent. It would serve as my own personal inferno, locked in guilt.

BARBARA MICHELLE

The second memory came to me in vivid detail. *The delivery truck rumbled in our direction as we faced each other, the striking redhead and me. I, a seething eighteen-year old stranger, traveled secretly to Elam's hometown. I knew I could make it there and back, he was busy studying for an exam back on campus, blissfully unaware of the event set in motion.*

He had mentioned her neighborhood offhandedly. I recognized her instantly, her splendor demanding center stage. I understood his attraction.

We both stood close to the curb. Jealousy grew thick as moss as I stared at her. She didn't know me. I stepped too close to the girl I loathed. At my advance, she retreated a step back. I loved Elam.

The redhead's eyes widened. She took another step back as if from a terrifying monster. She lost her balance and stumbled. As she struggled to stay upright, her foot slipped off the curb. Instinct tricked me. I reached out a hand to steady her, catching her clammy hand inside my palm. She tightened her fist around my hand. The next fleeting moment changed the trajectory of my future. I peered left, then right. No one noticed us standing together. I loosened my grip on her hand.

Her body tumbled backward; both arms flew out in a futile effort to gain solid purchase on something. Anything. Remorse kicked in. I tried to reverse my actions by reaching for her as she went down. I grabbed for Cam's arm, but her momentum caused her to slip away. It was too late.

Her fall was a strange catapult out into the street. Our eyes never lost contact. A dark malicious grin stretched across her plump lips as she sailed through the air. The oncoming truck skidded too late.

Neither Elam nor I knew she'd tricked him, that a friend had fathered the child in a secret affair.

Wrongs never to be righted, Camilla and the unborn infant could never be brought back. My jealousy and need to be good for Elam had caused the hellish effect. My callous selfishness had paved the way for me to take the bus ride and seek her out.

THE DECEPTOR'S CALL

The vicious deaths of my family members and Frank, a loyal protector, were irreversible. I wanted nothing more than to join them inside the barred windows. To share in the misery I deserved. Doomed and isolated from them, I resettled my head onto my crossed arms.

A tiny wave lapped over my aching feet. A new pain seared up through my back and into my neck. *Had their misery washed into me?* I lifted my head.

New, anonymous faces appeared. They thrust in between those of my family. The longer I focused on the nameless faces, I recognized familial characteristics shared with Camilla.

My vision's clarity dimmed slightly. Further understanding opened to me. Her loved ones had paid the price of her own deceitful choices.

Newer faces emerged, having no significance to me. The number continued to multiply, innocent souls forced to pay the price of others misdeeds.

The whispering voices had said I would walk alone. I longed for my own death.

I pushed onto my side, gasping with the effort. I forced my tortured joints to stand. Empty and secluded, I faced the island, the ocean at my back. My body was no more than the mechanics of a heart pumping and lungs breathing without substance. A vessel devoid of life.

With stunted steps and my back bent, I ambled as a vagrant without aim through the busy harbor and into the village. No one concerned with my safety, no one to care. The prisoners' torturous moans accompanied me, low and constant. I shuffled through the swarm of people in the village and past the busy shops. Bicycles and their bells buzzed around me. I shuffled on, hopeless under the sun's brilliance.

BARBARA MICHELLE

****

Villagers arced wide as I passed, avoiding my gaze. My directionless movements carried me adrift through the hubbub and on to the sandy street. I continued under the tangled canopy and the twittering of birds. I came to the end of the pier near the abandoned cottage. Bewildered at the reason I was brought there, I searched the water.

"Your journey is now complete." The grating voice sliced the jungle's calm. I recognized it at once. Camilla appeared, her bent posture filling the empty space before me in the middle of the bent pier. Elongated crow's feet etched her tired and reddened face. The sea shimmered behind her time-ravished body. Unlike me, she had meaning and purpose, if only for evil.

"You've lost it, Sandy, Your present. Your future."

"Were my grandsons real?" I had to know. I loved them wholly, unconditionally. "Did they ever exist?"

"Choices of the past alter the outcome of what lies ahead. Gifts of the future are beyond grasp or comprehension of what could be."

"Are you real? You smiled at me from the road that day. Right before the truck hit you."

"Camilla has paid her price for the selfish crimes she committed in her past. Her fate was determined long before Elam."

"So, you're not really Cam."

Without answering, the decrepit figure gazed at me.

"Whatever you are, you've accomplished what you set out to do to me. You've stripped away my family. Why not end me now?"

She stepped her crooked body painfully closer. "You are not finished here."

"There's nothing, and no one, left to take from me. What could you do to make my existence any more worthless?"

"There's work yet to be done. Always work."

THE DECEPTOR'S CALL

"So now I'm a slave? A slave for you?" My mind was empty, tired. I had no physical energy or desire to fight or take cover from any harm she planned. I didn't care what might happen to me. "You can't hurt me any more than you already have, no matter what you do to me now."

She nodded. "But there's much more."

"How? Will you never be satisfied with my suffering? If I have to walk circles around this island for eternity it won't make one bit of difference." I opened my empty palms to her. "I have absolutely nothing left. I am nothing."

"You have everything now. Previous ones before me have decided."

"What are you talking about?"

"Sandy is in your past. She no longer exists."

I disregarded what she had to say. I cared about nothing save for the love I held for my family.

"You will see." Camilla placed her wrinkled hand on mine.

We no longer stood on the creaky dock. My feet were planted firmly in the graveyard's sandy carpet, Camilla beside me. I read the names of my lost family members engraved in each elevated colorful crypt and cross stabbed in the sand. My husband rested in the spot I'd seen the men digging. Shauna, Ed, and my grandsons, Little John and his brother Elam II, were all located in graves nearby. For a reason I appreciated but did not understand, seeing their names gave me solace. They had been respected by being given a final home.

My heart flickered with affection for them. My place was here on this island, with the remains of my loved ones.

Camilla cut through my private thoughts. "Yes, you will remain here on Palm Isle. You've been chosen. This ancient burial ground has bestowed the responsibility on you."

"What do you mean, 'responsibility'?"

"My time has come. I have served my term. You now have control."

"Control?" I let her words sink in.

"Palm Isle is a place where requital finds triumph. My body will rest here. You will not use me." She spread her arms wide to the graveyard. "The others will rise at your call. They will serve faithfully."

"My call for service?" I shook my head. "I don't understand."

"Their bodies are here but their souls, their essence, are held safe and under guard by the birds. They are unspoiled by the sea."

She lowered her arms to her sides. "You are now High Priestess. The island passed the torch of reprisal from me to you. Someone with hidden secrets and has caused pain, as you did, as Camilla did. They reside anywhere in the world. No one is immune to the vengeance of Palm Isle. By use of those you call to serve, you will direct them here, to this beautiful tropical paradise."

"But I have no idea how to do this."

"Understanding is not necessary, it is an innate ability. The strength and abilities of the island and her original people will continue for eternity."

"I can't." I rubbed my swollen arthritic hands together. "I won't."

"Refusal is not a choice. The decision has been made. Sandy has shown strength, tenacity. Respect the ancient souls. Their own reprisals are realized through those who are led to Palm Isle." Camilla's worn body shuffled to the center of the burial ground.

"Wait," I screamed at her back. "You have to tell me more."

"Your penance will be paid as a ghost. Yet you will walk among the living."

Her wrinkled skin dimpled over her face, neck, and hands, the places where her dress did not cover. The dimples bubbled into a boil under the skin's surface. Rising steam from the boiling ended in long, coiled tendrils. Her skin disintegrated into black, tissue-thin pieces carried off on the breeze. Her naked, stooped skeleton stood before me then collapsed into a pile. The skull bounced on the top, open eye sockets and ghoulish teeth leered at me. The mass of bones faded to nothing. I studied the name carved into the headstone. *Camilla.*

I backed away from the gravesite, confused but not frightened, and passed through the entrance.

In soaked sandals, I plodded out beyond the village and into the isolation of the untamed forest bearing down over the lonely road. Island birds whistled and screeched in full voice, as if nothing had changed. I shuffled on and eventually followed the turn in the road. The rickety cottage where Camilla had lived taunted me. The steps appeared shabby enough to fall through. I struggled to the top, leaning heavily on the railing.

The front door creaked as I entered. The dilapidated dwelling was near empty except for a plain antique mirror hung on the wall near the door, the warped silver glass darkened with smoky spots. I waddled over and peered into it. With my new, dimmed vision, I bent closer for details.

I touched my fingers to my cheek. The woman staring back bore no resemblance to me. Hair snowy as dove feathers caressed a brown tinted face forty years older. The whites of my eyes had turned red streaked and watery. My pupils were dilated inside clouded blue irises. Creviced lines spreading from my lips, curved down in a frown. Deep grooves carved out from my cheeks, settling into sagging jowls. My aching shoulders slumped forward.

A loud knock echoed in the emptiness. I shuffled my newly kyphotic frame toward the closed door, a hand on my throbbing lower back. The door widened as the hinges creaked.

"Hello." A, willowy, middle-aged woman waited on the deck, her smile warm. I wanted to cling to her. "Are you the owner of the rental cottage around the corner?" she asked kindly.

Too stunned to answer, I stared.

She motioned her hand to her chest. "I'm Susan."

A well coifed lady waited at the bottom of the steps. "And this is my sister, Greta," Susan said. Greta stared up at the cottage from the ground, undisguised repulsion in her pout.

"I apologize for our late arrival to pick up the key," said Susan. "The airline had no record of our bookings or the flight. It was really strange. We were forced, last minute, to hire a charter plane to get us directly here." She paused.

What should I say?

She continued. "My cell phone refused to send messages here."

I knew my part like I had played it for years. It came naturally. Painfully, I reached my arm, the skin loose and paper thin, and took the key dangling from a metal hook on the wall. The pleasant woman offered her arm and patiently assisted me down the rickety staircase.

"Follow me," I said in a voice, rusty with age and the soft accent of the island.

"This is the first time Greta and I have seen each other in twenty years. We decided to take the opportunity and get reacquainted."

I trudged in front of them as she chattered on.

"We had plans to vacation on another island. But something told me this was the perfect place to relax in the peace and quiet. Catch up on lost time."

I observed Greta's frown. Darting inspection of the enclosing jumble of mangroves and banana trees, she resembled a victim expecting to be clobbered by a hidden creature. Blinding rays of sun glinted off the diamond on her left finger.

"Greta recently lost her husband." Susan whispered loudly in my ear as if we were old friends. Greta jerked her head, from staring intensely at the confusion of woods, to her sister's back.

Susan, unknowingly, continued. "And both our parents recently passed away."

THE DECEPTOR'S CALL

"I am sorry for your loss," I said. We stopped on the road in front of the rental cottage. Greta swatted at mosquitos swarmed up from the surface of the dark pond in the lawn.

A stray she-dog sniffed around the yard, the water covering her paws. Her nipples draped low; thin flanks defined the shape of her ribs. I recognized the poor soul from the day of my arrival onto the island. "Keep fresh water out for her," I said as we passed the pathetic creature. Ignoring Greta's disgust when the dog nuzzled her shins, I struggled up the stairs to the front door.

I silently cursed my veiny, inflamed fingers as they fumbled with the key in the lock. Finally, I pushed the door open. The cottage I'd shared with my husband hadn't changed.

Greta locked eyes with me on her way over the threshold. Revealed to me like an open book, I read her secrets. I identified why she had been brought to me.

"Welcome to *Paraiso*." I handed Susan the key and offered Greta my warmest smile. A dazzling emerald pendant glowed from the gold chain around her neck. Nose tipped up, she brushed by me.

As I made my slow descent down the steps, Greta's scolding words filtered out to me. "Susan, I will not spend one night in this rat-infested shack."

"Stop being such a princess, Greta. You never change."

I, the latest replacement, hobbled back to my new home; the old landlord's empty cottage for the deceptor's call.

BARBARA MICHELLE

Thank you for reading The Deceptor's Call. If you enjoyed the story, I'd love it if you could leave a review.

About the Author

Barbara Michelle is a native North Carolinian who discovers story through backpack travel experiences, morning beach walks, and soul-splitting thunderstorms. She dedicates writing hours to twisty tales and unexpected surprises. She loves pulling readers alongside characters on wild story-rides spiced with curiosity, concern, fear and shock. The Deceptor's Call is her first published novel.

Places to Stalk Me

Website/blog: https://barbaramichelleauthor.com
Facebook: https://www.facebook.com/BarbaraMichelleAuthor
X: @BarbaraAuthor
More to Come...

Milton Keynes UK
Ingram Content Group UK Ltd.
UKHW010801150524
442746UK00006B/254